Praise for Gary McMahon

"McMahon writes gritt
welcome antidote to
currently flooding the
urban existence

"Gary McMahon
Concrete Grove
it is gripping: a bl
you hardly dare look at what dark things hang
gleaming and winking in the branches of the trees."

– Graham Joyce on *The Concrete Grove*

"Gary McMahon is one of the finest of a new breed of horror writers. His work combines spare, elegant writing with an acute sense of the growing desperation felt by those having to deal with the crime and crumbling infrastructure of our urban centers. Illuminating these with a visionary's sense of the supernatural makes *The Concrete Grove* one exciting read."

– Steve Rasnic Tem on *The Concrete Grove*

"If you're a fan of slow-burn horror told in a strong and compelling way...
McMahon is one to watch."

– *Starburst*

Also by Gary McMahon

The Concrete Grove Trilogy

The Concrete Grove
Silent Voices

Hungry Hearts

Pretty Little Dead Things
Dead Bad Things

BEYOND HERE LIES NOTHING

GARY McMAHON

SOLARIS

First published 2012 by Solaris
an imprint of Rebellion Publishing Ltd,
Riverside House, Osney Mead,
Oxford, OX2 0ES, UK

www.solarisbooks.com

UK ISBN: 978 1 78108 020 7
US ISBN: 978 1 78108 021 4

Map artwork by Pye Parr

10 9 8 7 6 5 4 3 2 1

A CIP catalogue record for this book is available from the British Library.

Designed & typeset by Rebellion Publishing

Printed in the US

This one's dedicated to my cousin Linda, who told me all about the scary movies she'd seen at the cinema when I was much too young to go and see them for myself.

I never forgot that – it meant a lot to me at the time.

Acknowledgments

I wrote this novel more or less in isolation, so there aren't many acknowledgements to make. But a huge note of thanks must go, as always, to Emily and Charlie, my beloved little family. You keep me going. Thanks also to the usual suspects – mainly Mark West, Sharon Ring, Simon Bestwick, Jim Mcleod, Michael Wilson and Ross Warren – for their constant and gratifying support. Cheers to the writer chums who invited me to a terrific working weekend in Matlock: it really helped me get started on this book. A special doff of the cap must go to Steve Volk, Tim Lebbon, Adam Nevill, Joe D'Lacey and my good mate Mark Morris for being so bloody inspirational. Finally, thanks again to Jon Oliver and the brilliant team at Solaris. I literally couldn't have done all this without you.

NEAR GROVE

BEACON GREEN

BEACON GROVE RISE

SHOPS

UNICORN'S HORN PUB

GROVE TERRACE

GROVE ALLEY

GROVE STREET

GROVE CRESCENT

BACK GROVE CRESCENT

THE ROUNDPATH

NEEDLE

GROVE STREET WEST

DERELICT HOUSES

GROVE LANE

BACK GROVE ROAD

GROVE ROAD

THE DROPPED PENNY PUB

GROVE COURT

Grove Court Flats

GROVE MOUNT

GROVE NOOK

THE NAG PUB

GROVE STREET

GROVE SIDE

GROVE ROAD

THE EMBANKMENT

GROVE RISE

Seer Park

GROVE CORNER

GROVE DRIVE

GROVE DRIVE WEST

Grove End Primary School

GROVE END

GROVE ALLEY

Far Grove Skateboarding Park

FAR GROVE WAY

Waste Ground

Abandoned Factory & Warehouse Units

Railway Line (disused)

N

FAR GROVE

Captain Clickety
He's coming your way
Captain Clickety
He'll make you pay
Once in the morning
Twice in the night
Three times Clickety
Will give you a fright

– Traditional children's skipping song
(origin unknown)

I has been sent to bed by mummy and daddy. they dont want me to hear them fight. my name is jack. I want to keep a dairy and this is it. daddy thinks people who rite are funny in the head. he says I should be playin outside with my football or on my bike. I like my bike. but daddy wont let me play outside when it dark. that the scary time. nasty man mite take me away like that boy in the news before. my sister is daisy like a flower. I think somebody hates us. he is in the house all the time but we cant see him. he makes niose when nowbody else is here. he wants to hurt us. we hide under the bed when mummy and daddy are in the pub. he canit see us there. we ~~inibible.~~ inbisevil. he canit see us. but he is there. in the walls and under the floor. he creeps about and peeps threw the gaps to try and see me and daisy flower. I am scared. I can here him now. he goes clikcety clikcety like when I spilt my marbels on the kichen floor. clikcey clikcety clikc.

– From the diary of Jack Pollack, April 1974

PART ONE

The Gone-Away Girls

"Promise me that you won't try to save me."

– Abby Hansen

CHAPTER ONE

It starts, for him, with an ending...

In fact, it begins with a funeral.

Death is a constant in the Concrete Grove, just as it is everywhere else in the world. People come and they go; they live and they die, blooming and then withering like seasonal flowers on the stem. This natural cycle perpetuates, bringing existence and extinction and joy and sorrow, and everything else in-between, into sharp focus. But in the Grove these fundamental truths are pushed even closer to the surface, like a spiritual hernia; it is a place where the cycles of life and death are played out at an intimate scale across an epic canvas. A million different beginnings and endings, each with their separate details, their intimate little secrets...

But for Marc Price, it begins with an ending...

CHAPTER TWO

MARC WATCHED THE short funeral cortege as it made its way off the main road and into the grounds of the Near Grove Crematorium, following the narrow tarmac road past the gravestones and monuments. Most of the cars were old, outdated models, but kept in good shape by their mostly aged owners. None of the old man's friends had been what anyone might call well off. They were normal people, with normal amounts of cash in their pockets.

He sat in his car outside the front gates, watching through the grimy windscreen. He recognised not one of the cars in the small queue of vehicles. In fact he didn't know anyone who'd known Harry Rose apart from his uncle, but his uncle was dead too, five years in the grave from cancer of the liver. Uncle Mike had introduced Marc to Harry Rose, but only from beyond the grave – his name had been enough to convince the old man to talk to him. The two men had once drunk together. They'd been long-ago beer buddies.

The stereo was playing softly; the CD was a compilation of Ennio Morricone's film scores Harry Rose had given him not long after their first meeting. Marc closed his eyes and listened to the music, trying not to think about the immediacy and inevitability of death.

When he opened his eyes again, the final car in the grim little procession was inching its way through the crematorium gates. Bright shards of sunlight broke through the clouds and made patterns on the shiny roof and bonnet, which were a direct contrast to the dirty, dented bodywork of his little Nissan. He stared at the layer of dust on the dashboard, a light scattering of grey. The torn seats, the battered interior... somehow the poor condition of the car represented a facet of his lifestyle that he didn't like to think about. It had been new once, this vehicle, but now it was old. Not a profound insight, but one that moved him deeply on this particular day at this grim hour.

Marc turned off the engine, removed the ignition key, and opened the car door. He stepped out onto the road, glancing to the side to make sure there were no cars speeding towards him, and locked the door (he used the key; there was no central locking on this old beast). He pulled up his collar against the slight autumnal chill and jogged across the road, towards the iron crematorium fence. He had not been here for a long time – not since they'd cremated Uncle Mike. The place made him feel uncomfortable, exhuming memories that he'd rather stayed buried. Conflicting images and sensations almost overwhelmed him: the smell of booze on his uncle's breath, the man's strong arms lifting him off the ground when he was a child, his harsh voice, the way the skin around his eyes had creased when he smiled, almost covering his eyes.

He stood at the fence and stared through the trees. People were moving around in there, climbing out of their cars, milling around like geese in a field before the service began. He could see some of them shaking hands or speaking softly to one another, and others lit up cigarettes to smoke away the minutes before they were allowed to enter the small redbrick crematorium building. The weight of the dead was heavy here. Marc could feel it everywhere, even on the oft-trodden footpath outside the fence.

Marc wasn't sure what he was doing here. He had not known Harry Rose for long, and he had not known him too well. Yes, the two men had forged a bond of sorts over the past few months, but it was based on Marc's desire for information and the old man's need for company in the long, dim days before he died. They had been convenient companions, nothing more.

Yes, Harry had once known Marc's Uncle Mike well, many years ago, but Marc had known neither of the men beyond the superficial.

He reached inside his pocket and took out his mobile phone, checked it for messages, and then switched it off. He rarely received calls or texts. He led a deliberately friendless lifestyle, preferring to spend time on his own. He didn't know why he chose to ostracise himself from others, but isolation agreed with him. That was all he needed to know, the only justification he required.

He started towards the main gates, reluctant to enter, yet knowing that it was the least he could do – to pay the man his respects, say a final goodbye before the flames took him. He didn't need to hang around afterwards, and the strangers here would not press him to do so.

Loose stones crunched under his feet as he walked along the path, between grubby monuments and grave markers. The air was chill, the sky bright and open. Traffic noise dimmed behind him, as if he were in the process of entering a sealed environment.

Marc stood at the edge of the small group of mourners, trying not to be noticed. He wished he hadn't given up smoking; that would have given him something to do with his hands as he waited.

"Excuse me."

Marc looked up, resisting the urge to sigh. He had been staring at his feet, so failed to notice the man's approach. "Hello," he said, holding out his hand in an instinctive gesture that he didn't really mean.

The man shook his hand and smiled. "You must be Marc." His face was lined, his hair was thin and grey; he looked as if he was in his early sixties. "I'm Vic. Victor Rose... Harry's brother."

Marc nodded. Of course; Harry had told him about his brother, and the falling out the two men had experienced several years ago – some family thing, a silly argument that had stretched and changed into a longstanding estrangement. "Ah, yes. I'm pleased to meet you." When the man let go of his hand he didn't know what to do with it, so he just let it hang at his side, the fingers clasping an imaginary cigarette.

"I suppose Harry told you about me. About what happened between us?"

"A little bit, yes. Not in any great detail, though." He felt awkward, not really knowing what to say to this man. He hated small talk. It was meaningless.

"I wish we hadn't been so stupid. If I knew what was going to happen... how ill he was... well, you know." He smiled, sadly. His pale blue eyes were moist. His face was like parchment paper stamped with the signs of loss.

"I know. And I'm sure Harry felt the same." He had no idea what Harry had thought about the matter. Even if he'd been told, he had not retained the information.

An awkward silence descended between the two men, pushing them apart. Again, Marc wished that he could smoke. He hadn't felt the craving this strongly in a long time, perhaps for a couple of years.

"If he'd have told me how ill he was, I would've gone round, made up with him. He was my only brother... I loved the old bastard, even though I don't think I ever told him how I felt."

Marc was just about to say something – he didn't know what; just anything to break the uncomfortable, candid moment – when people started to shuffle inside the building.

"Looks like we're on now," he said, smiling at Victor Rose. "Please, after you."

Rose nodded and began to walk towards the entrance, hanging back enough that he didn't get too far ahead of Marc. *He doesn't want to go in alone*, thought Marc. He increased his speed and drew level with the older man. "Okay if I sit with you?" He was unsure why he'd made the offer, but once he did he felt better. Perhaps in this situation, a companion would help ease the tension.

Rose looked relieved. "Yes... yes, that would be fine."

Marc placed a hand on Rose's shoulder and guided him inside. He hoped that he would never get so lonely that he needed the company of a stranger at a family funeral – then he realised that he was already there. If he was called to the interment of some distant family member tomorrow, he'd have nobody to take with him.

Perhaps he'd ask Victor Rose.

They followed the other mourners inside and took their seats near the front of the narrow room. Marc looked around and concluded that there must be no other family members present. Not one person acknowledged Victor; no-one even looked in his direction. Either the trouble between the brothers had been worse than he imagined, or Victor had become so detached from his older sibling's life that he did not know these people.

Whichever reason were true, it was a sad state of affairs.

They stood when the service began, sang half-heartedly along with the hymns, and listened to the vicar as he described someone Marc barely even recognised. After what felt like a very short time, the velvet-draped coffin began to move on its roller towards the furnace door.

Marc felt unmoved by the brief ceremony. He was unable to connect with anything that had happened, any of the words the man at the front of the room had said. It all seemed too generic, so homogenised, that it might have come out of a can. Instant funeral service: just add water.

Before long, the mourners started to file outside. Their faces were unchanged; nothing had penetrated the façade.

"Can I offer you a lift?" he asked Victor Rose, as they were standing outside, waiting for something that had already happened.

Rose nodded. "Thank you. I came here on the bus... it would be a rather depressing ride back to Harry's patch on my own."

Marc said nothing. He just led the way to the car, walking slowly to enable to other man to keep up.

Once the car was moving, he switched on the radio, keeping the volume low. The local news was reporting more job lay-offs and a story about yet another company going into liquidation. Times were hard; people were struggling. It was the same old story told in a different way, or a sequel in which every move could be predicted on the evidence of what had gone before.

"Back there in the crematorium." He glanced to the side, at his passenger's profile. "It didn't seem like anyone knew you. I mean... not one of those people spoke to you."

Rose sighed. "My brother and I led very different lives. To be honest, I very much doubt those other mourners even knew who I was. Even before we fell out, Harry and I were distant. We always have been – ever since we were children."

Marc didn't respond.

"I suppose you think that's strange?"

Marc shook his head. "I really wouldn't know. My own lifestyle isn't exactly what you'd call conventional." He thought of his ex-wife, who was now living with a female tattoo artist in Singapore, and his nomadic existence as a freelance reporter for a variety of newspapers and magazines; his self-imposed exile from the human race. He'd never settled down, never made a mark of any kind in the world. Even the stories he reported faded a day or two after they were told, impermanent, not mattering to anyone for longer than the minutes it took to read them.

"We were very different people, my brother and I. My friends don't know he exists, and I daresay his friends never knew much about me. It's how we worked. We didn't need to be close in order to feel close. That probably doesn't make much sense – I know it doesn't to me – but it's just how we were. Who we were..." He fell silent, as if tired of the sound of his own voice.

Marc followed the route from Near Grove to the Concrete Grove, feeling as if he were chasing a long, dark thread through the corridors of a familiar maze. He always became downbeat when he approached the area. It made him feel so low that sometimes he wished he'd never heard of the place. The closer he got to the heart of the area, the more dilapidated the buildings became, the more potholes appeared in the road, and the shabbier the people on the street began to seem. Part of this was psychological – his reaction to the location – but not all of it. This place was dark; it was well shadowed. Things had always been different here.

Marc had a theory that some places were always in shadow, no matter how hard the sun was shining. The Concrete Grove was a joyless estate. Apart from the poverty and the criminality that bred here, there was another layer of darkness that could be sensed rather than seen. He thought of a dark sea lapping against concrete pilings, the waves occasionally slopping up onto the land and breaking it away, slowly encroaching. But that wasn't quite right.

The analogy was close, but not precise enough to communicate exactly what it was he felt.

He drove the car along Beacon Grove Rise, following a couple of other vehicles that had left the crematorium just before them. As he drove, he was struck by the way things never changed around here. It was like a film set that had not been taken down when the production company moved on, and people had moved in to set up home inside the two-dimensional backdrop. There was a sense of impermanence, yet also the belief that everything would remain as it was now, as it had been since the estate was built.

He parked the car on Grove Terrace, in a spot opposite the small row of shops. When he glanced over at the newsagents, a short Pakistani man with thinning grey hair raised a hand in an informal wave. Marc smiled and nodded. The man turned away and went inside his shop.

"I suppose we have to go in, don't we?" Rose was staring along the street at the Unicorn pub. His eyes were narrow and his lips were pursed.

"We don't have to. I could take you home if you like." Suddenly Marc was afraid. He didn't know what had caused the fear, but it was there, gnawing away at him and unsettling his emotions.

"Thank you, but no. It wouldn't be right. I should at least show my face." He turned towards Marc, a tentative smile now playing at his lips. "Could I buy you a drink?

"No," said Marc. "But I'll buy you one. Come on, let's get in there and raise a glass to your brother, the miserable old bugger." He smiled and patted Rose's arm.

They got out of the car and walked slowly along the street, not saying anything, just content to be silent. A few people entered the pub ahead of them, and when the door opened Marc heard the sound of many voices speaking at once, competing for attention, before it swung shut again.

They reached the pub doorway. Marc glanced at Rose. The old man nodded and Marc opened the door and stepped into the Unicorn.

He'd been inside the Unicorn a few times before, with Harry Rose. The old man had enjoyed a drink, and this place was just a few doors along from his house so had served as his local. Those times, clientele had been thin on the ground – just a few old men sipping bitter and studying racing forms, or the occasional young wannabe gangster spending his drug money and trying to play the big man in an infamous watering hole. Marc knew of the Unicorn's reputation. Even in Far Grove, where he'd been raised by Uncle Mike, the place was spoken of as a roughhouse bar filled with hard men and aging prostitutes who'd take you to a nearby side street and gobble you for the price of a pint.

These days the place had lost its edge, but the essence of that hostility remained, wedged like ancient mortar into the brick joints. Even today, packed out with old men and women who were seeing off an old friend, there was the sense that violence might kick off at any given moment, triggered by nothing more than a change in the temperature or a rogue air current drifting in through an open window.

"What are you having?" He turned to Rose and leaned in towards the man, so he could hear a reply over the clamour.

"Whisky, please."

"Double?"

"Well, I wouldn't say no."

Marc elbowed his way through the crowd and towards the bar. The two members of staff on duty were struggling to cope with the rush, so he had to wait a while before catching the barmaid's eye. She raised her eyebrows to signal that she'd made a note of his presence and finished off pulling a pint of mild for an old man who looked drunk already.

The man paid for his beer and staggered away from the bar, slopping half the contents of his glass down the front of his shabby suit jacket. The barmaid moved over to where Marc was standing.

"Aye?"

"A double whisky and a bottle of Becks, please."

She turned and bent over to the low-level cooler box, opened the glass door and took out a cold bottle. Marc stared at her enormous backside, unable to look away. The thin waistband of her tight black trousers had slipped down to reveal the lacy edge of her underwear and the flesh of her ample waist formed a bulging muffin-top around the beltline. She straightened and poured the whisky from the optic: two aggressive jabs with the glass.

"Anything else?" she asked as she turned back to him and placed the drinks on the wet bar. She had a pretty face but her dyed blonde hair was tired and dried out. Her makeup failed to hide the scars of a hard life.

"That's all, thanks." He took a sip of his beer straight from the bottle. It felt good, like a soothing balm for whatever might ail him.

Marc paid for the drinks and made his way back over to Rose. The man wasn't standing where he'd left him and he felt stranded for a moment, gripping the two drinks and scanning the interior for a sighting of his companion.

Rose waved to him from across the room, where he'd managed to squeeze onto the end of a long seat at the edge of a table cluttered with empty pint glasses. Marc made his way over to the table, dodging elbows and spirited hand gestures. He reached the safety of the table without spilling a drop and set down the drinks before spotting the low three-legged stool Rose had commandeered for his use.

"Thanks," he said, grabbing the stool and sitting opposite Rose at the narrow wooden table.

"Cheers," said Rose, raising his glass. "Here's to Harry."

"To Harry," echoed Marc, lifting his bottle and taking another drink.

The level of conversation inside the pub had settled to a lower volume. Now that everyone had a drink they were beginning to settle in and find a rhythm.

"I'm glad you called me to let me know about Harry," said Rose. "I'd never have forgiven myself if I'd have missed his funeral." His eyes were glazed. Marc wasn't sure if the whisky was working already or the man was holding back tears.

"It's okay," said Marc. "To be honest, I was only doing what Harry asked me to do."

Rose put down his glass. "What do you mean?"

"He'd asked a couple of times that I call you if anything happened to him. He knew he was ill. His heart wasn't good. The doctor had told him that he shouldn't make any long term plans." He took a drink, licked his lips. "So he gave me your number and asked me to make you sure were informed when it happened."

"Shit," said Rose, wiping the back of a hand across his eyes. "We really were stupid... stubborn and stupid and intractable." He gulped down the rest of his whisky. "My round," he said and rose to his feet. "Same again?"

Marc finished his bottle. "I might join you in a whisky," he said.

"Good lad."

He sat and looked around as he waited for Rose to return with the drinks. Making mental notes, he studied the other people in the pub. It was the curse of a writer, this constant logging of minor details. He was unable to be anywhere without mentally listing character traits, quirks and twitches, even the dun colour of the wallpaper behind the heads of a chatting couple.

Most of the customers were the wrong side of middle age, but there were a few younger people present. Only about a third of the people here had been at the funeral, so Marc assumed that the rest of the group was made up of regulars and those who knew Harry but not well enough to attend the service. A bunch of kids in their early twenties occupied the bay window, talking in low tones, their faces hidden by the peaks of baseball caps. He watched a man and a woman as they kissed in the corner by the cigarette machine; her lips mashed against his teeth and Marc caught a glimpse of her tongue as it snaked into her partner's mouth.

He wasn't quite sure when he felt her gaze – even later, when he thought back to this moment, he could not be certain of the exact moment that he noticed her – but he gradually became aware of a vague warm sensation at the back of his head. Turning, he looked past the crowded bar and saw a tall, thin woman leaning against the wall by the jukebox. He'd caught her eye just as she looked away, but he knew that she'd been staring at him.

The woman's face was long and narrow, vaguely horse-like, with a long nose and a wide, appealing mouth. Like a lot of women on the estate, she had dyed blonde hair, but hers was pulled back into a severe ponytail. Her black suit was cheap and in need of ironing but the blouse she had on underneath the jacket looked as if she'd spent a bit of money on it back when it had been in fashion. She looked at him again but this time she didn't look away immediately; she held his gaze for a long moment and a smile played at the edges of her broad mouth.

"There you go." Rose was back. He pushed a shot glass into Marc's hand and slammed down two bottles of Becks on the table. "I dunno about you, but suddenly I feel like getting pissed."

Marc raised his glass. "I'll drink to that."

CHAPTER THREE

THE AFTERNOON WORE on in a comfortable haze of whisky and beer. The craving for tobacco was almost crippling at times, because Marc kept seeing people nip outside for a smoke. He was drawn to follow them, as if some invisible umbilical were tugging him in that direction. But he fought the urge and managed to get through the worst of it. He drank more alcohol instead. It seemed to numb the craving.

He and Rose talked about a lot of things but they didn't discuss anything of importance. Their conversation lurched between football and politics (Rose was a life long supporter of Newcastle United; Marc was a Sunderland fan. They both voted labour but Rose was in favour of a return to a more rigidly socialist doctrine), women and wine, friendships lost and broken and relationships renewed. The old man soon became maudlin and the effects of the whisky were showing. At some point after 3 pm, he announced that he was going to call a taxi and rose unsteadily to his feet.

"Here," said Marc, all too aware of the slurring in his voice. "Use my mobile."

"Thanks." Rose thumbed the number and ordered a cab. He was told that it would arrive in about five minutes.

"I should've left earlier. I can't take the booze like I used to." His face was loose on the bones, the skin sagging. "But I'm glad I had someone to drink with, Marc. You've saved me from an afternoon sat in a corner drinking alone and wallowing in self-pity." He smiled and showed his teeth, which were so white and even they could only be dentures.

"I'll keep in touch," said Marc. "Harry was a good man, and it would be a nice tribute if his death meant that we stayed friends." He was surprised to find that he actually meant what he said.

"I'd like that. I know I can't take back what happened between me and Harry, but the fact that you spent time with him in his last days is comforting. Right then..." He stood, swayed, and steadied himself against the table, clattering the glasses. "I have to go. My cab will be here soon. I'll speak to you next week?"

Marc nodded. "I'll give you a call. We can go for a pint."

He watched as the old man wove across the floor, managing not to walk into anyone, and then pushed through the door and went outside.

Marc had about an inch of whisky left in his glass and the beer bottle was only half full. He knew that he should drink up and go, but the urge to keep drinking surged within him, a throwback to his younger days when he'd struggled with an addictive nature.

Just one more, he thought. *One more drink after this one, and then I'll leave.*

The room seemed to shimmer around him. He knew he was drunk, of course; but what he didn't realise was *how* drunk. He hadn't stood up for about half an hour, and his legs felt strange, as if they'd blended with the table and the chair and were conspiring to keep him seated.

He finished the whisky without really tasting it and picked up the Becks bottle.

When he put the empty bottle back down on the table it was like coming out of a trance. He knew that only seconds had passed between his last thought and the act of replacing the green bottle on the table, but it felt like he'd somehow fallen asleep and lost at least a couple of hours. The air in the room felt different, heavy. The quality of the light had changed, as if the sun outside had moved across the sky without him noticing the passage of time. He was familiar with this sensation of dislocation from drinking bouts in the past, but still it troubled him. It was as if he'd emerged from a lacuna, a blank spot. Anything could have happened while he was away.

Panicked, he checked his pockets. His wallet and his phone, his car and house keys... they were all still there. He hadn't been pick-pocketed during his mini fugue. He had no idea how anything like that could even have occurred, yet it made him feel calmer to confirm that everything was still in place about his person. The world might have changed fractionally, but he was still the same.

He glanced up and around and realised that the Unicorn was a lot less busy. People had drifted away, perhaps going home to their families or seeking a cheaper method to bring on oblivion by raiding secret stores of black market beer and spirits kept in the space under the stairs or beneath the bed.

The woman he'd noticed earlier was still in her spot by the jukebox, but now she was pushing coins slowly and methodically into the slot, one after another. He'd been aware of music playing but only now that the volume of the drinkers had lowered could he identify a tune. Neil Diamond: *Sweet Caroline*. That song, he knew, was one of the many that formed the soundtrack to the lives of people who drank in rough pubs and social clubs. Songs like this one – sad and sweet and with an instant hook – were sung by club singers throughout the country. The performance was always the same – a low-rent crooner on a low stage belting out bygone hits through a dodgy sound system. An overweight man in an ill-fitting black suit with white sweat marks under the arms, singing songs about divorce and heartbreak; always delivered in a fake American accent in a small northern town, a desperate attempt to delineate the boundaries of even smaller lives. To Marc, it was one of the most depressing experiences the world had to offer.

"Jesus," he muttered. And he fought the urge to laugh at his own bleak musings.

He needed to do something to break his mood, so he slowly rose from the chair and started moving in a crouch towards the bar. At the last minute he jinked to the right and walked along the length of the bar, following its curve towards the jukebox.

The woman picked that exact moment to stop feeding money into the machine. She turned around and faced the room. Marc was too close to her by now to back out, so he kept going and only stopped walking when he was right in front of her.

Suddenly this seemed like a bad idea. It was as if he'd entered another of those drunken fugues and only come out of it when it was too late to make any difference to the situation.

"Hi," he said, aware that he was swaying gently.

The woman stared at him. Up close he could see that she was wearing too much makeup. The dark rings around her eyes looked like week-old bruises. Her lips were thin and her skin, beneath the layer of foundation, was slightly rough, as if it had been sandpapered. But her eyes were beautiful: ice blue, piercing, holding within them the promise of something that he couldn't define. Staring into those eyes was like catching sight of a cold, quick, elegant movement; the flickering of something living encased within an iceberg.

"I, erm... I noticed you earlier. Thought I'd come over and say hello."

She didn't stop staring at him but she looked bored, barely even interested in what he had to say. Not that he could blame her: his patter was as stale as the air inside the pub, and as lifeless as her stoic face.

"Okay... sorry. I'll go away." He started to turn, his cheeks burning. He wasn't usually this awkward around women. In fact, he usually found it easy to turn on the charm; faking was simple, it was honesty he found a difficult trick to pull off. But there was something about this woman that disturbed him – the same thing that drew him to her.

"White wine and soda," she said, without moving. She had her back to the wall. The glass in her hand was almost full. Slowly, she raised the glass to her lips and swallowed the contents. Her eyes never left his face.

She handed him the glass.

He struggled to think of a witty response, but there was nothing left to say. He turned around and walked over to the bar, ordered the drinks. Then he returned to her side, feeling as if he'd been trapped somehow, or manipulated into doing something against his will. Not a big thing, just a tiny act of coercion, something unnoticeable to everyone but himself: a minuscule defilement of his sense of self, or a minor mutilation to a part of his body that would remain unseen.

He handed her the drink and waited. Why was he acting like this? What the hell was wrong with him?

"What's your name?" He couldn't stop looking at her eyes. He wanted to see that movement again, to try and discern what had caused it.

"Abby." Her voice was cold and hard, the inflection flat. The vowels were truncated, as if she could barely be bothered to form the words.

"I'm Marc."

"Oh." Her thin lips twitched apart as she spoke. She took a sip of her wine.

"I'm not usually this crap with women," he said, thinking that honesty might be the way forward. "You make me feel uncomfortable. Do you know that? The effect you have. Are you aware of it?"

"Do I look like I give a shit, Marc?" Those icy eyes, that tough voice.

"Listen... you're obviously not interested. Enjoy your drink and I'll –"

"No." That was all she said. Just one word. But it was enough to keep him there, as if someone had applied quick-setting glue to the soles of his shoes.

"You don't want me to leave you alone?"

She shook her head. "You can hang around for a bit. Talk to me. Nobody else does around here, not these days. It's like they're afraid they might catch something off me."

Puzzled by her choice of words, he wondered if she perhaps had some kind of disease. She looked thin enough that something might be eating her away from the inside. The suit jacket hung loosely on her frame and her legs beneath the hem of the skirt were so thin that he was afraid they might buckle if she stepped away from the wall and put all her weight on them.

Cancer? Was that it? It might explain her demeanour, the way that she didn't seem to care, and that faintly hostile coldness behind her eyes.

"It's nice to see a new face around these parts," she said, as if continuing some conversation the precise details of which he'd missed. "You get sick of these mardy bastards around here." She twitched her head, indicating everyone else in the pub. "Sometimes I want to smash their faces in just to see what they'd do." She smiled at last, but it was a bitter expression that didn't quite suit her long face. "Do you know what I mean, or am I scaring you?" The question was a challenge. He could feel it. She was testing him, feeling him out.

"No, I knew exactly what you mean. Sometimes I get like that myself." But it ran deeper than that. He knew it even if he was unable to vocalise his feelings. This place – it lent force to the everyday negative emotions people had, and it amplified them. He didn't know how, or why, it happened, but here in the Grove bad thoughts took on substance, became even worse deeds-in-waiting. All it took was a trigger, and sometimes the finger pulling that trigger was the last one you expected.

There was a pause, then, and she looked around the room, her face resuming its previous set expression of mild distaste. Marc tried to judge the true shape of her body underneath her clothing, and he was left with the off-putting impression of skin and bones. Usually he was attracted to women with a fuller figure, and he failed to understand what it was about Abby that he found so appealing. Was he simply drunk and horny and had seen an opportunity here, or did the attraction run deeper than merely the possibility of a quick fix of empty sex? He couldn't be sure; his thoughts refused to settle and his emotions were unfamiliar.

"How about another?" he said, draining his bottle. He'd abandoned the whisky in favour of sticking to beer. He was already too drunk to repair the damage, but at least he could prevent drinking himself insensate.

"Yeah," she said. "Thanks." Gratitude – this was new. He felt like he might be getting somewhere.

His journey to the bar this time was fraught with anxiety. Although the pub was quieter now, and he knew that he wouldn't collide with anyone, he felt too exposed. His drunkenness was a badge of dishonour; it was difficult putting one foot in front of the other without stumbling.

He made it to the bar and clung on for dear life. He looked down at his hands. The knuckles were red.

"Yer in there, mate."

He turned to his left and examined the owner of the voice. It was a short, fat man dressed in jeans and a ripped black T-shirt that was pulled out of shape and faded from being washed too many times.

"Sorry?"

"The lass," said the man. "She'll go with anyone, her. Yer in for a shag the neet."

Marc blinked. His eyes felt gritty. The man's smile was wide and vaguely threatening, as if he were pushing for a fight.

"We're just chatting," he said, wondering why he felt the need to justify his actions to this stranger. "You know, a bit of harmless fun."

The man shook his head. The muscles in his neck bulged and there was a blue tattoo of a swallow on his throat.

How witty, thought Marc, resisting the urge to grin.

The man turned slightly, so that he was facing Marc head-on. He was broad; his biceps were large and hard. More tattoos snaked down his wide forearms. "Don't worry, mate. I'm only havin' you on. Bit of a laugh, like. But, seriously, if you play it right she'll take you home with her the neet. Game on, like."

The barmaid – a different one this time; they must have changed shifts – came over and Marc ordered another bottle of Becks and a white wine and soda. He glanced back at Abby. She was slumped against the wall, her eyes heavy-lidded, starting to close, and her hips swayed gently to the music. She was even drunker than he felt. Now that she'd let her guard down, he could see how far gone she really was.

He carried the drinks over to the jukebox. Johnny Cash was singing about a Ring of Fire. Behind him, the short, fat man and his friends started to laugh. Marc was too tired, and too drunk, to even care.

"Ta," said Abby, straightening her spine and attempting to smile. The expression was lopsided. Marc thought that it was an apt metaphor for how he felt.

"Listen," he said. "We're both a bit pissed here." He glanced out of the nearest window. It was getting dark. "I haven't a clue what time it is, but I haven't eaten a thing since breakfast. How about going for something to eat? My treat."

She slid a few inches down the wall and then forced herself to stand straight again. "How about a takeaway?" she said. "We could go back to mine and order one in."

"Yeah, okay."

The men at the bar laughed again.

"Come on, then," said Abby. She gulped at her drink, draining the glass in seconds. Her eyes were glassy. "Let's fuck off out of here."

CHAPTER FOUR

Royle sat in his car and watched the estate, hoping that he didn't see anything nefarious go down. He was off-duty, half-drunk, and incapable of acting professionally if anything did happen. He watched as a couple of young boys made their way towards Grove Alley, laughing. They walked with the stylised gait of chimpanzees: bow-legged and with their arms bent and swinging as if they were carrying rolls of carpet under their arms.

Wannabe hard men; trainee gangsters. This place was full of the fuckers.

Royle switched on the police radio and listened to random call-ins: a possible burglary in Cramlington, a domestic in Near Grove... all the usual night-time scenarios. He switched it off again and stared through the windscreen. The boys had gone. The street was quiet and empty. It was late. Some of the lights in the houses were still on but others lay in darkness. He could hear the steady rhythmic thud of bass-heavy dance music coming from somewhere across the estate.

He got out of the car and nipped along Grove Street, then followed the Roundpath until he came to the gate in the hoardings that surrounded the old concrete tower block. He stood outside and stared in at the Needle, at its cruel walls and its boarded windows. There was a light on in the security cabin that squatted in the building's shadow. He turned and walked a few paces along the Roundpath, stopped and bent low to the ground. He reached down and ran his hands over the loose gravel; small stones and wood chippings passed beneath the tips of his fingers.

This was where it happened. The man, Simon Ridley, had been stabbed to death by a person or persons unknown. His two friends had been standing with him when it happened, but they were unable to identify the assailant. Ridley had died almost instantly. Royle remembered coming out here to see the body. A young constable had already been on the scene, making the area secure with police tape. The body had been covered by a white sheet that was too small to hide everything and Ridley's legs from the knee down had been visible. There had been a lot of blood on the ground; it had stained the sheet.

He'd lifted the sheet to look at the man's face. The victim had been smiling.

Even now, over three months later, he could not forget that smile. He dreamed about it regularly; it followed him through the darkness. At the time he couldn't be sure what it was about the corpse's facial expression that had disturbed him so badly. Only afterwards had he realised that it was because it was a smile of pure irony.

Royle didn't usually become emotionally involved with cases, and his level of obsession in his work was manageable – at least most of the time, and apart from one special case. But this one was different; he wanted to know the real reason behind that smile. He needed to find out who had stabbed Simon Ridley, and why they'd done it. Royle knew that his thought process was flawed, but for some reason he couldn't help thinking that if he answered these questions he might be able to understand more about his own life, and about the ghosts that haunted him.

He rose to a standing position and took one final look at the Needle. The place had always made him feel uncomfortable, as if the cold, grey structure hid something that wasn't quite ready to be seen. He'd worked this patch long enough to know that strange things happened in the Grove. The estate was like some kind of locus for negative energy; in Medieval times it would have been considered cursed. Once he had read an article in a magazine about something called the Hum – low level electro-magnetic waves that some people were able to hear in the form of a low-frequency humming noise. These people heard it all the time; whenever they were close to electricity pylons, the sound became more apparent. One theory was that the Hum originated from all the electrical goods people pack into their homes. It had even driven one or two people insane.

There was something like that operating here, in the Grove. But it wasn't a discernable sound. More like a feeling, a sensation; like the slow, burning sensation at the nape of the neck when you feel like you're being watched. He felt that all the time. It only ever went away when he left the estate.

Royle had a name for it: he called it the Crawl. Because that's how it felt: as if invisible insects were crawling across his skin, wandering around all over his body. The sensation wasn't exactly invasive, but it was persistent. Sometimes he wanted to rip off his clothes and leap into a river to wash it off – anything to be rid of the terrible feeling that things were crawling all over his body, treating him like a patch of ground.

The Crawl.

He could feel it now; he could always feel it, when he was here, on these streets. Thinking about the Crawl made it seem worse, because it drew his attention to the sensation.

He turned away from the hoardings and walked back to his car, head down, skin crawling, shoulders hunched, and with his hands stuffed deep into the pockets of his coat.

Royle drove out of the estate towards Grove End. He passed very few people, apart from a couple making their way along the street from the direction of the Unicorn pub. The woman was tottering on her high heels and the man looked pensive, slightly out of place in his surroundings. He thought he recognised the woman, but he couldn't be sure.

The farther Royle travelled from the source, the less bothered he was by the Crawl. Eventually, when he was roughly a mile away from the Needle, the feeling stopped completely and he was able to relax. The three whiskies he'd enjoyed earlier that evening no longer warmed him. He reached out and turned on the car's heating system, listening to the slow suction of air into the interior of the vehicle.

When he arrived at his flat he sat there still waiting for the car to heat up. After a couple of minutes he got out and walked to his door, fishing his keys out of his pocket. He let himself in, climbed the stairs, and went straight to the drinks shelf. He took a sip of whisky before taking off his coat. It felt good, like an old friend.

The off-license downstairs was still open but he had enough supplies to see him through most of the following week.

He supposed that it had been stupid to rent a flat situated directly above so much temptation, but he'd long ago realised that it was impossible to fight his cravings. He could manage the problem, but would never defeat his addictive nature. Vanessa wanted to arrange for him to attend AA meetings, or see a counsellor, but he wouldn't accede to her demands. He knew that he was drink-dependent – he wasn't an idiot, locked into a cycle of self-denial – but the basic fact was that the dependency sustained him. If he didn't have the drink, he'd lose his ability to cope with the job he did. Almost everyone he knew on the force had a drink problem. Nobody talked about it out in the open, and as long as it didn't affect the way you did your job, it was simply accepted as part of the territory.

He walked across to his tiny stereo and flicked on the radio. There was a late-night phone-in programme about street crime. He changed the station to a sports discussion show and sat down in his chair by the window. He liked to watch the streets at night. It gave him a sense of the mechanics of how society worked. There were phases of activity after nightfall: the early evening crowd of street kids marking out their territory, then the after-pub crowd staggering home, followed by an emptiness that seemed almost holy.

Sometimes, when he sat and stared out of the window, he saw signs of something bigger than himself, a vast conscious energy that stirred the litter in the gutters, the leaves on the trees, the swings in the playground opposite his flat.

Royle had never been a religious man, but as he got older he became more aware of his burgeoning spirituality. He wasn't sure what he believed in, but he knew that he believed in something – or that he *wanted* to believe.

In his trouser pocket, his mobile phone began to vibrate. He took it out and opened the text message. It was from Vanessa.

Are you awake?

It was a system they'd worked out between them. He struggled with insomnia and the pregnancy was causing her to sit up late at night, unable to sleep. So if one of them wanted to talk, or simply to listen to another voice on the phone whatever the time of day or night, they'd send a quick text to see if the other was amenable to a chat.

He reached over and retrieved the landline phone from its spot on the windowsill and dialled her number. She answered on the second ring.

"How are you?" she said, without preamble.

"The usual. Can't sleep, mind refuses to shut down. You know..."

He pictured her smile and the way she always ducked her head slightly, as if to try and hide her chin.

"What about you? Baby keeping you awake?"

"Yeah. Baby's been restless tonight. I don't think it enjoyed the mushroom sandwich I had earlier. Maybe Baby's getting a bit sick of mushrooms."

"The way it got sick of cooked meat?"

"Yes." She paused, and he sensed some minor apprehension on her behalf. "I know I shouldn't say this, but I'm missing you tonight. Sorry. No... I definitely shouldn't have said that."

He adjusted his position in the chair and rested his fingertips on the edge of the whisky glass. "No, it's okay. I know what you mean. I'm feeling a bit down myself, and kind of wish that I had someone here in the flat. Just another presence around the place."

"Uh-hum. That's it. That's exactly it. I wouldn't want you to speak to me, or do anything. Just be here. Be around, to make it less lonely."

He felt an ache in his chest. Nothing major, a slight twinge that was gone just as quickly as it had arrived. "Yes," he said. "Yes."

They both stopped speaking, then. It was a comfortable, companionable silence. If they'd been sitting in the same room, one of them perhaps reading a book, it would have felt natural. But on the phone it was slightly strained. Royle listened to the static on the line and thought about the Hum. This thought led on to the Crawl, and he shut his eyes to try and disperse the negativity it brought. He was out of its range here; the Crawl could not reach him.

There was a crackling noise in his ear – or was it more of a clicking sound? Then the low-grade white noise surged back in and drowned out the other sound he thought he'd heard.

"This is awkward, isn't it?"

He nodded and then remembered that she couldn't see him. "It isn't usually like this," he said. "It's probably me. I'm tired and frustrated."

"Is it that young man, the one who was stabbed?"

"Yes... it's always about him, lately. I can't seem to shake it. I need to find out who did it, bring them in, and file it all away neatly."

"Life isn't like that. You know it isn't. How many unsolved cases have you been involved with? How many dead people were buried without the answers to why they ended up that way? You know better than anyone that these things can't be tied up in a bow and put away on a shelf somewhere, all neatly packaged. It doesn't work like that."

She was right. She was always right. About this, and about everything else. About them, their relationship, the way they had to live apart if they were to stand any chance of getting back together.

"How's the drinking?"

He knew she'd ask. She always did.

"The same." He waited for the sigh but it didn't come.

"But are you working on it?"

He looked at the whisky glass perched on the arm of the chair. The amber fluid glimmered with light reflected from the window.

"Yes," he said. "Slowly. I'm working on it slowly."

He heard a soft smacking sound as she pursed her lips or sucked her teeth. He imagined her small, pink tongue poking between her lips.

"We'll get there," she said, and for a moment he wasn't quite sure what she meant. "You and I, we'll get there in the end."

"I hope so. This can't go on – not once Baby's born. We tried so hard, we were so desperate for a family, and now that it's happened we have to make sure that we *are* a family." He felt like crying. The force of emotion was staggering; it made his body ache, filled up his head with acid.

"We're getting closer, Craig. I can feel it. Things are changing and that can only be a good thing. The fact that we both want to be together makes me confident that we will be."

His hand clenched around the glass. He stared at the hand, as if it belonged to someone else. He had no sense of trying to make a fist; he could barely even feel the hand as the fingers tightened around the glass. He wondered if it would break, and he'd cut himself on a shard, bleeding onto the chair.

"I'll let you go now." Her voice sounded so incredibly far away, a distance that could not be measured by common means. The words meant so much more than she intended, and for a moment he wished that he could explain to her exactly how he felt. Then he realised that he couldn't do that, because he didn't understand it either. There were no rules of engagement in the war he was waging against himself. He was making it all up as he went along, hoping that the casualties would be slight. He felt like the walking wounded, travelling along a road towards a salvation that might not even be there when he got to the end.

"I love you," he said, his voice trembling with emotions that were so new to him they didn't even have a name.

"I know." She hung up the phone.

Royle returned the handset to its home on the sill and once again stared out of the window. The empty play park opposite looked different, as if subtle changes had occurred. The swings rocked slowly, the roundabout turned as if it had been pushed gently by an invisible hand; the climbing frame seemed as if it were tensed for movement, like a large spider waiting to pounce.

Five years ago, on this day, a seven year-old girl called Connie Millstone had disappeared from that park. Royle was in charge of the case – his first high-profile assignment after he'd been promoted to Detective. There was a big fuss made in the press at the time, articles in the red-top papers about predatory paedophiles, low-rent journalists calling for citizens to unite against a perceived societal threat. It had been absurd; a witch-hunt.

Despite the case having never been solved, Royle had been praised by his superiors for the way he'd handled the media-created outrage.

But little Connie Millstone was only the first of what soon became a spate of disappearances. The press began to call them The Gone-Away Girls.

Over the next year, three other kids went missing, all young girls. The disappearances were linked by a similar M.O. and the demographic of the victims. The only child to be linked directly to the Grove estate was a girl called Tessa Hansen; the rest had lived outside the area.

These were all children aged between seven and ten. Each one went missing from a supposed safe place (if anywhere in the Concrete Grove could be called that). A playground, a supermarket car park, the Far Grove skateboarding park, and in Tessa Hansen's case a corner sweetshop on Far Grove Way – a street which formed part of the unofficial boundary between the estate and the district of Far

Grove. There were never any witnesses, and no reports of anyone suspicious hanging around. The kids just... went away.

Connie Millstone, aged seven.

Alice Jacobs, aged eight.

Fiona Warren, aged nine.

Tessa Hansen, aged ten.

They were all in the same approximate age group. Each of them had fair blonde hair, a slight build, and was said by relatives to have a certain dreamy aspect to their personality and a loner's ability to enjoy their own company. There was a link between them, but Royle had never discovered what it was. Other than the superficial similarities in their appearance and the fact that they each lived within a two or three mile radius of the Concrete Grove, there didn't seem to be anything that connected the girls. They didn't even know each other; they all went to different schools and moved in separate social circles. The fact that each subsequent girl was a year older than the last might be relevant – some kind of pattern – but he couldn't see how or why. It was simply another part of the puzzle whose meaning eluded him.

It was maddening.

Like Simon Ridley's smile, those disappearances still haunted Royle, and with this being the five-year anniversary of the first incident he was unable to rid his mind of the memories. He saw the places where those children had been, the holes they'd left in the fabric of existence, wherever he looked. Child-shaped gaps in the world. The Gone-Away Girls didn't seem to be coming back, and every drink he took was a reminder that he'd failed them, failed their families, failed everyone, including himself.

Peering out into the darkness, he spotted something in the playground. There was something perched on the bottom of the slide. From this distance, it looked like it might be a bundle of clothing someone had dumped there, or a particularly small vagrant sleeping on the slide. He stood, leaning closer to the window, and tried to make out further details.

The bundle was about two-feet long. It could be a child, lying there on the end of the slide. Was it happening again, or could this be one of those missing children returning?

No, that was impossible. They'd be teenagers by now, if they were even still alive.

He blinked and then refocused his vision, hoping that the image would be gone. But it wasn't. There was somebody on the slide.

Somebody.

Some body.

A body.

He moved quickly across the room, grabbing his coat, and was out the door, down the stairs, and in the street before he realised that he had not brought along his mobile phone. He'd left it by the chair after reading Vanessa's text. There was no way to contact the station if this was in fact a dead body, or if he got into any kind of trouble investigating the scene. He could have run back up to the flat and grabbed the phone, but he experienced a sense of urgency that would not let him turn back.

He ran across the road, stepped over the short fence that surrounded the playground, and moved towards the slide. As he watched, the bundle began to move. It twitched several times, rolled over, and slipped off the edge of the slide, out of view. He felt the Crawl upon him – on his skin, like beetles.

Royle slowed his pace. The situation was so strange, so unlike anything that he could think of, that he was suddenly too afraid to move. So he stood there in the centre of the playground, wishing that he'd paused to pick up the phone.

The air was cold. The night was quiet. He couldn't even hear a distant siren or an alarm. Not even the noise from a car or motorcycle. He stared at the slide, but the bundle was still out of sight. It had fallen to the side furthest away from him, and the darkness prevented him from seeing underneath the slide.

Slowly, he moved forward, ready to run or defend himself if something were to occur.

When he reached the slide there was no sign of the bundle – or the body, as he'd first imagined it was – so he made a quick inspection of the area. There was nothing on the ground nearby. The breeze had dropped so there was no movement from the swings or the roundabout.

He heard a rustling sound behind him, followed by a soft clicking noise. He turned around and looked at the trees bordering the northern edge of the playground, forming a boundary between the area where kids played and the tiny pavilion where old ladies and workers from the office a few streets away liked to eat their packed lunches. The leaves nearest the ground were moving, as if something had just crawled under there.

The Crawl, he thought. *It's the Crawl, and it's come to get me.*

His skin tingled.

He walked over to the spot and waited, trying to hear another sound. There was only silence – a silence so intense that it was almost like a new form of sound. He bent his knees and lowered himself into a squatting position, looking intently into the shadows under the trees. The leaves were no longer moving, but from deeper inside the undergrowth he heard a soft rustling, as of something moving away from him in the direction of the pavilion.

He spotted a fallen branch nearby and picked it up. Shuffling forward, he used the stick to prod at the area where whatever he had seen must have scuttled through and into the bushes. He lifted the hanging leaves and peered into the darkness. Nothing moved. There were no more sounds to indicate that anything might be in there, hiding from him and watching his every move.

The Crawl.

He stood and threw away the branch. Walking backwards, he moved away from the trees but kept watching them, looking for signs of movement. When he was satisfied that there was no longer anything there, he turned and headed back towards the road.

Behind him, something made a single clicking sound. He stopped, didn't turn around. Waited.

The sound was not repeated.

This time, when he started walking, he had to fight the urge to run. If there was something (why did it have to be a thing, rather than a person, that he imagined back there?), he would not show it that he was afraid.

Because if the Crawl smelled his fear, it might come after him.

CHAPTER FIVE

Abby lived in a small two-bedroom semi-detached house at the south end of Grove Rise, overlooking the old railway embankment. They walked side by side along the wide footpath but didn't touch one another. Marc thought that he should at least reach out and hold her hand, but it didn't feel right. Even their proximity felt awkward, as if there was something wrong with the dynamic.

Abby stumbled on her two-inch heels and then righted herself. "It's just along here," she said, slurring only a little. The buttons on her jacket had come undone and it flapped open, displaying the small humps of her breasts beneath the blouse and the excess material at her flat stomach. The top two buttons of the blouse were also undone. Her sternum was prominent, with only a scant covering of pale flesh.

She's so thin, he thought. *Almost emaciated...*

Again, he was confused by the strength and source of his own desire.

Curtains and blinds were shut at the windows of most of the houses they passed, but pale light bled around the edges and through the gaps. Marc caught sight of the occasional red eye of a lit cigarette as someone smoked on their doorstep. There was a feeling of mute desolation, a sense that behind this façade there was nothing but a deep, black emptiness. He had no idea what time it was, but it felt late. Too late to turn back, anyway.

When they reached the house, she stopped underneath a streetlight. The sickly light made her look ill. Marc waited to see what she would do, and when she reached for him he twitched in shock. Then, as she leaned in close and opened her mouth, he let himself go with the moment, enjoying the seedy glamour of her overly made-up face closing in on his.

When she kissed him, she did it with such force and urgency that he feared she might leave bruises. It felt as if she were trying to eat his face without breaking the skin. Her thin lips were hard; her large mouth was soft and wet and tasted of wine and soda. When she forced her tongue into his mouth it felt like an invasion, the prelude to a rape. He almost gagged but then he got the reaction under control, stopping it before it went too far. His stomach flipped. The muscles in his thighs tightened.

Abby's long, firm tongue explored the inside of his mouth and he brought his teeth together softly, nibbling gently.

They came apart slowly. She wiped her mouth with the back of her hand. His crotch was aching. She reached down and brazenly cupped his balls, and then rubbed her hand across the front of his trousers, pressing her palm so hard against his erection so that it began to throb. "Let's go inside," she whispered.

He followed her through the gate and along a narrow concrete path. The lawn on each side of the path was overgrown and filled with weeds. The curtains were open at the large front window. There was a standing lamp switched on inside the lounge, shedding weak light across the carpet. The TV was on and showing scenes from a 1970s action movie: Clint Eastwood, Sondra Locke; cops and criminals in grey suits with flared trousers running through the grimy streets of downtown San Francisco.

She opened the door and stepped inside, kept going along the hallway. She'd left the door open, so Marc assumed that he was meant to follow her inside. He shut the door behind him and continued towards another door at the end and on the right: the living room. When he went inside, Abby was closing the curtains. She'd taken off her jacket; the thin material of the blouse clung like crepe paper to her slight form. Her arms were painfully thin.

She turned around and smiled. She seemed more relaxed on her own turf, as if she'd also taken off a layer of the armour that had been so apparent in the Unicorn.

"Drink?" She moved gracefully across the room, running a hand across his chest as she passed him on her way to the door. "Or should I try to find a pizza menu, or something?"

"To be honest, I'm not really that hungry anymore." He took off his coat and threw it onto the sofa.

She smiled. "Beer okay?" She walked out of the room before he had a chance to answer.

Marc sat down on the sofa and watched the muted television. The film had come to a break. Adverts for banks and supermarkets played out before his eyes, not even touching him.

"Here," she said, opening a can of bitter and sitting down beside him. "It's cold but I don't know what it tastes like – I never drink bitter."

He barely paused to wonder why she had cans of the stuff in her fridge.

He sipped the bitter and felt her place a hand on his thigh. When he looked over at her she was sitting staring at him, a strange, unreadable expression on her face. She seemed to be looking inward, staring at something that lived inside her. That was the only way he could think of to describe how she looked.

He put down the can on the floor and leaned in towards her, knowing that it was what was expected of him. He kissed the side of her neck and she moaned softly. He pulled away, feeling as if he was doing something wrong. Nothing felt right. He was simply going through the motions and feeling nothing of any substance.

He looked around at the living room. There were a couple of cheap prints on the wall, framed landscapes of places he didn't recognise. On the mantelpiece above the electric fire was a small plastic model of the Angel of the North. Shoes were scattered on the floor in one corner. On a small occasional table to one side of the television there were photographs of a little girl. These were all held inside pretty little silver frames. One of the photographs was of the girl in school uniform. Another showed her smiling on a desolate beach. There were at least seven or eight of these images: it was like a small shrine.

"My daughter," she said, noticing his interest. "That's our Tessa."

"She's a beautiful girl," he said.

"She was. She was very beautiful... my little Princess."

Marc knew what was coming. He should have known that the woman's damage must have come from something like this, but he'd been too drunk and aroused to stop and think about what he was doing, who he was really with.

"She went missing five years ago. She was only ten years old."

He looked again at the photos. Placed among them were other items: a few crude, childish examples of arts and crafts. Perhaps they'd been created by the girl when she was at school or attending a day nursery. There was a fired clay saucer, a primitive pottery figure, and two small macramé animals. This was the art of loss, bespeaking all manner of private grief.

"Should I go?"

She shook her head but remained silent. The television flickered like a faulty god from across the tawdry room.

"Are you sure?"

She nodded. Her eyelids fluttered in the gloom. She slid across the sofa so that their thighs were touching. This time the contact was electric; he imagined sparks flaring between them, forming an arc of white light. She leaned in close. He felt the soft warmth of her breath against his cheek. She closed her eyes and opened her mouth, and this time when she kissed him it was less hungry, more relaxed and intimate. This time it felt like she knew exactly who she was kissing.

He embraced her, running his hands across her back, feeling her bra strap through the thin blouse.

She was breathing heavily. He felt constrained, wanted to get out of his clothes and feel her naked skin against him. He moved his right hand, bringing it around to the front and slipping it between them. He cupped her left breast. She took a sharp breath and smiled into his kiss.

They were upstairs before he'd even registered that they'd moved off the sofa. They picked at each other's clothing, pulling away garments like hunters skinning an animal. That's how it felt: primal, necessary. An act born out of need rather than want.

Her body was so thin that she was made up of angles. Her elbow bones were sharp points in the dark and her kneecaps stood out from the skin. Her breasts were small, with large nipples and dark areolae. He bent forward and kissed them, one at a time, teasing the nipples erect. She tugged his trousers down to his knees and he backed away from her to take them off and throw them across the room. She slipped off her knickers and displayed the darkness between her thighs. He knelt like a supplicant, moved his head forward, and began to lap at her crotch, feeling her open up for him. She reached down and pushed the back of his head. He tensed his tongue, jabbed the tip into her clitoris.

She moaned something under her breath but he couldn't make out the words.

The sex was both hard and soft, it was desperate and yet it was also strangely rhythmic. They felt their way towards separate climaxes, and then, after a short and silent period of rest, they made love again. This time it was slower, more relaxed, and although lacking the same urgency it was no less intense.

Afterwards, Abby fell asleep in his arms, her head resting against his chest. It was uncomfortable but he didn't want to move in case he woke her. After several minutes she shifted, turned her back to him, and curled up with her spine bent, the bones prodding her skin. He reached down and touched her flesh. She was hot to the touch.

He was sober now, and unable to sleep. The sex had invigorated him, washing the tiredness from his system. He stared at the ceiling, and then at the walls. In this room, too, there were several photographs of Tessa. She was a pretty girl with a wide smile. She looked a lot like her mother, with a similar long face and thin lips. She had the same ice-blue eyes.

The walls were covered with a type of wallpaper that had been in fashion half a decade ago. The ceiling was plastered with ridged white swirls of Artex. The furniture in the room – the double bed, a built-in wardrobe, a dressing table and chair – looked inexpensive, mass-produced.

Gently, he slid out of bed and went to look for his trousers. He found them near the door and put them on. He didn't bother looking for his shirt. The heating must be on; it was warm inside the house.

He glanced back at the bed but Abby hadn't moved. The skin of her back was white in the darkness, like dead flesh. He could make out the individual bones of her vertebral column through the papery flesh. Her shoulders were so narrow that she could have been a child lying there on the mattress, sleeping uneasily in her parents' bed.

He opened the door and left the room, closing it gently behind him. He padded across the landing and paused at the top of the stairs. There were two other rooms up here – one must be the bathroom. He moved further along the landing and tried the first door. It opened onto the second bedroom. This must have been where Tessa had slept. There were posters of ponies and fairy tale characters on the walls. The bed was covered in a pink duvet. There was a small TV, a stereo, an Xbox, and all the books on the shelf above the headboard were storybooks about princes and princesses and faraway lands.

Abby must have kept the room exactly how it had been when her daughter went missing. He was again reminded of the small table-top shrine in the living room. At the centre of the bedroom there was a large, roughly triangular pile of what at first he took as random objects. Then, when he moved further into the room to take a closer look, he realised what the objects were. Broken toys, the pages from what might have been her favourite books, stuffed animals that were missing an arm or a leg, and in one case even a head. There were doll parts, oversized jigsaw pieces, fractured board games, foreign dolls in national dress, and the remnants of a destructed playroom: all the sad parts from the broken toys that nobody ever got around to fixing.

The pile of discarded playthings formed a small pyramid, the apex of which was level with Marc's mid-thigh. He stood before it and wondered how long it had taken to build. Had Abby created it all in one go, or had she added to the mound gradually, forming a kind of homemade monument to her memory over the past five years since her daughter had disappeared?

He put out his hand and let it hover above the totem. That was how he'd begun to think of the weird construction: with each layer of toys representing a period in the girl's life. The older toys were nearer the bottom – baby things, the mobile from above her crib, perhaps even her first stuffed toy – and the newer stuff was at the top.

As he stepped around the mound, he noticed a photograph attached to the top of the pyramid. A small monochrome portrait of the girl, possibly taken not long before she'd gone away: her last school photograph, or maybe one taken by Abby on their final family holiday? The background was a greyish blur, so he couldn't make out where the picture had been taken. It wasn't even clear if the girl had been indoors or outside in the open air.

When he looked closer he realised that her eyes were shut. What he'd at first assumed were the girl's eyes were in fact drawn on; somebody had sketched false eyes onto her eyelids. He bent down to inspect the photograph closer, to try and understand what it was he was looking at.

Was it an image of a dead girl, like Victorian post-mortem photography? Or was she simply asleep, and whoever had drawn the eyes had been playing a joke? There wasn't enough detail to be sure, but the image disturbed him. Perhaps if the photograph had been in colour, he might have been able to discern more detail. As it was, this was just a girl with eyes drawn onto her closed lids.

He backed out of the room slowly, trying not to make a sound. He could not turn away from the grim totem, and now that he'd seen the photograph he was unable to think of anything else. Even when he closed his eyes, he saw that face: the drawn-on eyes stared at him from the red-tinted darkness.

He shut the door on the dreadful image and went to the next door along the landing. It was the bathroom. He locked the door and sat down on the toilet, trying to clear his mind. But all he could think of – and all he could see, like a flash against his retina – was the girl's small, white face and those crudely drawn eyes.

He stood and lifted the toilet lid, took a piss and stared at the clean white tiles above the cistern. As he washed his hands, he tried not to meet his own eyes in the mirror above the sink. He knew that they would look haunted, just as this house was haunted by something that was not immediately apparent – a quiet spectre, a ghost of sadness and decay. He wasn't afraid, he was mournful. The death of this child – if she even was dead, and not simply being held somewhere by another haunted and tormented soul – permeated the bricks and the mortar, the very fabric of the building in which he stood. Her absence was like a physical thing, taking up space that it did not own.

He dried his hands on a frayed towel and left the room, shutting the door and walking back to Abby's room. He paused outside the door and listened, trying to make out if she had woken or if she was still sleeping. There was no sound from behind the door, so he opened it and went inside.

Abby was in the same position she'd been in when he left the room. She hadn't moved, not even a fraction, as far as he could tell.

"Abby?"

There was no answer. Either she was fast asleep or faking it. He wasn't sure which of these options he preferred.

He walked over to the bed and slipped beneath the covers, pulling them down to his waist. He was still warm, despite the chilling sight he'd stumbled across in the second bedroom. He turned over onto his side and stared at the base of Abby's neck, where the bone was most prominent. She had a small tattoo on her right shoulder; her daughter's name in a fine, looping script. He moved closer and kissed the opposite shoulder softly, just allowing his lips to rest there for a moment. Her skin was warm and clammy. The thin layer of sweat there tasted of smoke and Chardonnay.

CHAPTER SIX

MARC WOKE LATE the following morning. His head was aching and his hands felt numb, as if he'd been punching walls in the night. He sat up in bed, resting his head against the pillows, and was glad that Abby was not lying next to him. He tried to clear his head. A patch of sunlight moved across the floor towards the bed, as if hunting him. He glanced at the window, and saw that it was bright outside. The day looked new, as if it might turn into something glorious.

He smelled frying bacon and his stomach began to twist and grumble. He couldn't remember the last time he'd eaten. They'd not got around to ordering takeaway last night and he'd consumed a lot more alcohol than he was used to.

He rubbed his head, clawed at his cheek with his bitten fingernails, feeling the stubble there.

Sounds drifted up the stairs and into the room, through the open door. The radio was playing and Abby was humming along to the tune.

Marc got out of bed and slipped into his clothes. He didn't want to have a shower; it would be best if he just ate and ran, leaving the woman downstairs to come to her own conclusions about last night. He remembered the ferocity of their lovemaking, as if the act of sex had stripped away her grief for as long as it took her to come. He wasn't quite sure how he felt about Abby, and even less sure regarding how she might feel about him. She gave little away; her defences were impressive.

He left the room and walked towards the bathroom, glancing over at the other door – the one that led to the absent child's room, where that bizarre structure was hidden. He tried not to think about it and went into the bathroom. He opened the cupboard door and found a spare toothbrush still in its wrapper. Next to it, on the shelf, there was a packet of cheap men's razors, a half-used bottle of aftershave, and some shaving foam. He wondered who they belonged to, or if in fact they were there for anyone who needed them. For some reason, Abby didn't strike him as the kind of girl who said no often. He recalled the comment he'd heard in the pub yesterday, when that pissed-up bloke had told him that she'd sleep with anyone who bought her a drink.

He stared at his face in the mirror above the sink. His eyes were red, the skin around them swollen. His lips were dry and his teeth looked yellow.

"Morning, handsome," he said, tilting his head and grinning.

He brushed his teeth, took a piss that seemed to last forever, and left the room. This time he'd managed not to look over at the other bedroom door. He went straight for the stairs and walked down them silently, as if afraid to be heard.

He turned at the bottom and saw her through the kitchen doorway. She was bending over the table, setting out a couple of plates and some cutlery. Her short dressing gown had hitched up over her thighs. There were old, faded scars there that he'd failed to notice the night before and faint marks like old bruises that had never healed.

Marc felt like running, but he told himself not to be stupid, not to judge this woman before he even knew her.

She turned around and saw him, a smile appearing briefly on her face before it was swallowed by some other expression, one that he could not read. Was it regret? Dread? Terror?

"Morning." He walked towards the kitchen doorway.

"Hi," she said, turning away. "I made bacon and eggs. I hope you're hungry."

"Cheers," he said, sitting down at the table. "That would be great."

"Coffee?" She didn't turn to look at him when she asked the question.

"Black, thanks. One sugar."

She nodded, but still didn't turn.

He watched her as she poured hot water into two mugs Her shoulders were narrow, her arms were thin. She was tiny, breakable. Like a porcelain doll. Last night she'd seemed more like a warrior.

"Here." She turned and set down one of the mugs on the table. The handle of the spoon stuck up above the rim. He grabbed it and began to stir, slowly. "Food's nearly ready."

"Thanks." He stopped stirring. "How do you feel this morning?"

She tensed. "What do you mean?"

"Well..." He wished he hadn't started this; he should have just kept his mouth shut, or maybe talked about the weather. "You know. After we... what happened between us."

"After we fucked, you mean?"

He was shocked, but what stunned him more was his reaction to her words. He'd expected her to be like this, so why did it have such an impact? "Yes," he said. He took a sip of coffee.

"I feel fine. I'm used to it. You'll probably hear this anyway, so I'll tell you now." She turned to face him. Her eyes were large, glaring. Her cheeks were tensed. "I'm a slag. I'll fuck anyone, me. It's what I do, just so I don't feel so alone. It doesn't make you anything special."

Marc wasn't sure what he was meant to say, so he went with a joke: "You say the nicest things."

There was a pause, and then she smiled. Even her eyes lit up. "Thanks." She turned back to the cooker and started serving up the bacon and scrambled egg. She'd made too much, but she piled it onto the plates anyway.

"This looks good." He stared at the plate of food. He wasn't lying. It looked fantastic. The bacon was well done, just the way he liked it, and the eggs weren't too soft.

"Eat up, then," she said.

He took one mouthful and his stomach began to ache. He answered this by shovelling in more food, unashamed at how ill-mannered he was coming across. He was starving. Ravenous. He'd never felt so hungry in his life.

"I like to see a man with a big appetite," she said. She hadn't touched her own food. Clearly she preferred to watch him eat.

Marc took a break halfway through, gasping for breath. He swigged his coffee like a navvy on a tea-break, enjoying the way he almost choked on the now lukewarm liquid. He wiped his mouth with the back of his hand, almost slobbering. "Jesus... you must think I'm a pig."

Abby shook her head. "I worked you hard last night." Beneath the table, he felt her bare foot touch his leg, rubbing along his shin bone. "You need to replace that energy."

"About last night..." He shook his head when the cliché came out of his mouth. "Fuck, that sounds crap. I'm sorry. I'm trying to be original, I really am."

She shook her head. "Don't worry. I've been here before, too many times. I know the script by heart. It was a one-night stand. You don't want to see me again. Don't even want my number."

"No, wait..."

"It's fine. Really, it is. I don't want to give you my number anyway. I'm not after a boyfriend, or even a fuck buddy. I don't need anybody permanent in my life."

"Listen, that's not what I meant."

She stopped talking, started pushing the eggs around her plate with a fork.

"I meant the opposite, actually. I... I would like to see you again. I do want your number."

She raised her eyes and stared directly into his face, as if examining him for facial scars. Her eyes narrowed, her nostrils flared.

"My daughter wasn't the first one to go missing. She was the fourth. The final one."

Marc said nothing. He didn't want to break the spell. That's exactly how it felt; as if some kind of magic was being weaved, some form of urban witchcraft.

"The Press called them the Gone Away Girls. It has a nice ring to it, doesn't it? Like poetry, or a song lyric. They loved that fucking name, the reporters. They used it all the time...I think they were gutted when my Tessa was the last and they didn't get to use it again, except whenever they resurrected the case to sell some extra copies." She was rubbing her hands, as if soaping them at the sink, trying to scrub off the dirt.

Marc put down his knife and fork. "You don't have to tell me any of this. It's okay. I understand. It's personal."

She stood, carried her plate to the sink, and left it there. Then she sat back down at the table. "Tess's father is still around. He lived in the area. Not in the Grove, not anymore, but nearby. He comes round here sometimes. I don't know what he's looking for, but he always wants to have sex. He cries when he comes. He weeps like a baby into my shoulder."

Marc sat and stared as she spoke, unable to focus his thoughts. Was this a brush-off, or something else? The woman was maddening. She always made him feel as if he'd not quite understood what she'd said, or had missed the crucial point of the conversation.

"I think he wants to save me," said Abby, looking down at the table, still wringing her hands. "But that's the last thing I need. They always, always want to save me, and not once do they stop to even think that I might not want to be fucking saved." Her eyes were shining. She blinked several times before continuing. "Just promise me one thing, Marc. Promise me that you won't try to save me."

He could not fight her. The will was too strong.

"I... I promise," he said, not entirely sure what kind of promise he was making. It felt so much wider, deeper, than what she'd asked.

She nodded her head. "That's the only thing I'll ever ask of you, and if you break that promise I'll ask you to leave and never come back again." She stood and went to a cupboard, opened the door and took out a cardboard box file. "Every man I've ever met seems to think I want to be saved, when all I want is a nice fuck and a warm body next to me at night."

She dropped the box file onto the table and stepped back, folding her arms across her tiny chest. "There they are. The Gone Away Girls."

Marc reached out and opened the file. Inside was a sheaf of newspaper clippings, each one reporting the disappearance of a young girl. By the second one – Alice Jacobs – they were already using the collective title Gone Away Girls. Abby was right; they'd been in love with their own invention.

He flipped through the clippings, not reading them but skimming, noting the similar details of each case: a young girl, taken from a place that was considered safe, never seen again. He wondered why he'd never heard of this, especially since he was a journalist. But he'd been working freelance at the time of these abductions, and living in Birmingham for much of the time. Five years ago... where exactly had he been then? It was difficult to pinpoint because he'd moved around so much, chasing stories, looking for the big score that never came. Maybe he'd even been in London, on one of his regular trips to the city? He could never quite settle there, but he always stayed at least a month, sleeping in friends' spare rooms or on their floors. But he always returned to the north; he always failed to find the big story, the one that would set him up for life...

He wished he'd been the one to coin the term Gone Away Girls. It was a classic, the kind of epithet that lasted, sank deep into the consciousness of everyone interested in the case. He didn't even feel bad about his envy. He was used to having thoughts like these, and so familiar with the mercenary thought processes of journalism that he'd moved far beyond any vestigial sense of shame years ago.

He put away the clippings and closed the file. Abby was still staring at him. Her eyes were flat; her mouth was a tight little line. "I don't know what you want me to say."

Abby unfolded her arms. She reached down and took the file, clutching it tightly against her chest. "Just remember my little girl's face, and appreciate that I don't need saving." She turned back to the cupboard and put away the file, pushing it right to the back. When she straightened up again, she turned around and leaned the small of her back against the work bench.

They stared at each other in silence.

Somebody began to knock on the front door, quietly at first but with increasing vigour.

Abby glanced over towards the open kitchen door, and the hallway beyond. The knocking continued. Marc looked along the hallway. At the front door, he could see the fuzzy outline of a head beyond the frosted glass.

"Aren't you going to answer that?"

She shrugged. Her fingers were fidgeting with the buttons on her dressing gown. She crossed her legs at the ankle, one over the other.

Marc finished his coffee.

The knocking grew louder. Then a man's voice said, "Open the door. I know you're in there."

Marc pushed his chair a few inches away from the table, wincing as the legs screeched across the cheap laminated floor covering. He stood and turned towards the back door. "Maybe I should go."

"No," said Abby. "No, it's okay. I'll deal with this. You just sit down and have another cup of coffee." She reached for the kettle and flicked the switch to set the water to boil again. "I won't be a minute." She moved quickly across the room, closing the door on her way out. The edge of the door bounced when it hit the frame, opening again, but just a couple of inches. He moved across the front of the table, positioning himself so that he could see through the gap. He watched Abby's white-gowned figure as she approached the door. She smoothed the gown across her hips, flicked her head to shift the hair from out of her eyes, and opened the front door.

Marc couldn't quite see the man clearly. The doorstep was set down lower than the hallway floor, and Abby's thin body further obscured his view. They spoke quietly. The man must not be annoyed after all. Perhaps he was merely concerned. Abby glanced over her shoulder a couple of times, as if she were talking about him. The man attempted to manoeuvre his way past her and through the doorway, but she angled her body to block him.

"Come back later," he heard her say. "I'm busy."

"Who's in there?" The man's head, with his close-cropped hair, bobbed up and down, back and forth, trying to see past her and into the house. He had a thick neck. He wasn't tall, but he was broad through the shoulders.

Marc jumped in shock when the kettle clicked off. He turned and watched the steam as it rose in a smooth line from the spout. He walked over and made himself another cup of instant. His hands were shaking. Behind him, the door slammed shut. Footsteps padded along the hallway, towards the kitchen door.

Let her be alone, he thought. *I don't want any trouble.*

When he turned to face the door, she entered the room and sat down at the table. Her eyes were red, as if she'd been crying, or fighting tears. Her face was white but there were pink streaks on her cheeks.

"Are you... are you okay?"

"Yeah." She looked up, trying to smile, but it didn't quite work. "I'm fine."

"Who was that?" He wished he hadn't asked, but the reporter's instinct never let him down: he always, always asked the questions that came into his head, as if he did not possess a mental cut-off switch.

"Just an ex-boyfriend... He pesters me sometimes, wants me to have him back."

"Oh." He blew on his coffee. Suddenly he didn't want the drink.

"Listen, I'm sorry but that bastard's upset me. Can you go?"

He put the mug down on the work bench and stepped away. Suddenly he didn't know what to do with his empty hands. "Yes, I'll go. Give you a bit of peace."

"Thank you," she said, as if she really meant it.

"Can I have your number?" Again, he wished he'd never asked.

She stared at him, her eyes boring into his, her lips parting slightly. "Are you sure? Are you really sure you want it?" She was challenging him, making him prove that he was man enough.

"Yes. I'm sure."

She nodded. There was a fruit bowl in the centre of the table. As far as he could tell, it contained nothing but a couple of apples and several dried-out tangerines. She reached into it and withdrew a stubby little betting shop pen, then wrote down her number on a slip of paper she produced from her dressing gown pocket – as if she'd been carrying it around with her for this exact moment.

Marc stepped forward and held out his hand.

She placed the folded paper on his palm. "Give me a call," she said. "But remember what I said."

"Don't worry. I won't try to save you." He could see by the look in her eyes that she didn't believe him, but she was willing to give him a chance.

"I'll call you a taxi," she said, standing. Her dressing gown gaped below the waist, flashing her narrow thighs, the unkempt patch between her legs. Marc felt himself grow hard again.

He gritted his teeth. "No thanks. My car's parked near the Unicorn. I can walk over and get it."

"Whatever," said Abby, and turned away.

They stood in the hallway, standing with their backs against opposing walls, facing each other, with a foot or two of carpet between them. Even in her bare feet, she stood a few inches taller than him.

Marc wanted to reach out his hand and unbuckle her dressing gown. She didn't say a word; she just watched him, her eyes examining every inch of his face, his eyes, his mouth, his throat... looking for his all-too-visible flaws.

Marc was lost in the moment, falling into her seedy little world and drowning in whatever it was he found there.

"Well," he said, softly.

"Yeah," she replied.

He left the house without saying anything more, and did not look back. He couldn't. If he turned around and saw her there, standing on the doorstep in her short white dressing gown, he might just turn back and go inside. But he wasn't ready for that; he needed to think things through, to decide if he really did want to use the number she'd given him.

He walked in the direction of the Unicorn and read the number. Abby had not written a message, only the digits. Finally he turned his head and looked back. She was still standing in the doorway, a tall, white figure with painfully thin legs.

She lifted her left hand, waved once, and then turned around and went inside, slamming the door behind her.

CHAPTER SEVEN

ERIK BEST SAT in his car and watched the man leave. He gripped the wheel with his scarred hands, staring through the windscreen. The man moved away slowly, as if there was all the time in the world. Erik knew otherwise; experience had taught him that time was a limited resource and had to be used sparingly.

Just before the man reached the end of the street, he turned back to look at Abby. She was standing on the doorstep waving, her free hand clutching her dressing gown at the throat. She turned and went inside. The door slammed shut.

He remembered when he used to love her, and wondered what those feelings had now changed into. What he felt for Abby these days wasn't love; he had no idea what it was. He supposed it might even be described as a form of hate. He couldn't stand seeing her but he always went back; he hated the way she looked these days but he kept dreaming about making love to her, lying with her beneath clean satin sheets. Nothing made any sense. His emotions were like the colours in a kaleidoscope, constantly changing and blending and making new patterns.

"Bitch," he said, starting the car. He pulled out from the kerb and slowly followed the man around the corner, staying far enough back that the bastard would not guess that he was being followed.

He reached out and switched on the radio – a local station discussing the big Premiership match in a few days. Erik shook his head and changed the channel. He'd stopped caring about football when the game changed so much that it was barely a contact sport, and all the players became prancing millionaires. He preferred boxing, or martial arts. Sports in which real men challenged for dominance, not overpaid prima donnas with overactive libidos.

Erik watched the man climb into a boxy little Nissan and drive away. He followed the Nissan off the estate and towards the A1. He had no idea where it was heading, but he was going to follow until it got there. He'd grown up in this area, knew its roads and highways by heart. Wherever this car stopped, he would be familiar with the location in some way. He'd probably done business nearby. Erik Best had done some kind of business everywhere in the northeast.

The Nissan eventually headed into Gosforth, along the High Street towards the Gosforth Hotel pub, where it turned right and continued up the slight hill. Erik had a couple of mates who drank regularly in the pub, and he'd enjoyed some good nights there, getting pissed and picking up women, often getting into a fight after last orders was called at the bar and they were forced to relocate to some other late-night drinking establishment.

The Nissan pulled in at the kerb outside a small terraced house with dingy curtains. The tiny patch of garden outside the front door was overgrown with weeds. The door itself was dirty and weathered. There was a To Let sign stuck in the tiny patch of soil underneath the front window, as if nobody had bothered to take it down because these properties went up and down for rental so often.

Erik stopped the car a little further along the street and waited, watching in the rear-view mirror as the man got out and started fumbling in his pocket for his house keys. He was about medium height, but skinny. Erik would have no trouble with this one. He gripped the wheel with his hands and emptied his mind of distractions. This was it: he needed to be turned on, tuned in, and ready to dance. This was his comfort zone; he only ever felt at home when he was about to do violence.

He got out of the car and walked briskly towards the man. He'd done this so many times before, and his timing was always immaculate. Just as the man inserted his key into the lock, Erik glanced behind him, just to check on the surroundings. The street was clear. Nobody was standing outside their house or at their front door, watching the street. There was a sense of quiet abandonment, as often there was in suburban streets in the early morning.

The man opened the door; Erik increased his pace and went right up behind him, pushing him against and then through the opening door and into a cramped hallway beyond. He reached behind him and shut the door, forcing the man right inside. He said nothing. He let his muscles do the talking.

The man staggered, regained his footing, and turned to face Erik. He looked shocked but still under control. He had no idea who he was looking at.

"Hello," said Erik, smiling. He'd practised the smile for hours in front of the mirror when he was younger, and knew that it made an impression. The smile made him look slightly insane, but just about sane enough to make whoever it was turned upon do whatever he said. At least until the shock wore off.

It was the smile of a killer, and he was proud of being able to summon it to order.

"Go inside. I'm right behind you." He made the smile wider. "Don't try anything silly."

The man did as he was told, walking slowly but tensely along the hallway and through a door on the left.

Erik entered the small living room behind the fucker, stopping in front of the door, blocking the exit. Behind the man – who had turned to face Erik as he entered – there was another doorway that led into a sunken galley kitchen. There would be a back door in there, one that led out into the yard, but it would be locked. Even if this dude bolted, he wouldn't get the door open in time.

"Who are you? What the fuck do you want?" The man was regaining his composure. He clearly felt embarrassed about obeying a stranger's orders in his own home. Bravado was beginning to take hold.

"My name is Erik Best. Now shut the fuck up and tell me your name, and what you're doing with Abby Hansen." He waited, staring at the man. Still smiling, his hands open but ready for action.

"I don't have to tell you anything. Get out, or I'll call the police."

Erik sighed theatrically and looked over at the phone. "Go on," he said. "Try it. I reckon that phone's about ten yards from where you're standing. I'm five yards away from you. If you think you can make it across the room, pick up the phone, and tell them what's going on before I get to you... well, you're welcome to try it. I could do with the workout." He shifted his weight from one foot to the other. It was done for effect, but it also made him feel ready to pounce, like an animal in the wild. His leather shoes creaked. The clock on the wall ticked away the seconds.

The man shifted his gaze away from the phone and looked back at Erik. "My name's Marc Price. Now, would you please just leave?"

Erik shook his head. "I'm not planning to hurt you, Marc. Not this time, anyway. All I want is information. Understood?"

Price nodded. He backed away; just a step, but it betrayed his intense fear. "I don't know what you're after, but I have no money. Look at this house – it's a shithole. I don't even own it. There's nothing of value here."

"Right, let's just relax. Now tell me what you're doing hanging around Abby Hansen's place, marra. Can you do that?"

"We... she... we're friends." He looked down, at the top of his shoes. His cheeks flushed. He'd been caught out and he knew it.

"So you picked her up last night, went back to her place and had a good shag?"

Price nodded. He didn't look up.

"It's okay. Like I said, I'm not going to hurt you. This is simply a warning. Okay, marra?"

Silence; the slow *tick-tock* sound of the clock on the wall; the gentle creak of leather as Erik took a soft step towards the other man, his feet moving lightly across the carpeted floor.

Price looked up. His eyes were wide. His mouth was open, the lips slightly apart. Those lips were trembling.

"Leave her alone, marra. She's had enough trouble over the years and doesn't need any more. You don't know her. You have no idea what she's been through. She doesn't need fly-by-night fuckers like you stuffing one up her and taking the piss out of her grief."

Price tried to inflate his chest. He took a deep breath. "Listen, mate, I'm sure Abby can make her own decisions. She's a big girl. She doesn't need someone like you looking after her. Let me guess... are you the ex-boyfriend that came round there earlier? Maybe one of those sad bastards she told me about, the ones who won't take no for an answer." There was sweat on his brow and his upper lip. "The kind of bloke who follows her around like a lost puppy, trying to catch a sniff of her so he can wank about it later."

Erik sighed; he shook his head.

Was he going to have to use violence after all, simply to get his point across to this idiot?

He planned the moves in his head: a brisk step inside, throw a quick, short uppercut to the chin; step back out again, deliver a hard right hook to the side of the head. Easy, so fucking easy... The kid wouldn't get back up for a long time.

He smiled. "This is a friendly warning, marra. Next time I won't be as gentle." He clenched his hands into fists, raised them to stomach level. It would be good to knock the fucker out, but that wasn't his purpose today, not if he could help it.

"Next time I won't come to your house. I'll wait somewhere else for you, the place you'd least expect to see me. In fact, you *won't* see me. You won't even feel it when it comes."

"I don't want any hassle." Price's posture was loose now; he'd finally lost his nerve. He wanted to run; it was obvious in the way he was carrying himself. No violence was required, after all. "We just fucked, mate. That was all. It was a one-night stand. I believe she's had a few others in the past... that's what she told me. I'm not the first... no way will I be the last."

Erik winced, and he hated himself for showing his emotions to this stranger.

Abby was so easy; she always gave herself away so damned cheaply, and to men who didn't even realise how special she was. He clenched the muscles in his jaw, ground his teeth together. "Just let that one fuck be the last, and then we won't have any problems, you and me. Got that, marra?"

Price's gaze flickered back and forth, as if he were looking for a weapon. Part of Erik hoped that he spotted one and tried to use it. He didn't like the way the bastard was talking about Abby; he showed no respect for her, as if his night in her bed had meant nothing.

"Yeah..." Price's shoulders relaxed. He deflated fully; his shoulders slumped, his chest shifted inward. The bravado was fading; the fight was leaving him quicker than it had arrived. "Yeah, okay. I don't need this shit. Not for the sake of an opportunist fuck."

"Now, tell me what you're doing sniffing around the Grove."

Price ran a hand through his hair. He was a good-looking guy. This made Erik dislike him even more. "Listen, I'm a freelance reporter. I've been researching a book. That's all. Nothing suspicious about that, is there?"

Erik laughed. "You're writing a book about the Concrete Grove?" His anger dissipated; there'd be no blood spilled today. He wasn't even in the mood. "Jesus Christ, marra, that's a good one."

"No, no... Not exactly. I'm writing a book about the Northumberland Poltergeist. Ghosts are back in fashion – I'm just trying to jump on the bandwagon and make some quick cash." He shrugged, still afraid but calming down a little, realising that he was not going to be beaten up.

Erik shook his head. "Man, that's fucking priceless... The Northumberland Poltergeist. I haven't heard that name in years."

"Now," said Price, raising his open hands, pointing at the door. "Would you mind getting the fuck out of my house? You've done what you came here to do: I'm scared. I'm terrified, actually, if it makes you feel any better. I won't be messing around with Abby again. Now, just leave me alone."

Erik paused, and then he turned and walked out of the room. When he reached the door he opened it, turned around, and said "Remember what I said. Oh, and don't even think about doing anything daft, like phoning the police." He took the silence as an affirmative response and shut the door behind him as he left the house.

Walking back towards his car, he looked up at the sky. The clouds were dark, troubled. He knew how they felt. His entire life was nothing but trouble – one long succession of bad things, queuing up to make their mark. Situations like this one happened to him all the time. It often felt as if he was dogged by bad things, like stray cats following him in a line along the street.

Erik unlocked the car and got inside. He turned on the engine and killed the radio, and then just sat there, staring at the sky, at those grumbling clouds, waiting for more trouble to come for him.

CHAPTER EIGHT

Marc took a bottle of whisky from the cupboard in the kitchen and opened it. His hands were shaking; his mouth was dry. He didn't like violence, never had. Before the accident, his old man had been quick with his fists, especially on points of honour. He'd even hit Marc a few times when he was a small boy, but he was certain it didn't run in the family.

Some people thought of Marc as a coward, but that wasn't quite true. Hadn't he just stood up to that psycho who'd forced his way inside the house? Well... sort of. Until his nerve had gone.

No, he wasn't a coward. He just hated physical violence. He was terrified of it. He'd seen the results of true violence a lot in his job, particularly when he'd worked on the crime pages. Beatings, murders, suicides... he'd reported all kinds of messy situations. He knew what a gunshot wound looked like, and had examined stab wounds at close range. Once he'd even stood there while a young woman who'd thrown herself in front of a truck on a busy motorway was scraped up off the road by policemen armed with snow shovels.

He poured an inch of whisky into a glass, and then added another inch because he knew the first wouldn't last long. He took a swallow and felt the pleasing burn in his throat. It felt good, purifying.

He'd always liked the taste of good malt whisky, and right now it tasted even better than ever. The drink was good medicine for whatever ailed him.

He thought about Abby Hansen, and asked himself if she was really worth this kind of hassle. The answer, he was sad to discover, was yes. He tried to convince himself that he was mistaken, but it was no use: he was becoming mildly obsessed with her.

But what was it about her that drew him? Why could he not stop thinking about the woman? She wasn't his usual type – he liked hefty, athletic brunettes with big thighs and even bigger chests – and she could hardly be described as a great beauty. Her hair was badly dyed and in terrible condition; her skin was dry; her body was wracked by alcohol and the effects of borderline malnutrition.

So why the hell was he so keen to go back there, to see her, to fuck her again – no matter what Erik Best had told him? Why did he want to climb back into her bed and spend another night with her, clinging to her slender form in the darkness of her grotty little house?

He drifted from the kitchen to the living room, running a hand across the dust on the top of the television. There was a photo on there, held in an expensive frame. It showed Marc aged six; and there were his parents, flanking him and smiling at the camera. His dad looked stocky and aggressive, even when he grinned. His mother just looked tired. She'd always looked that way, right up to the day that they both died. He couldn't remember a time when she hadn't looked exhausted.

He recalled the day he'd lost his parents as if it were only yesterday: the memory was imprinted on his brain, too perfect, as if it had been put there by someone else.

He'd been in the car with them, strapped into the back seat and reading a comic – *Superman*, of all things. The car had skidded on the wet road. It had been nobody's fault, just one of those fluke accidents that happen every now and then, as if God was getting a bit bored and needed some entertainment, so he decided to wipe out somebody's folks in the rain.

His mother had been driving, and when the wheels locked she didn't know what to do. The car had moved slowly, as if it was on a conveyor belt, edging sideways towards the edge of the road and the sheer drop into a farmer's field below. He remembered looking out of the side window and watching the drop approach, and then glancing into the front to see his parents holding hands and staring into each other's eyes. Again, this memory was more like a movie than something that had actually happened. It was simultaneously distant and up-close, as if he were separated from the image by a sheet of glass.

Still, they could have survived the crash. That's what everyone told him, even now. It was a fluke, a crazy accident. The car had tilted and the outcropping branch of a tree had smashed through the passenger side window, almost taking off his mother's head, tearing away her chin and smashing her teeth, causing her to choke to death on fragments of her own skull. His father had been turned to face her at the time, and the branch had slowly sheared off his face as he screamed his life away.

Marc's mother had died comparatively quickly – the collapsed red ruin of her head was proof of that.

But it had taken his father a long time to go because the car was falling so slowly... Marc had seen it all, and he still saw it now, whenever he dreamed. His mother's sunken, partially crushed head, his father's red-screaming skull... another film; a succession of images that played out on a mental screen whenever he closed his eyes.

At first he didn't like to dream. For a long time, he'd taken drugs to stop the dreams from coming. Then, when they stopped working, he simply accepted them, imagining them his penance for surviving the accident. He almost welcomed them now, and it scared him that he did this so willingly.

They hadn't been very good parents, not particularly. But they'd been the only ones he had, and after that he had none. He was left with no one, except a distant uncle who at first had treated him like a lodger who rented a room in his home rather than an orphaned family member. After a while – as he developed into a young man – Uncle Mike's attitude had softened. He'd started to show affection. They became a small, weird family unit for a short while, at least until Marc was old enough to leave and go to University. After that, he'd lost touch with Uncle Mike, until he'd received a call one Saturday afternoon telling him that the man was dead.

He took another drink and sat down on the sofa, trying to clear his mind. Images of his dead parents mingled with those of Abby's naked body, and the effect made him feel dirty and ashamed. Her bony body; his father's fists; her tiny breasts; his mother's smile; blood and semen; love and hate; sex and death. He blinked, rubbed at his temples, and leaned back against the sofa, allowing the cushions to grasp him. He leaned forward again to pick up his glass and then back again to try and relax. He felt like he was being pushed and pulled in every direction but the one he wanted to move in. He always felt like that; his life was a series of manoeuvres designed to shove him one way and then the next, without taking into consideration his desires. He was always dodging something – the past, the present, or simply himself – rather than moving with any clear direction in mind.

"Fucking hell..." He reached out and grabbed the remote control, flicked on the television to distract his thoughts. He picked a music channel and turned up the volume. Some ragtag indie band he'd never heard of capered across the screen, playing toy instruments and wailing about lost love. He let the music wash over him. It wasn't bad; he'd heard worse. He even started to hum along with the chorus, once he picked up on the tune.

Who the hell had that guy been, the one who'd invaded his home? Erik Best. The name meant nothing to him. He wasn't the biggest man Marc had ever encountered, but he was certainly the scariest. Not too tall, but broad through the shoulder, his hair buzzed down to a skinhead cut. He exuded a sense of menace like no one else Marc had ever met.

Marc had come across dangerous people before, and had even interviewed a few gangster types when he was working on stories for the cheaper red-top papers. He remembered speaking to convicted murderers, rapists, drug addicts... but none of them had possessed the sense of barely repressed violence that his visitor had sweated from his very pores.

The man was terrifying. He didn't even have to do anything to generate fear; all he needed was a few words, a simple gesture, a calmly worded warning... that was more than enough to get his point across.

"You idiot..." He knew that he was going to see Abby Hansen again, despite what the man had said. He kept picturing her naked, or on all fours on the mattress, pressing lazily against him as he thrust into her. She'd made love the same way she acted outside of the bed: unbothered, nonchalant, she couldn't give a damn.

Jesus, was that it, just because she didn't seem to care? Was that why he wanted to see her again – to try and force her to care, or even to pretend? Was he really so shallow? Or so desperate to make her like him, want him?

None of this made any sense. He'd acted strangely in the past, often embarking upon relationships with unsuitable partners, or starting situations that he knew would end badly. But this was another dimension entirely. He didn't even like the woman. Nor was he attracted to her, not really. But he wanted to fuck her so much that he felt the desire as a constant ache in the pit of his stomach.

He'd heard stories from some of his wilder drinking buddies about affairs with what they called "dirty women" – back street slappers, rough trade, even full-blown whores – but not once had he been tempted to follow their lead and go after someone he deemed that kind of person. And was Abby really like that? Was that how he saw her?

No; she wasn't a dirty woman. Abby was damaged, she was almost crippled by her loss and her grief, but she wasn't one of those women some of his nasty-minded friends prized as perverse trophies.

Perhaps he was simply attracted to her pain. He was self-aware enough to realise that he'd done this before, forged a relationship with someone who had experienced a similar kind of loss to his own. But that had been years ago, when he was young and didn't understand his own motivations. He was older now; he knew what he was doing and why he did it. These days he tended to deliberately forge bonds with people who were well balanced, emotionally centred... or not forge bonds at all. His own pain was enough. He no longer needed to mix it with someone else's.

Except now all that was changing... and he had developed this strange infatuation with a women which whom he'd only spent a single night. Was that really enough to justify this level of craving?

Craving.

It was an interesting word. It sounded the way it felt: hard, sharp, and dangerous.

He finished his drink and stood up to get another. He'd left the bottle in the kitchen rather than bring it through into the main room. He didn't want to get drunk. He knew that if he did, he might just get out the piece of paper with Abby's number written on it and give her a call. Say hello. Beg her to let him go round there.

The phone rang as he was entering the kitchen. He put down the glass and turned back into the living room, trying to remember where he'd put his mobile. His jacket; it was in his jacket pocket. He moved across the room, picked up his jacket from the arm of the sofa, and started prodding at the pockets. He felt the hard rectangle of the phone through the material, grabbed it, and answered.

"Yeah."

"Hello... Marc? Is this Marc Price?"

He recognised the voice but couldn't place its owner. "Yes, this is Marc. What's up?"

"Marc, this is Vince... Vince Rose, from yesterday. I'm sorry to call like this... I hope I'm not disturbing you."

Marc remembered the old man, and how they'd promised to keep in touch. "Oh, yeah... Hi. How are you?"

"Listen, Marc, I'm at my brother's house. I'm at Harry's place. I've found some stuff that you might like to see. Are you free at all any time today?"

He looked at his watch. It wasn't even noon. "Tell you what, offer me some lunch and a couple of cans of lager and I'll be round in half an hour. How does that sound?"

"Splendid," said Rose. "That would be fine. I'll pop out to the shop and get us some booze and sandwich makings. There's tea and coffee here, but not much else." He paused, as if he couldn't quite select the right words he needed to continue. "I think it's in your interest to see what I've found... there might be something useful here. Perhaps even something that'll help you with your book. I'm not sure what most of this stuff is, but I think it'll mean a lot more to you than it does to me."

The book: Marc had almost forgotten about the fucking book.

The project had really started to come alive for him when he'd met Harry Rose, and he was afraid that it might die along with the old man if he didn't make an effort to carry on with his research. But this phone call seemed promising; it might lead to the book actually being finished. He already had a publisher interested, and if he managed to show them something interesting the advance would pay his bills for a few more months of freedom while he weighed up his options.

"I'll see you soon, Vince. We'll talk more then. I can't wait to see what you've found there." His lips were dry. He hung up the phone and headed back towards the kitchen.

Just one more drink, he thought. *It wouldn't hurt. One more little drink for the road...*

CHAPTER NINE

THE LIGHTS ARE off. The house is silent. A solemn gloom fills the empty rooms, making them seem occupied by something patient and unmoving; a thing that lies in wait.

Abby Hansen is flat on her back, naked, in the bed that she once shared with Tessa's father. Her eyes are open, but she does not see. Her legs are parted and her hands are cupped there, over her pudenda, in a protective gesture. The bedroom curtains are closed, filtering out the light, but the room is nowhere near dark at this time of day.

The house creaks and settles. Other noises sound outside: car engines, yelling children, somebody calling loudly for a dog or a child named Socrates. Far off, a police helicopter prowls the skies, its unseen occupants looking for wrongdoers.

Abby does not move. She hears none of these sounds. The only noises she registers are internal: trees and brushes rustling within the confines of her mind, the gentle thrumming of a tiny bird's wings, a small animal padding through undergrowth, and a light breeze stirring close to the ground.

She sits up jerkily and stares at the wall – *through* the wall, to whatever it is that dwells in the places nobody else can see, the gaps in the world that only a few people can discern. She stays that way for several minutes, not moving, barely even breathing, just staring blindly through the solid brickwork. She does not even blink.

Abby Hansen has one foot in this world and one in another, far stranger place.

She is conscious but she is not awake; nor is she asleep, not really.

Whatever she does during this fugue-like state, she will remember nothing of it later. She will simply assume that she took a nap; that the previous night's exertions tired her out and she's been catching up on her rest. After all, a woman like Abby needs all the rest she can get these days.

A car radio booms outside the house; tinny dance music fills the street. Somebody starts to shout and swear; another voice joins in, but softer, less aggressive. Laughter. A car wheel-spinning away along the road, churning up loose stones. The music fades into the distance, becoming an imitation of itself, just another sad piece of aural flotsam cast adrift on the currents of life.

Still Abby Hansen does not blink. She does not move. She grips herself between the legs, as if she needs to urinate, or masturbate – perhaps she's caught between the two acts, unsure of which is the more appropriate response.

After a short while, she twitches. It is just a slight jerk of the head, which she then tilts to the side, like a dog listening to its master's call. She removes her hands from between her thighs. Her fingers are wet; her pubic hair glistens. The muscles in her thighs are twitching rhythmically, as if a weak electrical current is passing through them.

She slides her legs across the duvet, placing her feet on the floor and twisting to face the door. She sits like that for quite some time, as if waiting to be summoned into another room. Her face is blank, expressionless; her hands are open at her sides, as if she is balancing an invisible item in each palm. She rubs her still damp fingers together, then raises her hands and licks away the residue.

She freezes, her head still tilted to one side.

Finally, she moves again. In one smooth, clean motion, she stands and turns to face the door. Her movements are much more graceful than usual, like those of a dancer. She steps lightly across the room, her bare feet making little sound on the carpet. She walks slowly and softly, barely making an impact on the world – either this world or the other, the one contained within her. As her reflection passes across the glass of the long mirror on her dressing table, she does not even glance that way. She walks through the door and out onto the landing, not noticing that her reflection is fuzzy, faded, as if she is barely there at all.

She knows who she is – she is aware of her name – but that is all. She has no past, no future; all that exists is the present, this moment. Nothing else matters; it isn't there, doesn't touch her at all.

She reaches the stairs and descends them silently, heading down and towards the kitchen. She walks across the kitchen floor, to the cupboard under the sink. Bending her legs in a fluid motion, lunging so deeply that her bare buttocks almost brush against the floor tiles, she opens the cupboard door. Her head does not move; she keeps it fixed straight ahead. The muscles in her neck are tensed and bunched, standing out like cables beneath the skin.

She takes a small plastic bag filled with candles out of the cupboard, closes the door, and stands up straight. The candles are the type used for decorating cakes. These are all she has in the house. She turns around and goes into the living room, where she picks up a photograph of Tessa. The one she took in the park, a few days before the girl disappeared. In the photo, Tessa is wearing her bright red quilted gilet over a grey long-sleeved fleecy top, and her favourite dark jeans and running shoes. It is the same outfit she was wearing the day she vanished.

Abby moves across the room, not caring that she is naked. Her thighs are soaked; she's been secreting sweat from her skin and fluid from her vagina, as if her waters are breaking prior to giving birth.

The curtains are open but nobody is passing by in the street outside. She opens the bureau beside the bookcase and takes out a brown package. She unfolds the paper package and removes the old pair of Tessa's pyjamas, the ones the girl was wearing the night before she went away. They are still stained with her urine. She wet the bed that night for the first time in years, as if she was afraid of something or experienced a premonition of what was to come.

She returns to the stairs and ascends, holding tightly onto these items. She turns right at the top of the stairs and stands outside Tessa's room, gazing at – no, *through* – the door with her thousand-yard stare. If she is aware of anything around her, she does not betray this on her face. Her eyes are still open, but they are like the eyes of the blind: wide, empty, unseeing. Glazed. For all she sees of her surroundings, they might as well be shut tight.

She reaches out without looking and opens the bedroom door. She steps inside and closes the door behind her.

The curtains are closed to ensure that the room is dim; she always keeps it this way, as a form of tribute. This room is not meant to see the sun again until her child returns.

She approaches the shrine she's made and kneels down beside it. She places the photograph on the floor, and then begins to arrange the candles around the base of the crude pyramid. Inside the bag where the candles were stored is also a box of kitchen matches. When she's finished setting out the candles, she lights them one by one with a match. She does not look down, but she doesn't burn her fingers. Her body knows exactly what to do. This is not the first time she has carried out this homespun ritual, despite the fact that she has no memory of doing so before or afterwards. Like an athlete's muscle memory, her body stores the information and carries out the task without even bothering her mind.

Once the candles are lighted, she takes hold of the pyjamas and presses them against her face, inhaling the smell of her missing daughter's dried piss. Still there is no expression on her face.

She puts down the pyjamas and tucks her legs and feet beneath her bottom, drawing in her knees tight in front of her. Slowly, she begins to rock on her knees and calves, back and forth; a small, rhythmic movement. She smells wet grass and hears the rustling of tree branches. Somewhere beyond the grove of ancient oaks, a small figure is waiting. She cannot identify who this person is, but it seems familiar.

More liquid leaks out from between her legs.

She feels the wet grass under her legs. The wind blows against her skin, rising slowly. Branches creak; tiny animals move in the undergrowth. It is dark within the protective circle of the trees. She is outside, naked, but does not feel the cold. The light of the moon keeps her warm, even though it is a cold light, a dead light whose warmth can never reach her. Menstrual blood runs down the inside of her thighs; the animals hiding in the trees smell it and began to whine, like wolves scenting fresh meat. They are hungry. They need to feed.

Abby opens her mouth and begins to chant:

"*Tessa, Tessa, Tessa... bless her, bless her, bless her... come back to me.*"

Her voice is dull, flat. There is no sing-song quality to the chant, but still it is a song of sorrow, a short chorus of mourning.

"*Tessa, Tessa, Tessa... bless her, bless her, bless her... come back to me.*"

She rocks faster on her knees, hearing footsteps crunching towards her on the fallen leaves. The quality of the air changes subtly; someone is approaching from out of the thickest trees. Somebody is coming. The rich blood she spilled has called whoever it is to the scene.

She chants the rhyme over and over, a litany, a calling.

In front of her, the trees part; in front of her, the makeshift shrine shifts, one of the objects that form it moving slightly to create a small opening.

"*Tessa, Tessa, Tessa... bless her, bless her, bless her... come back to me.*"

The cold, dead moon shines down its pale light, making her milky skin shimmer.

Something moves in the opening, emerging from inside the shrine. It is a short, scrawny tree branch – not much more than a sapling. It moves sinuously, curling and twisting as it quests forth, tasting the air of two worlds that have momentarily become one.

Abby keeps chanting. She continues to rock back and forth on her knees. Her bladder fails and urine pools around her legs, soaking along with the blood and other fluids into the weave of the carpet. The smell is sharp, pungent, as it finally reaches her nostrils, like a spilled chemical.

The scrawny sapling reaches out further, towards her face. Like a small arm, its tip spreads out into four spiky wooden fingers and a thumb, and it makes to caress her cheek. Then, quickly, it changes direction and whips briskly against her flesh, making a minuscule nick and drawing a spot of blood below her right eye. Abby does not even wince; she does not pause in her lament.

"*Tessa, Tessa, Tessa... bless her, bless her, bless her... come back to me.*"

She rocks and chants, chants and rocks. The two worlds begin to merge more fully, and then to separate before the culmination of these events can take place. The grove of oak trees dims, becoming shadow and silhouette, and then the harsh light of the world outside the house seeps gradually back into the room. She stops speaking. She becomes still. Her eyes – although already open – snap into focus as if she is opening them for the first time.

SHE LOOKED DOWN, at the candles, and then threw down onto the floor the pyjamas she was clutching. The carpet was wet with blood and piss and ejaculate. The room smelled like a hospital toilet. She started to cry, silently but deeply. Her entire body shook with grief as it remembered giving birth to her child, her Tessa.

Once she managed to stop the tears, Abby reached out and snuffed out each of the candles with her forefinger and thumb, like a vicar putting out the votive candles in a church after prayer.

She put the candles and the matches back inside the plastic bag, gathered up the rest of her things, and left the room. She didn't bother getting dressed. She went back downstairs and put the stuff away, then filled a plastic bucket with hot water from the tap, squirted washing up liquid into the water and stirred it with her hand. She returned upstairs, to Tessa's room, knelt down once again, and scrubbed the carpet clean. She did not weep again. When she was finished, she rinsed out the bucket in the upstairs bathroom and left it on the floor. She took a long, hot shower to clean her body and dried herself with the oldest, toughest towel she could find in the airing cupboard. Like a hair shirt, it punished her, making her skin turn red.

She returned to her room, to her bed, and sat there, staring at the wall.

She was unsure what had just happened, but something inside her felt broken. It was a familiar feeling, one that had kept her connected to her emotions for such a long time; she remembered experiencing a sensation just like it when she lost her virginity at the age of fifteen to a family friend, and then again, when she pushed out Tessa into the world.

She picked up her cigarettes off the bedside table and lit one, drawing deeply from the smoke. She opened a drawer and took out the small whisky bottle she kept there; it was half full. She drank the whisky straight from the bottle and smoked the cigarette down to a stub.

Only when the whisky bottle was empty did she allow herself to lie back down on the bed, on top of the cheap duvet.

She thought about the guy she brought home last night and ran her hands slowly along her thighs, feeling strangely aroused. He had touched her there, too, but he did not touch her inside. Nobody could, not now. Not ever again. Other forces were at work inside her womb. She was sure of it. The desire passed, like a cloud crossing the sun.

She closed her eyes and thought about a grove of ancient oak trees, a high, cold moon, and the sound of approaching footsteps in the undergrowth. In the darkness behind her eyes, she saw a small, skinny arm with four claw-like fingers, and wondered if it was real or just a dream she'd once experienced.

She reached up and felt the small nick below her right eye. It had stopped bleeding but it was still sore. The slight pain was a comfort; it meant that all the things she struggled to remember might just be real after all.

Daisy like a flower got bad sleep. we hear noises in teh nite. bad nioses. bashing on walls. laffing. crying. I don't now what happnin anymore. she cried lots and I hugged her. mummy and daddy didn come. clickety sound under my bed and I want it to stop. bird face man stand besides my bed. in the walls an under the floor. he there. he evawhere. captain clickety he evawhere. he even in places we hide. under the bed and in the cubod. I seen him. he see me. he smilez with his birdy mask. I write in this dairy cos I donno what else to do. words mite make him go away.

– From the diary of Jack Pollack, April 1974

PART TWO

THE CRAWL

"Always ask for me."

– DS Craig Royle

CHAPTER TEN

Royle was making a coffee when the call came in.

His office at the Far Grove police station was small and cramped, filled with loose files and notebooks, but the one thing he could not do without was a decent coffee machine. He didn't let anyone touch his machine – *his* machine; it was his personal property and he made sure everyone knew it – and often found himself the butt of station jokes because of his possessive attitude towards the appliance.

But Royle didn't care. He liked his coffee, and that was all. He needed it to get through the day, and a few cups of Nescafe just wouldn't cut it. His coffee had to be freshly ground, freeze-packed, and preferably from deepest Columbia.

He answered the phone, glancing at the machine as it dripped evil-looking black fluid from the filter into the misted glass jug. His mouth was watering. "This is DS Royle speaking. Can I help you?"

"Sir, it's Sergeant Barnes here. We've had one of those calls."

Royle focused completely on Barnes' voice. "Okay, I'm all ears. Tell me what you've got." It might be something; it was probably nothing. They usually turned out to be nothing.

"Mrs Millstone. She rang in five minutes ago. I'm not quite sure what the problem is, but she was scared. Upset. Something about a scarecrow… that's all I managed to get out of her, I'm sorry. She wasn't making much sense. She asked for you by name. Demanded I get you, actually."

Royle thanked Barnes and hung up the phone. His coffee would have to wait. He was needed elsewhere. He rubbed at his cheek with his hand and felt the stubble rasping against his fingertips. He was tired, strung out, and needed some rest. The coffee was no longer enough. He was craving whisky. This was a first; he usually suffered these cravings later in the day, when he was weary and irritated. It was way too early to want a drink.

But there was a reason for his response: it had been one of those calls… that's what everyone called them, on the rare occasions that they came in. One of *those* calls.

Basically, Royle had let it be known that he was to be informed if anyone with even the slightest connection with the Gone Away Girls case called in, no matter what the reason might be for the call. He realised that everyone on the force thought he was obsessed, and on his darker days he would agree with them. But this was both more and less than mere obsession. He'd promised each of the families that he wouldn't rest until he found out what had happened to their girls, and he intended to make good on that promise.

He realised that this kind of honour was outdated, that it only ever seemed to feature in fiction – crime novels and Hollywood movies, stories about broken down cops trying to solve one last case before they retired. He also knew that it was a mistake to make such an impossible promise to a victim's family. Yet still, it was what drove him. That promise – the fact that he'd made it in good faith and it had been accepted like some kind of lifeline – made it real. He wouldn't stop until he found out what had happened to those girls. It simply was not in his nature to forget about them. Somebody needed to remember, to act as a witness, and the task had fallen to him.

Like a festering wound, the knowledge that they had been taken and nobody knew – or even cared – why or by whom burned inside him night and day.

He left the office and cut through the operations room, trying not to catch anyone's eye. A few people nodded; one or two even said hello. Royle knew that he wasn't well liked, and that he was only hanging on here because of his longevity and connections higher up the chain of command, but he didn't really care. He'd stopped caring about things like friendship and career-building a long time ago. The only person who meant anything to him now refused to live with him, and that summed up how much of a mess he was in.

Outside, he climbed into his car. Reversing out of his space in the car park, he looked at his face in the rear-view mirror. His eyes were streaked with red; black smudges circled them. He looked like he hadn't slept for weeks. In truth, he had not. The only time he ever managed to close his eyes and slip into unconsciousness was with the aid of alcohol. He was drink-dependent, maybe even an alcoholic, but the drink was what helped him at least get some form of rest. That was the real reason he was afraid to do something about the addiction: if he didn't have the drink, he might never sleep again.

He drove north, through Far Grove and towards the Concrete Grove. His skin prickled with the

Crawl as he crossed the invisible geographical border between the two districts, as if his blood were answering some strange call. He knew the sensation was psychological rather than physical, but still it didn't mean it wasn't real. This place, it had became a part of him. He knew that he could never leave, even if he wanted to.

The truth was he didn't want to leave the Grove.

Vanessa had tried to convince him to apply for a transfer on several occasions, but he'd never taken her seriously. Even when she left him, six months pregnant and not really wanting to go, he had dug in his heels and told her that he would never turn his back on this place – these people, the parents and siblings of the Gone Away girls. Even a transfer to nearby Newcastle was out of the question. It was only a few miles south, but Royle felt that it was too far away from the locus of whatever strange things had been happening round here for years.

He'd never discussed his suspicions in public, but he knew that there was something deeply wrong with the fabric of the Grove. Too many bad things happened; there was a lot of darkness under the skin of the estate. Royle didn't believe in ghosts, or magic, but he did believe that a place could be *wrong*. Some places attract darkness, and this was one of them. Some places are seething with the Crawl.

The Concrete Grove, Royle knew deep inside his heart, was a Bad Place.

He slowed as he drove along Grove End, past the old primary school. He watched as school kids laughed and played, remembering that those poor girls had once done the same, oblivious to the darkness that was coming for them. But nobody would ever hear their laughter again; their innocent games would forever go unseen.

He parked on Grove Crescent, outside the Millstones' tiny two-bed semi-detached house. He didn't get out of the car immediately. Instead he sat there for a few seconds, trying to centre his energy, to focus on what was important. He recalled the disturbance in the park the night before, and wondered what he'd almost seen there, moving through the bushes like a living embodiment of the sensation that he felt right now.

It had been yet another example of the badness that festered here, growing like a malignant tumour. He was certain of it; there was no doubt at all.

"Nothing," he said. "It was nothing." But he knew that he was lying to himself, just the way he lied to everyone. He could not speak aloud about his feelings, even to himself. Something was gestating here, and had been for a long time: something that wanted to be born.

He thought about Vanessa's stomach and the life that was growing inside her. They didn't know what she was having; Vanessa had wanted it to be a surprise. Royle was too scared to even imagine which gender the baby might be. He feared that if he thought too much about it, the baby might not come out right. It might be deformed. Or dead. What if the badness here had infected Vanessa, tainting the foetus? What if his seed had been bad, even before the baby was conceived?

What if the baby Crawled out instead of being pushed?

"Jesus..." He shook his head, closed his eyes. Why did he always have to be so dark? His thoughts were never optimistic. Perhaps that was the fault of the Grove, too. Vanessa had often said that the place – along with the job he did – had eaten away his insides, leaving behind an emptiness that he could never quite fill, no matter how hard he tried. Was she right? Was that what had happened to him? Were all of his strange thoughts about the estate nothing but the imaginings of a twisted mind, a brain attuned to darkness?

He got out of the car and approached the front gate. A figure was standing in the window, watching him. The curtain fell back into place and the figure glided away. Seconds later, the front door opened.

"Good day, DS Royle." Tony Millstone was a ruined man. Before his daughter had vanished, he'd been something of a long-distance runner, competing in local road races and even in a few marathons. Now he was old, withered, and decrepit well before his time. He was only forty-seven but he looked at least a decade older. He dressed old, too, favouring dull, colourless cardigans and creased slacks over the jeans and colourful shirts he used to wear. His running shoes gathered dust in a cupboard somewhere, his dreams mothballed up with them.

"Tony." Royle walked up the path and shook the man's hand. His bones felt brittle, like bread sticks.

"Come inside. Margaret's put the kettle on... she needed something to do with her hands." He shrugged, smiled, and led the way inside.

It wasn't just Tony Millstone who looked worse for wear. The house itself seemed stuck in a time warp; it hadn't been decorated since Connie's disappearance and judging by the dust in the corners and the cobwebs up near the ceiling, it was barely even kept clean anymore. Royle imagined that the inside of the Millstones' hearts must also look like this: dry, empty, filled with dust and cobwebs and silence.

Margaret Millstone was standing in the kitchen doorway. She was wearing washed-out, shapeless jogging pants and a sweatshirt that had once fit her previously statuesque figure perfectly but now hung on her scrawny, malnourished body like an old potato sack. Her hair was thin and dirty, greying at the temples. She wore no makeup. Her eyes, he thought, were like piss-holes in the snow.

"Hello, Craig." It was always first name terms with the mothers. The fathers all seemed to prefer to address him by his official title, as if that afforded them some distance from what had happened to bring him here. He'd often wondered why it worked that way and not the other way around, but had never been able to come up with a satisfactory answer.

"Hello, Mrs Millstone. I believe you called the station and asked for me." He took the cup of tea she offered, sipped it and nodded his thanks.

"Of course I asked for you. You always say to ask for you if we ever need the police." Her hands were shaking. "You've been good to us." She did not smile. She didn't even hold his gaze as she spoke.

"That's right. Always ask for me. I'll always drop anything else that I'm doing for you – you know that." He took another small sip of the tea. It was stewed; the teabag had been left in the water far too long. "What is it? What's the problem?"

She glanced at her husband. He nodded. "It's probably best if we show you... here, come through. It's outside, in the back garden."

He followed her into the kitchen, gratefully setting down his cup on the table as he passed by. The kitchen was cold, the white goods old and battered. A few tiles had come off the wall near the door and not been replaced. The lino floor was peeling away from the concrete floor slab in one corner. There were crumbs all over the place, but at least it was proof that the Millstones were eating and not slowly starving themselves to death.

Mrs Millstone opened the back door and stepped outside, into the unkempt garden.

Royle followed her, looking up at the clearing sky. The day was unseasonably mild, the sunlight bright and surprisingly powerful now that the dark clouds had dispersed. He walked close behind her and when she stopped abruptly he almost collided with her.

"Sorry," he said, resting the tips of his fingers at the base of her spine, but she hadn't even noticed the contact.

"It's over there." She raised a hand and pointed. Her fingernails were bitten right down to the quick. The cracked cement path was flanked on either side by small, overgrown lawns, which were populated by broken stone gnomes. Connie had loved those gnomes: she had even painted them, but now the colours had faded.

To the left, there was just the length of timber fence that separated the Millstones' property from the one next door; to the right, at the bottom of the garden and attached to the fence on that side, was a low garden shed. The roof was full of holes, the tarpaper covering was ripped. The weather had hammered at the wooden panel walls and the single glass window had been shattered and covered over with a black plastic bin bag. The bin bag was flapping slightly in a gentle breeze and distracting him, so at first Royle didn't realise what he was meant to see.

Then he understood.

Peering around the edge of the shed there was a stocky figure. It was wearing a wide-brimmed hat and a black and red striped Dennis-the-Menace sweater. Royle took a step backwards, more surprised than afraid, and went instinctively into a fighting stance: fists raised, back leg taking his weight, shoulders hunched. Later, he'd be impressed by his presence of mind, but now he just stood there, wondering if there was going to be an attack.

"It was there when I came out here to hang up the washing. Just... just peeping round the corner like that, watching me. Creepy bloody thing..."

Royle lowered his hands and walked forward, closing the distance between him and the figure. The day's warmth seemed to fade. The breeze became a little stronger, and colder.

It wasn't a real figure, of course. It was some kind of bonfire guy... or, more accurately, a scarecrow, just like Barnes had said on the phone. He'd recognised within seconds that it wasn't a living person, and yet still he'd readied himself for action. It was the face that had caused him such an extreme reaction. At first glance, it had looked real, like a person's features staring at him... but now that he was drawing closer to the scarecrow, he could see that there was simply a photograph attached to its head.

The scarecrow's jumper was torn in places, so the stuffing was hanging out. The torso was stuffed with what looked like old newspapers, bills and receipts, and even a few tattered old one pound notes – a monetary unit that was taken out of commission in 1984. This stout upper body was mounted on a stick that was as broad as a man's calf, one end of which had been sunk deep into the earth to support the strange, jerrybuilt figure.

Royle stood before the scarecrow and examined it closely. The stick was in fact a tree branch. The bark had been stripped away to reveal the pale timber beneath, but the wood was untreated. He could still see the faint marks from whatever blade had been used to lay bare the natural wood grain.

He was trying not to look at the photograph that was plastered to the front of the scarecrow's head until he'd calmed down, but still it drew his gaze.

The photograph was a portrait of little Connie Millstone, the daughter of the house and the first of the Gone Away Girls. But this was no ordinary photograph: it was old, faded, and sepia toned. Royle thought it looked stylised, like the Victorian death photographs he'd once seen in a book but never forgotten because they'd been so disturbing. But even worse than the still pose and the mordant tone of the shot, was the fact that Connie's eyes were closed, and upon the lids someone – perhaps even the missing girl herself – had drawn in a thick black pen a crude representation of eyes.

Royle stared at the photograph.

It was a startling image.

His vision blurred; tears filled his eyes. For a moment he thought he might even faint.

He wiped his eyes with the back of his hand and took a minute just to clear his head. He had to focus on what was in front of him and ignore any other references or connections his mind came up with. This was not a Victorian death study; it was a photograph of a missing little girl, perhaps the last one ever taken of her. In the photograph, Connie looked the same age she'd been when she went missing. So it wasn't a recent shot; this had been taken at least five years ago.

He tried to remain calm. He owed the family his full attention. He owed them that, at least.

Was this some kind of sick joke, carried out by local kids on the anniversary of the girl's disappearance? The idea was feasible, but to Royle it just didn't feel right. There was more to this than what was immediately on show, some kind of reason hiding beneath the surface. Why would anyone go to the trouble of constructing the weird scarecrow and obscuring its face with the image of the missing girl? It didn't make sense; it was overly complicated for some nasty practical joke.

But who else could it be? This family had no enemies. Quite the opposite, in fact; they were well liked, and most people in the area empathised with them for what had happened to their only daughter.

"Craig..." Mrs Millstone's voice was still quite far behind him. She was afraid to come any closer. Maybe she expected the scarecrow to come to life and start hobbling along the path towards her?

"Just a minute..." He let out a long breath and stared at the image pasted over the scarecrow's face. He committed the face to memory, even though it was already there, along with the rest of them, burned into his brain like a brand.

He turned around. "The photo... Is it one of yours?"

She shook her head. "I haven't been too close, but I was close enough to know that I didn't recognise it. Why would we have a photo with scribbles on her eyelids, anyway? It's... it's awful, like something out of a horror movie."

"I'm sorry, but I had to check."

She nodded. "Can we go inside now?" She turned away without waiting for an answer. "I'll make another cup of tea." Her voice was tiny, like that of a child. She was clinging to the everyday rituals of making tea, offering her guest refreshments, and in truth she was clinging to her sanity.

Royle followed Mrs Millstone along the uneven cement path, resisting the urge to look behind him to check if the scarecrow had moved.

He knew it hadn't. That was silly. It would be impossible.

But still he couldn't bring himself to look and see.

CHAPTER ELEVEN

"OKAY, MARRA. JUST keep me posted. You know you're always welcome back here." Erik Best stared at the wall, distracted, as he spoke on the phone. There was a crack there, in the plaster. He'd never noticed it before, but it started at the corner of the double door frame and made a rough diagonal line up towards the ceiling. There were ragged cobwebs around it, but there was no sign of any spider.

He said goodbye to his friend Marty Rivers, who was now living in London for the foreseeable future, and walked across to the doorway. He peered at the crack, wondering how it might have formed. The house wasn't new, but it was in good repair. He'd spent a fortune on having that doorway widened and glass doors installed, about six years ago, when he decided to invest some money in the property. It shouldn't be damaged. The workmanship had been top notch. He'd handpicked and supervised the workmen himself.

He stood on his tiptoes but was still too short to reach the top of the door frame. He shook his head and turned away, pacing across the room to the front window.

"Marty, Marty, Marty..." The guy had been his best bare-knuckle fighter and one of the most reliable men on his payroll. Something had happened a few months ago, up at the Needle – one of Marty's old school friends had been stabbed by a piece of shit kid from the estate. He'd died on the spot. Marty had gone down to London to speak to the friend's pregnant missus, and now he'd decided to stay there, to become some kind of surrogate dad to the imminent arrival. Erik had put out feelers to see if any names came up regarding the stabbing, but so far nobody was talking.

He looked out at his garden and tried to gain pleasure from what he saw. The plot was huge; the boundary fence adjoined a small wooded area, beyond which was a private field. Erik had made a lot of money over the years and this place was his haven from the stress of his business world. He knew a lot of dodgy people, consorted with all kinds of low-life criminals and high-class scumbags, but he'd not once invited any of them into his home. It was out of bounds, and hopefully out of reach. A man like Erik Best tended to make enemies, and the less those enemies (or even friends) knew about his private life the better.

Private life... now there was a phrase. These days, the only private life he had time for consisted of sex with the kind of slappers who worked in the low-rent pubs and clubs where he arranged security, or the occasional orgy with some punters from the fights. The middle classes; they always got horny after watching bloodshed. In the past, he'd enjoyed a lot of action that way, but these days all he wanted was safety and security, someone to hold in the night.

Abby Hansen had once offered him the kind of lifestyle he now craved. When she'd been raising

Erik's daughter, little Tessa, he'd kept his distance, but as soon as the kid went missing he wanted to be part of their lives. It was just like him to want everything after the offer had been withdrawn. His timing had always been off in matters of the heart.

We never know what we've got until some fucker takes it away, he though, watching a small grey squirrel run across his lawn. He wished he had a gun in his hand, just to shoot something that was alive. Make it dead. It was a primal urge; a deep-rooted instinct. To kill. To destroy.

Few people had known that little Tessa Hansen had been Erik's child until she went missing. Even the bloke Abby had been living with at the time of her disappearance – his name eluded Erik, like so many other things lately – didn't have a clue. He thought the girl was his own. The truth had only been let out into the open because of a traumatic event. They'd only fucked a few times, and she'd fallen pregnant easily. One drunken night when she puked up her pill; a tiny life conceived during a booze-inspired grapple. More of that bad timing, he supposed... what he would give to be able to be her father now, to raise her and teach her about the world. But it was not to be.

He turned away from the window and sat down in his favourite armchair, craving a few grams of coke. He was trying to cut down on the drugs, but the opposite seemed to be happening: he wanted more and more, relying on pills and powders to give him succour from the shitstorm around him. He knew it was bad form, and that his body would be suffering, but somehow he just couldn't manage to kick those bad habits. Indeed, ones he thought he'd overcome years ago were returning with a vengeance.

When his mobile started to ring, he almost ignored it. But it was one of the business phones, and he tried to make it a rule that business always came first – even before his so-called fucking private life.

He took the phone from his shirt pocket and thumbed the answer button. "What is it?" No pleasantries for Erik Best; no pleases and thank yous. Just straight business talk.

"Erik... I mean, Mr Best. It's Hacky."

One of his little lapdogs; a scruffy kid on the Grove estate he sometimes paid to keep an eye on things. One of the many; just another small cog in the mighty Best machine, each one oblivious of the rest yet working in harmony to protect him and to keep the wheels of commerce nicely greased.

"What is it, Hacky? I'm busy, so this had better be fucking good."

A pause; then someone whispering in the background, rushed and excited. "Aye, it's good. I *think* it is, anyway. For you, like. The thing is, I'm not even fucking sure *what* it is..." Another pause, this one longer.

"Go on, Hacky. Tell me about it." He settled back into the chair and closed his eyes, still thinking of Abby Hansen. But not as she was now, all thin and haggard and defeated; no, Abby as she had been a few years ago, before grief got hold of her and turned her into a listless punch bag. The Abby who had always been the boss in bed and who'd never put up with any of his shit.

"You know you always tell me to ring you if I see something weird?"

"What do you mean by weird, Hacky?"

"You know. *Weird*. Dead strange, like. Anything out of the ordinary on the estate... you always tell us that however small it might seem, a weird growth can sometimes have long roots. That's what you say, innit?"

Erik sighed. "Yes, son. More or less."

"Okay, then. I got summat weird. One of them things... the things you want to know about."

Erik opened his eyes. He glanced again at the crack in the wall. It was just the same; it hadn't grown, or moved.

Moved? How the hell could it do that?

His mind wasn't straight. He was drifting off into irrelevant areas, focusing on stupid, pointless concerns. He needed to concentrate, to live in the now and not the back then. "Come on, marra, spit it out, will you? I have better things to do." But did he? Did he really?

"The thing is... the *thing*... oh, fuck, man. Listen, if I tried to describe it you'd think I was tripping or summat."

"And are you?" Erik leaned forward, ready to end the call and organise a little beating for Hacky, just to warn him not to waste Erik's time. "Were you laying it on a bit heavy last night, you and the boys? Did one of you cook up a batch of cheap smack?"

"Nah, I'm clean. Had a few beers and a smoke round me brother's place, but nowt else. Nowt daft, like." He sounded proud, as if this short period of abstinence meant something important in his broken life.

"Listen, Hacky, tell me what the fuck this is all about or I'll have your legs broken."

This time the pause was longer and held an intensity that had not been present before. Erik listened to the static on the line. He thought for a moment that he could make out other voices in there; voices and a soft slow clicking sound, like distant maracas. But then it faded.

"Remember Monty Bright?"

That got Erik's attention. "Yes. Of course I remember Monty." They'd been friends and sometime enemies, comrades and occasionally business rivals. Theirs was always a complex relationship, but one that often created a lot of mutual wealth. Monty had run a loan sharking business, and Erik had been known to fund some of Monty's bigger deals. They'd been silent partners many times, mostly in security companies and anything where hired muscle was required. They'd drawn blood together, fought hard men, and shared slutty women. They'd even organised a few boxing bouts, matching local fighters for a cash prize. On the level. Everything above board. Just for the hell of it.

"It's got something to do with him… with Monty."

"Monty's dead, Hacky. He died in the fire when his gym burnt down, remember? My gym, now, that is if your fucking brother and his mates hurry up and get that fit-out job finished."

"Just come to the estate and take a look. Meet us at the gym. There's nobody working there today. You really need to fucking see this, man. It's… it's… shit, I don't know what the fuck it is, man. It's weird. Weird, with fucking long roots..."

Erik checked the time; it was past lunchtime but he hadn't eaten a thing. He wasn't even hungry.

He had nothing better to do. It was a depressing thought, but it was true.

"Okay, I'll be there in half an hour. If this isn't good, you'd better run hard and run far, Hacky my boy. If I'm wasting my time here, it won't just be your legs that get broken. And I might just break your brother's, too, for slacking on the job."

"I know," said the kid on the other end of the line. "Just come and see." Then he ended the call.

Erik's mind was still on Abby Hansen. If he had business on the estate, then it wouldn't be out of order to maybe pay her a little call. See how she was. Find out if she needed anything. He knew that he was being stupid, that she'd pussy-whipped him without even trying, but still he could not stay away. She was like a drug; he needed her, even if it was like this: brief, unwanted visits, during which she usually verbally abused him. Stolen time. Tense, bruising moments spent in her company when she didn't even want him there, not now.

He locked up the house, checked the dogs – two border collies; Rocky and Apollo – in their kennels and set off for the Grove. On his way there, through the winding roads of the Northumberland countryside, he wished again that Abby would wake up and see what it was he had to offer, how good it could be for them both if she dropped her guard, let him back in.

Erik had never lived on the Grove. He'd been born in Byker, in the east end of Newcastle, and from a very young age had demonstrated that he could take care of himself. His father had enrolled him in a boxing academy when he was five years old. He'd beaten everyone they put in front of him, and graduated through the age and weight classes with ease.

His teenage years had seen him go off the rails and he began street fighting rather than using his craft in the ring. Erik was always bright enough to know that, unless you were truly dedicated, the fight game would never make you rich. He lacked the application and willpower to become a champion; his skills were purely natural, and a wide lazy streak coupled with habitual indiscipline meant that he could not stick to any kind of training regime.

So he used his skills in other ways.

Years ago he'd realised that he didn't have to fight every battle himself. He surrounded himself with tough guys, men who were strong and fast but lacked his cunning and intellect. He set up illegal fights and made a fortune. When he'd made enough money he bought an old farmhouse a few miles from here and started hosting bare-knuckle bouts in the Barn, a small outbuilding with thick stone walls and neglected horse paddocks – he'd employed Hacky's brother and his gang to do the building work there, too.

He also ran a security firm that provided pubs and clubs with trained door staff, big blokes who knew exactly what to do if trouble started. Erik saw himself as a primitive renaissance man; a facilitator; an entrepreneur: he was the Donald fucking Trump of the mean streets and even meaner housing estates.

Now, at the age of fifty-one, he was what his younger self would have considered wealthy. He owned a large, beautiful home, several other properties, two well-trained dogs, had three cars in the garage, but lacked someone to share it with.

There was a time when Abby Hansen would have walked over broken glass to live with him, but that time was long gone. These days she'd rather cut herself on the scattered shards than stand by his side.

The Concrete Grove... why would she want to stay here? Their daughter wasn't coming back; she would never come home. This place was the dark centre of a universe Erik could barely even understand. He cruised through it, that alien universe, and he used it and its denizens for personal gain, but he had no idea how it really worked. Like a black hole, it sucked everything towards it, bleeding them dry: Monty Bright, his absent friend Marty Rivers, the once beautiful Abby Hansen... all of them drawn inexorably towards the black centre of this place, screaming silently as it ate them alive.

He drove through the estate with these dark thoughts on his mind. Part of him hoped that Hacky was taking the piss; he had the urge to commit violence, and that useless kid would do as target practice. He guided the car along the grubby streets, along Grove Road and onto Grove Street, where Monty Bright's old gym was situated. He'd acquired the building and was having it fitted out; it would be a gym again, and this time *his* name would be above the door... as long as Hacky's brother got on with the job, of course, the work-shy little bastard.

He parked at the kerb and got out, walking quickly to the front door. He opened the door and stepped inside. Three young men stood at the bottom of the new timber stairs, huddled around the bottom step. Hacky looked up and smiled. He raised a hand and walked over.

"So, I'm here."

"I'm sorry to make you come all the way here, Mr Best. Really. But there was no other way... this has got to be seen. You wouldn't believe it otherwise."

The other two boys nodded, looked away, staring at the fire-damaged walls. They were guilty; all of them, guilty of so many petty crimes that it would be difficult to pin a single one on them. He could see the badness dripping off them like sweat. He was covered with it, too, but he was clever enough to construct a barrier. The black hole wouldn't suck him in. He would never allow it to get a good enough grip on his soul. These fuckers were already halfway inside; it was consuming them like space debris.

"What the fuck is it, Hacky?" He stepped forward, grabbed the kid's upper arm with one big hand, and knocked his baseball cap from his head with the other. The cap was old, faded, and had a decal featuring Scooby Doo smoking a spliff. "I'm really not in the fucking mood for any of your bullshit."

"Please." Hacky cowered; he actually stepped back and hunkered down a few inches, as if he were a dog trying to subjugate itself before an alpha. He bent down and picked up his cap. "Honest, we have summat to show you."

The other two nodded. They wouldn't hold Erik's gaze. They were too afraid even to speak.

"Show me." He let go, pushed the kid away. "Show me before I change my mind and knock you out just to release some tension."

"It's at Beggy's place." Hacky motioned towards one of the other young men – a tall, thin streak of piss with acne scars all over his long neck and thin throat.

"Yeah," said the one called Beggy. "I didn't know what to do with it, so I put it in my old man's lock-up. It's on Grove Drive. One of them old garages past the Corner... you know?" He looked down, inspecting his oversized trainers. He blinked too much; it was making Erik angry, grating at his nerves.

"So take me there. Go outside and get in the car. Now."

He watched them troop slowly out through the door and then glanced up the stairs, at the partially repaired upper floor. The walls were bare, some of them still stained by smoke. He locked the door on his way out. "Give me your keys," he said to Hacky. "I don't want you letting yourself in there ever again, not unless I'm around. Oh, and when you see your brother, tell him to get back here and finish the job."

The kid handed over the keys without looking at Erik's face. He nodded.

Erik unlocked the car. "Get in the back – all three of you. I don't want any of you fuckers in the front with me. And try not to dribble on the upholstery." He watched them squeeze carefully onto the back seat, three unwise monkeys, and got in the front, then started the car. It took them less than three minutes to get to Grove Drive. The garages stood in a row opposite the waste ground beyond the primary school. Seven squat, graffiti-covered buildings, none of them ever used to park a car. They were all utilised for storage instead, and the police turned a blind eye to whatever was kept inside, and to whoever rented them. Nobody cared about this place, as long as there was no serious trouble. Things ticked over in the Grove; crimes were done; people got paid; the status quo was maintained.

The black hole kept on sucking, hungry for more.

"Which one?"

Beggy spoke, but quietly. "The third one from the left."

"Get the fuck out and show me."

They all climbed out of the car. Erik waited until they were walking towards the garages, and then he got out, too. He locked the doors and followed them across the footpath and onto the tired grass verge, wondering what the fuck could be so important that Hacky would disturb him and ask him to come here. He'd known all along that it must be something major; the kid was too afraid to fuck with him over trivialities.

Beggy bent over and unlocked the up-and-over garage door. He opened it and the three of them stepped back in the same movement, as if they were afraid of what was in there. They stood and waited for Erik to move.

"You going to tell me what I'm here to see, or do I have to guess?"

Beggy shook his head. Hacky coughed; a harsh dry sound. The nameless third member of the group looked away, trying to pretend that he wasn't here. He hadn't spoken a word so far and didn't look like he was going to change that habit any time soon.

"Well?"

"You do it," said Beggy. "I can't go back in there... I've seen enough." He was pleading, not ordering, and Hacky nodded.

"You're more afraid of whatever's in there than you are of me?" Erik took a couple of steps forward, interested now. He was standing close to Beggy. The kid nodded, but didn't raise his head. The footpath was obviously fascinating; he was inspecting it like it was the most interesting thing he'd seen so far that day. The acne scars on his throat were livid, bright red welts. They looked painful, like aggravated wounds.

"Okay, I'll show you." Hacky moved reluctantly into the shadow of the garage, his slim body swallowed by darkness. The other two young men stepped to the side, away from the open door.

"Don't go anywhere," said Erik. He walked forward, stooping at the waist to get under the garage door, and looked around.

There wasn't much in there. In fact, it looked like someone had recently moved a lot of stuff out. Streaked dust marks decorated the internal surfaces; cobwebs had been disturbed in the corners. The oil-stained floor was scuffed in places, as if heavy objects had been pushed or pulled across it. Erik seemed to recall that Beggy's father was some kind of low-level fence, so he probably used this place to store stolen goods that he couldn't keep inside the house for some reason: furniture, plasma screen televisions still in their cardboard boxes, perhaps even a few large car parts that were too heavy to shift on his own.

A stack of rolled up carpet off-cuts had been pushed up against the wall on the left hand side. The right hand wall was clear, but someone had set up a small camping table, upon which there was a red and black tartan plastic flask and a set of pornographic playing cards. Erik walked over and looked down at the cards. They were vintage 1970s, showing scenes of blank-eyed women copulating with drugged farm animals. Nice.

He looked up and watched Hacky. The kid was staring at a large rectangular object covered by a dark, stained tarpaulin sheet. He was fidgeting; he shuffled his feet, picked at his fingernails, bit his bottom lip.

"Is that it?" Erik indicated the sheet.

"Yeah. It's under there... under that cover thing." He licked his lips. His eyes were wide. The gloom inside the garage had made his pupils dilate, unless he was strung out on drugs, despite what he'd said earlier.

"Take the fucking thing off, then. Show me what you've got."

A strange kind of tension had entered the garage with them. Erik knew that he should be losing his temper by now. The kid was stringing this out, making a fucking meal of the situation. But there was an atmosphere between these concrete walls that made him cautious. There wasn't any actual danger here – of course there wasn't, not for him anyway. No, not danger: something else, a sense of... weirdness. Something here was not entirely right. That was the only way he could think to explain what he felt.

Then he realised what it was: he felt like he was being watched. He was experiencing that sensation of eyes upon you when you walk across a room; the sense that someone is peering at you but you can't see them, not yet. A painting's eyes following you across a gallery floor; or the heat of a person's gaze burning a hole in the middle of your back from across a room.

Watched.

He was being watched.

Hacky bent over and tugged at the end of the tarpaulin sheet. He did it half-heartedly at first, as if he really didn't want the sheet to come off, but then he used both hands and pulled hard, shuffling backwards as he did so. The sheet slid away, dropping to the floor. Beneath it was a large glass tank with a heavy lid, the kind of container that was used for keeping tropical fish, or exotic lizards.

"What's the story with that tank, then?" Erik didn't move.

Hacky stepped further away, not taking his eyes from the tank. "Years ago, when I was little, I used to keep snakes in there. I had a couple of pythons. Dad got hold of them from some mate. The police came and took them away. They weren't legal, like..." He kept staring at the tank. "Dangerous, they reckoned..."

Erik paused for a moment, unwilling to move closer to the tank, and what might be lurking inside it. The shadows kept its contents hidden; all he could see was a large dark glass receptacle, with something bulky nestling behind the glass. It could have been discarded clothing; it might have been a dead animal. A cat or a dog.

Then the thing moved: a slight twitch, like a muscular spasm.

"It's alive," he whispered.

A snake?

"We thought it was dead," said Hacky. "We found it down on Beacon Green, in a little ditch, half-covered by leaves and shit. We were looking for a bag of pot we'd stashed there a few nights ago." Still he stared at the tank. Whatever was in there coiled lazily, moving a little like one of the pythons the kid had claimed to have owned before they were seized by the authorities.

"What is it?"

A snake...

Finally Hacky looked away from the tank. He turned to face Erik, and his features remained in shadow. His mouth barely moved when he spoke. Darkness writhed across his face like tar. "Honestly, I haven't a fucking clue."

Something thumped wetly against the other side of the glass, shifting again inside the tank. There was a moist slithering noise as it adjusted its position.

"Fucking hell," said Erik, and his feet moved forward as if they weren't under his control. He wanted to stop them but they refused to obey. He was walking towards the tank, and the living thing that was imprisoned inside.

"Is it one of those snakes of yours?"

Hacky didn't answer. He'd already gone back outside, too afraid to stay and watch.

CHAPTER TWELVE

It was lunchtime and Marc was craving a protein fix. He'd been drinking a lot lately – much more than usual – and seemed to exist with a constant hangover, seeing the world through a thin layer of gauze. He hoped that Vince Rose hadn't been serious about having a few cans of lager and instead wished for a nice cup of tea. A splash of milk. A spoonful of honey. Lovely.

He parked his car at the kerb and stepped out onto the street outside Harry's house. Even though the old man was dead, Marc couldn't help but feel as if he was waiting inside, watching through the net curtains, as he always used to when he had visitors.

Glancing at the grubby nets, he accepted the reality that Harry would no longer be there; his tall, thin form would never again stand in the window, looking out at the street and scowling at passers by.

"Hey, Marc!"

He turned around and saw Vince Rose walking along the street, a blue carrier bag clutched in each hand. He raised the bags to waist level and smiled. "Lunch."

"Good to see you, Vince." Marc moved towards the man and grabbed one of the bags – the one that looked heaviest – and stood to the side while Rose walked past him. He fell into step alongside the other man.

"I didn't get any booze. I hope that's okay. I'm trying to cut down and... well, if it's there, it's a temptation, right?"

Marc nodded. "Thank God for that. I'm thinking about going on a month-long detox because of all the drink I've been having lately. It's getting crazy."

They reached the front door and Rose set down his bag on the doorstep, took a bunch of keys from his jacket pocket, and opened the door.

"It's weird coming here when Harry isn't around." Marc stared through the open doorway, into the gloomy hall. "I've never been inside this house without him inviting me inside. He would always wait in the window, watching, and as soon as I got near the door it would open. He'd say 'Why don't you come in for a while?' and walk back inside, leaving me to follow."

"He's still here," said Rose. "In one way or another. You'll see." He stepped inside and walked towards the kitchen, bumping the carrier bag against the wall.

For a moment Marc didn't want to go inside. It wasn't the same; it wasn't right. This was Harry's house, and Harry needed to be there, to give his usual greeting and put the kettle on. There was a space inside this house, and its shape was that of Harry Rose. The old man had been cut out of the world but his absence was still here, permanent, like a scar in the fabric of existence.

When he stepped over the threshold and into the house, the sunlight seemed to pull back, moving away from him. He felt the temperature drop and the daylight vanished. The lack of Harry Rose was a ghost, a forlorn spectre. In that moment Marc realised that most so-called hauntings were not about what was there, but what was no longer in place. It was not the remains that mattered, but what had been taken away, removed from the living world and placed somewhere else, where nobody could see them.

Ghosts, he thought, *are simply absences made solid. They're holes in the world, holes that will never be filled again.*

He nudged the door shut with his shoulder, using his foot to make sure that it fitted properly into the frame. When the lock clicked, he followed Rose down the hallway and into the small kitchen, where the other man was putting away the shopping.

"I got ham and cheese. Is that okay? Some nice bread: fresh stuff, from the bakers."

"That sounds great," said Marc. He put the carrier bag on the table and sat down in one of the dining chairs. He blinked, trying not to draw attention to the fact that his eyes were moist. Not quite real tears, but almost... he missed his friend. He wished that Harry were still here, bustling around in the tiny kitchen, moaning – as he usually did – about some real or imagined slight.

"How do you take your tea?"

Marc shifted in the chair, turning to face his host. "White, one sugar, thanks. I usually take it with honey, but Harry used to laugh at that and call me a snob."

"Aye," said Rose, shaking his head. "The old bastard had some funny ideas about stuff like that. For years, he called me a traitor to my class simply because I attended university and went to work in insurance. He never let me live that down... never failed to twist the knife, either."

The kettle made a popping sound, signalling that the water had boiled. Steam filled the air between the two men, making it seem like a fog had crept into the room.

Rose didn't move. He stood there, veiled by steam, staring at nothing.

"Erm... the kettle's boiled." Marc made to rise, but when his host snapped back into the moment, lurching towards the kettle, he pretended that he'd simply been shifting his position on the seat.

"Sorry. I was miles away, there. Thinking about that stupid old fart." He looked down, at the surface of the work bench. "I miss him. Even though we hadn't spoken for years, I bloody miss him." He poured boiling water into the cups and waited for the teabags to brew. After a few seconds of silence, he fished out the used teabags with a teaspoon and flicked them both into the sink.

Marc said nothing. He didn't want to intrude upon the man's thoughts.

Rose added the milk and sugar to the mugs, and then handed one to Marc. "Cheers."

Marc raised his mug. "*Salute.*" It had been Harry's favoured toast; he even said it when he was drinking a glass of water.

Marc took a long drink. The tea was hot and sweet; strongly flavoured. "That's a nice bastard brew," he said, out of habit. He always used to say the same phrase to Harry; over time it became a kind of running joke. Their relationship had rested on things like that: quirks and mannerisms, phrases and peculiarities. Harry had been an awkward man, and sometimes he refused to discuss a subject in a direct manner. He liked to talk around things, to make Marc work for the information. Sometimes he could be morose and even uncommunicative, but he always asked Marc to come back and see him. He was lonely. He liked the company of another human being. Marc hoped that the old bastard hadn't been too lonely when he died.

"I miss him, too," said Marc. "He was a one-off: a true original."

They drank their teas and waited for the atmosphere to level out. Something had come into the room, perhaps it had followed him in from outside. It skulked around in the corners, watching them with envy. After a short while, it left them alone, and Marc was able to adjust to the house without Harry Rose. At first he'd wanted to leave; now he wanted to see why he'd been invited here.

"You hungry?" Rose began to open the bread.

"Yeah. A bit." Marc stood, crossed to the sink, and rinsed out his cup with cold water from the tap before placing it in the sink.

"Let's eat first, and then I'll tell you what I found."

Marc turned around, rested the small of his back against the edge of the sink. "Okay, that sounds good. I never like to solve a mystery on an empty stomach."

Rose laughed. "Oh, there's no mystery. Not really. It's just some stuff... Harry stuff."

"Yeah... *Harry stuff.*"

Marc knew exactly what was meant by that remark. One of Harry's habits had been that he often brought home random objects, bits and pieces of junk, old files and paperwork, books without covers, broken toys. Sometimes he fixed the toys and gave them away to charity shops. More often than not, he made something different out of them, perhaps combining the remains of two or three items to construct a third. Marc remembered the time he'd made a scale replica of the Needle out of old-fashioned foil milk bottle tops. He still had no idea where Harry had found the bottle tops, but one day when he'd come to visit, there'd been a cloth sack filled with them on top of the cooker.

Harry Rose had been a creative man, but a lot of the time that creativity had been focused on wasteful things, turned in the wrong direction. Sometimes it was even directed inwards, and had manifested in extended bouts of manic depression when Harry would lock himself away and refuse to see anyone.

Rose piled high a plate with sandwiches and set it down on the table. The two men ate in silence for a while, gazing at the food and chewing slowly.

A shaft of sunlight shone through the kitchen window, moved slowly across the table between them and then vanished; a ghost of light, a promise of something that could never be realised.

"How well did you know my brother?"

Marc glanced up from his plate and saw that Rose was staring at him intently, with a serious expression on his thin, weathered face.

"I know you spent a lot of time together over the last few weeks of his life, but did he open up to you?"

"You'll have to be more specific." Marc put down the remains of his sandwich and waited.

"Okay, let me ask you a question. How did you meet Harry? What brought you here, to him?"

Marc leaned back in his chair. He glanced at the window. The sunlight had dimmed; the patch of visible sky outside was flat and inexpressive. "My uncle used to know Harry, years ago. Uncle Mike died of a brain tumour while I was still at Uni. It was sudden. I'd always had a lot of time for the guy – he raised me when my parents died. He wasn't a real uncle... he was, well, just a friend of the family, I suppose. It seemed natural for him to look after me when my folks died." He paused, looked again at the window. It was slightly brighter: a rectangle of pasty light. Said out loud, his life story seemed strange, as if it was a fiction. The edges didn't quite fit together; there were gaps that he could not fill.

"So you already knew about Harry? You were aware of him?"

"Yes, I was. The reason I'm writing this book about the Northumberland Poltergeist case is because Uncle Mike used to talk about it all the time. He was kind of obsessed with what went on in the Needle all those years ago. I think he worked here, on the estate, and he knew a few of the people involved – maybe even the kids, the Pollack twins."

Rose nodded. "Yes. That sounds about right."

"You knew my uncle, too?"

Rose shook his head. "Not really. Even then, I'd cut my ties with this place. But me and Harry were still speaking back then. I used to come and visit him, and there were always all kinds of people in this house. He knew everyone. He loved to talk and to socialise. Christ, sometimes I wonder if we even came from the same stock." He laughed softly, but it was a strained sound, as if he had to coax it from his throat. "I think your uncle was one of the blokes Harry used to drink with. I remember a Mike – big guy, with masses of curly black hair?"

"Yes," said Marc. "That was him. People used to call him Stavros, after the sidekick from *Kojak*." He smiled.

"God, yes... now I definitely remember him." He shook his head.

There was another period of silence, but this one didn't last for long.

"Harry was a strange man. He collected information in the same way that other people like to collect stamps or books or little pottery figurines. He liked urban myths and tall tales. He collected other people's stories and kept them inside his head. I'm sure one day he intended to write a book of some kind, but never got around to it. But the older he got, the more withdrawn he became. Then he simply stopped being so sociable, as if he had too many stories in his head and there wasn't room for any more."

Marc smiled, remembering the way Harry Rose's face used to light up whenever he talked about things that had gone on in the area.

"He also collected... other things."

"What do you mean?"

"He was something of a kleptomaniac, my brother. He liked to take things that weren't his. Like a magpie drawn to shiny objects, he couldn't resist nabbing something that might have a story attached to it."

"I see."

"He kept a lot of this stuff in the attic rooms. Did he ever show you those rooms?" Rose glanced upwards, at the ceiling.

"No," said Marc. "He never even mentioned them."

"Okay." Rose stood, pushing out his chair, and crossed to the window. He stared out of it for a moment, and then turned back to face the room again. "So I went up there to see what he might be keeping. I thought that I might be able to return some stuff to its rightful owners, if there was anything valuable, or maybe even sell it." He paused, looked down at the floor, and then back up again, at Marc. "He'd got rid of most of it, emptied out the rooms. To make space."

"Space?" Marc stretched his neck. It was aching. He must have slept in a bad position at Abby's place. "Space for what?"

Rose walked across the kitchen, approached the table, but did not sit back down. "I think it's best if I show you." His jacket was hanging on the back of the chair. He reached into the inside pocket and brought out a folded A4-size manila envelope. "But first let me give you this."

Marc reached out and took the envelope. His name was written on the front. He recognised Harry's handwriting.

"I found it in his bedroom, on the bedside cabinet. He must have left it for you to find." He remained standing, watching Marc as he examined the envelope.

"Thanks," said Marc. He tore open the envelope and took out what was inside: a photocopied sheet of paper, folded down the middle. He straightened out the sheet of paper and saw that it was a copy of a brief extract from somebody's diary.

> I think somebody hates us. he is in the house all the time but we cant see him. he makes niose when nowbody else is here. he wants to hurt us. we hide under the bed when mummy and daddy are in the pub. he canit see us there. we ~~inibible.~~ inbisevil. he canit see us. but he is there. in the walls and under the floor. he creeps about and peeps threw the gaps to try and see me and daisy flower. I am scared. I can here him now. he goes clikcety clikcety like when I spilt my marbels on the kichen floor. clikcey clikcety clikc.

He read it through twice, understanding dawning upon him long before he'd finished rereading the words. "It's Jack Pollack… the little boy. It's the boy who lived in the Needle and was haunted by the Northumberland Poltergeist. He wrote this, didn't he?"

Rose did not respond. He just stood there, watching.

Marc grabbed the envelope again and peered inside. He'd missed something in his haste: a second sheet of paper, this one an original rather than a photocopy.

He gripped the sheet of paper by the edges with both hands, as if he were afraid it might burn or blow away. Upon it was drawn the crude representation of a figure. It looked like a man, but could also have been a woman. It was difficult to assign a gender because the figure was wearing a long, black cape that smothered its body and a white, beaked mask over its face. In its hand was raised a short, thin stick or wand with a pointed end.

This was obviously a child's drawing. The lines were jagged, the shading went outside the lines, and the overall effect was that of crudity, juvenile artlessness... and yet, the drawing held an element of horror that Marc found difficult to ignore. The face was coloured with white crayon, the cape shaded in broad, angry strokes of a thick, black pencil.

Underneath this character was written its name, in the same clumsy, misspelled handwriting as he'd read in the diary extract:

captain clikcety

"He never told me he had anything like this." He looked up, at Rose, and the room pitched to one side, causing him to shudder. He felt like a man on a little boat, yearning for the shore.

"Maybe he didn't have it then. He might have got hold of this stuff just before he died, and not had time to show it to you."

"I saw him in hospital several times before he died. We talked about a lot of things – my book included, to keep his mind off his pain. He would've said. He would've told me. I'm sure of it."

"Then I don't know why he didn't. Come on. Let me show you what else I found."

Rose waited for Marc to rise and then walked out of the room, to the stairs. He paused at the bottom, resting one hand on the wall-mounted wooden banister, and then began to climb.

Marc followed him up to the first floor, noting the sound of the stairs as they creaked beneath their weight. They walked along the landing to the second stairway at the opposite end – one that had been added after the house was built, when the attic space was converted into habitable rooms.

Rose took out a set of keys and selected one of them. He unlocked the sturdy wooden door that sealed the stairway, and pushed it open. He reached inside and flicked a switch. The light came on up the stairs; a single bulb hanging from the ceiling at the top.

"Up here," he said, redundantly.

Marc was glad he'd spoken. The atmosphere was starting to feel strange, as if there might be something up there at roof level that he might regret seeing.

He followed Rose up the narrow staircase. The timber creaked even louder than before, and Marc had the weird sensation that there were more people packed into the cramped space than just the two of them. He resisted the urge to turn around and see who was following them – he knew there was nobody there, but his body was trying to convince him otherwise. The back of his neck was prickling; his spine felt warm, as if a hand were rubbing it through his shirt.

At the top of the stairs there was a door on each side of the tiny landing, where the attic was effectively split in two. Both of the doors were closed. The single bare bulb on the ceiling between the doors struggled to illuminate the space, as if something were pushing back the light. Marc kept expecting it to flicker and then go out, but it didn't. That only ever happened in horror films, and not in real life. Or so he kept telling himself, just to dispel the slow-creeping dread that had followed him up the stairs.

"I'll show you the library first," said Rose, his voice seeming too loud in the stairwell.

"The library?" said Marc, just trying to fill the space with his voice.

Rose stepped up onto the small landing area and used another key to unlock the door on the left.

"Security conscious, wasn't he?"

Rose didn't reply. He simply nodded once. Then he opened the door and stepped inside.

Marc was reluctant to follow, but he knew he should. In fact, he had little choice in the matter. Despite what his body was telling him, there was nothing to be afraid of here, deep inside the house of his old friend Harry Rose. There was nothing to fear; nothing that could hurt him. And if he was lucky, there might just be something in the attic that would bring his stalled book project back to life.

CHAPTER THIRTEEN

Royle was scared to go down to the basement. It was an embarrassing admission, even if it was only to himself, but the lower level of the Far Grove police station had always made him afraid. Over ground, he was okay. He felt not a tremor of apprehension regarding the station. But once he was forced to go underneath, the fear kicked in. He was reminded of the Crawl, and how it made him feel.

The main building had been built in the mid nineteen seventies, but it had been constructed over the top of the former police station, which had been a lot older. The contractor had decided to keep the original basement and foundations, using it as a platform on which to mount the new station superstructure. The old basement had been where the cells were. Small rooms with rusted iron bars, each one containing only a tiny sink and with a metal bed frame bolted to the floor. The detainment facilities they used these days were much more modern and comfortable; those old Victorian cells were like something out of Bedlam. Whenever he was down in the basement, Royle imagined the people who'd been caged there. He felt their eyes upon him; he heard their screams ringing in the air. He could almost see them crawling across the floor towards him...

He knew it was just his mind creating an atmosphere that didn't exist in reality, but this knowledge did nothing to reassure him. Whatever he did, however hard he tried, he couldn't shake the nagging fear that this place was home to ghosts.

The elevator doors opened and he stood looking out into the main access corridor. He knew that he should just step out and make his way to his destination, but his body refused to obey the simple command.

The old stone basement walls had been rendered with plaster and painted what was meant to be a soothing shade of white, contemporary lighting had been fitted, and new rooms had been created within the underground space... but still, the place held a sense of dread and expectation. To Royle, it was like walking into a military bunker. As he passed open doors, he half expected to glimpse inside those rooms men in shirtsleeves leaning over table-top maps of war, moving little plastic flags around as they planned their invasion. White collars, small round spectacles, pale skin, peering eyes.

Royle finally stepped out of the elevator and turned right, heading for the small on-site lab. The facility wasn't much to brag about, but it was somewhere the two resident techies could examine evidence that was considered urgent or too sensitive to be shipped out to the technical team based in Newcastle. The apparatus they had was limited, but the technicians – Miss Wandaful and Charlie – were talented and dedicated; they worked until the job was done, and never gave excuses when things went wrong.

He approached the computer server room and paused to glance inside the open door. He listened to the humming of the big extractor fans as they sucked warm air out through vents and through hidden ductwork, keeping the machines cool. The air-conditioned breeze cooled his cheeks. A man in jeans and a blue police-issue polo shirt was examining the system, making notes in a small black book. The man turned around and smiled. Royle recognised his face but was unable to put a name to it, so he simply nodded in greeting and continued walking along the corridor.

The lab door opened before he could reach it and Wanda Harper – the head technician – came out, her fingers struggling to take the cellophane wrapper off a fresh packet of cigarettes. She didn't see Royle at first, but when she looked up her eyes opened wider, as if she were startled.

"Ah," she said. "Fuck it. I thought I had another fifteen minutes before the hassle arrived." She smiled to show that she was at least half joking.

"Sorry, Miss Wandaful, but you know me – always a few minutes ahead of the game." Royle watched as the woman slipped the cigarettes into the back pocket of her jeans, under the white lab coat. She ran her hands through her spiky dyed blonde hair and rubbed at her temples, as if trying to ward off a headache.

"Well, seeing as you're here..." Wanda reached back and made a big show of opening the lab door. "Age before beauty," she said, bowing her head in mock deference as he entered.

The small room was crammed so full of stuff that it could barely fit two people, so it was always a relief when one of the technicians was on holiday – as was the case this week. The tiled walls were lined with shelves, each one packed to breaking point with box files or rows of medical supplies – bottles, cardboard boxes, instruments in sterilising machines. The floor was littered with filing cabinets, small cooler boxes and portable freezer boxes. Everywhere there were random pieces of equipment, and Royle felt hemmed in, as if he'd entered a storage facility rather than an annexe of a functioning police station.

The scarecrow was laid out on a stainless steel gurney at the centre of the room, the left side of its torso covered by a creased white sheet. The gurney was usually meant for transporting bodies, or parts of bodies, and the strange, stiff, legless figure looked out of place beneath the harsh, bright lights of the lab.

"What do you have for me, Miss Wandaful?"

Wanda grinned. Everyone at the station called her Miss Wandaful. She'd spent a long time protesting against the occasional nickname when it first started up, until finally, after six months on the job, she made the mistake of telling a uniformed officer on a station night out that she actually liked to be called that. Nobody had called her by any other name since.

"Okay," she said, standing at one end of the gurney. She moved slowly around to the side, pulling the white sheet fully off the figure and placing it to one side. "What we have here is a scarecrow."

"Gee," said Royle. "Do ya really think so?"

She carried on, unperturbed. "As you know, there was a photograph of Connie Millstone attached to the scarecrow's head. From what we can tell, it looks like the girl might have been deceased when it was taken. I'm sorry." She glanced at him, her face tense. "I was hoping to be able to tell you otherwise, but... well. That's how it looks. We've sent the photo to the main lab for an in-depth DNA analysis. The results should be back in a few days. I can tell you now, though, there were no fingerprints present."

The too-bright light made Royle feel exposed. His head was aching and his eyesight was blurred. He blinked several times in quick succession, to clear his vision. "Is this an assumption, a hunch... or is it a fact? How do you know she was dead when it was taken?"

"It isn't fact," said Wanda. "But it isn't guesswork, either. From the photo, you can see that the girl's skin has begun to take on the soft appearance of death; her muscle tone is nonexistent. If it was in colour, you'd be able to see the slight bruising caused by pooling blood and necrosis."

"What else?" Royle wanted a drink. He was craving whisky.

"This is where it gets really weird." She reached out and touched the pole that formed the central support for the figure. "This is made of solid oak. The head's the same."

Royle moved closer and stared at the pole. The bark had been stripped away; the nude wood looked like it had been smoothed down badly with a low-grade emery cloth. He examined the length of the body, resting his gaze upon the smooth, burnished head. Someone had removed its hat. The wooden head was virtually featureless; only the grain of the wood was visible.

He was reminded of Pinocchio, and of a show that used to be on television when he was a kid: *Pipkins.* It had scared him so much that he wet the bed. From what he could recall, the kids' programme was set in an old toy shop where the stuffed toys and puppets were alive: raggedy old Hartley Hare, with his dead eyes and loose stitches; Pig, Topov, and the rest of the gang. Horrible, all of them – grinning dishevelled demons. Dusty, falling apart at the seams... the awkward puppets had populated his nightmares for years afterwards.

Wanda's voice cut into his thoughts: "There are no oak trees within a twenty mile radius of the Concrete Grove estate."

He nodded, backtracking from his shabby, flyblown memories. "Okay. I'll admit that is a bit weird. Why use oak particularly and why go to so much trouble in the first place? It doesn't make sense. It isn't logical."

"Oh, it gets better than that." She turned and lifted a scalpel from a steel dish on a nearby trolley. Bending forward, she opened the scarecrow's jacket and used the blade to make a long slit down the front of its charity shop shirt – the two halves of which were stitched together using some kind of thick, fluffy thread. "That's some kind of natural fibre. Maybe hemp. Again, we've sent a sample to the lab for proper identification."

Royle didn't speak. He was captivated. He watched as the scarecrow's innards were exposed.

"What we have here is a mixture of stuff, all kinds of rubbish. Burnt leaves, pieces of paper... all sorts of crap."

Royle noticed for the first time that Wanda was wearing surgical gloves. He stared at her hands, pale and bloodless beneath the tight rubber layer, and watched as she raked around inside the belly of the scarecrow. A sudden terror filled him: what if she withdrew her hand and was clutching human organs, or, even worse, Connie Millstone's hand?

"There are a lot of receipts in here – from local shops, petrol stations, that kind of thing. All used as stuffing. What makes them special is that they're all dated to the exact same time and date." She stopped and looked up at him. Sweat was beaded on her forehead. Her eyes were shining, eager. She loved her work. "Can you guess when that was?" Her teeth glistened beneath the lights.

Royle nodded. "The day Connie Millstone went missing."

Wanda nodded. "Bingo. There are also a lot of dried leaves: oak, maple, rowan, rosewood. Each one a species that isn't present in this area. You have Charlie to thank for that information, by the way. He's the nature buff. I emailed him some digital images and he looked at them on the beach in Mexico. Isn't technology wonderful?" She winked. "Rather than stuff this thing with any old kind of rubbish, someone was extremely specific about what they used." She lifted her hand. Leaves spilled between the fingers. "These things have a special significance to someone, but I'll be shagged if it means anything to me."

"So there's some kind of meaning here. A message. Perhaps even some kind of ritual, perhaps?"

"You tell me. You're the detective man."

"Have you sent samples of everything to the main lab?"

"Yes." She backed away from the gurney, slipping off the rubber gloves. They made a smacking sound as she peeled them from her fingers. "They're doing every kind of analysis they can think of: chemical, fingerprinting, DNA, the whole deal. We've done some of the basic stuff here, of course, but we couldn't find a thing. No fingerprints, no apparent residue. Nothing. We need to look deeper. They have a lot more sophisticated equipment in the city than our shitty little budget allows for."

"Sorry. I wasn't having a dig. Just being thorough. Like you always are."

She smiled. "I know. It just pisses me off that we can't get any decent kit in here. Charlie and I have all the skills but none of the resources. If I wasn't so stupid, I'd fuck off and work in the city. The big lab, where my skill set would be appreciated." She leaned back against the sink, opening the pedal bin with her foot and dropping the gloves inside. She wasn't wearing any shoes, just the paper slippers used in hospitals. And morgues.

"*I* appreciate you. Don't know what I'd do without you sometimes."

"Fuck off, copper," she said, but she was smiling again. The bags under her eyes were huge and dark, like bruises. She was putting on weight. Her bleached hair looked as dry as straw. The teeth she'd recently spent a lot of money on having repaired and capped looked fake, plastic. The job was taking its toll, showing up like minor injuries or subtle deformities on her body.

Mine, too, thought Royle. *This fucking job, it's killing us all.*

He looked again at the scarecrow. He could have sworn that the head had not been turned that way, facing in his direction, the last time he looked, but it was difficult to be certain. There were no eyes, so it couldn't be looking at him; no mouth, so it was unable to grin. But he felt like it was doing both of those things. The smooth, bare wooden head that lacked even the merest hint of a face was watching.

And it was laughing.

CHAPTER FOURTEEN

ERIK SAT ON a dining chair and stared at the cat box. He'd found it in the lock-up garage and used it to transport the... the what? That was the big question, wasn't it? Just what the hell did he have in there anyway? What the fuck kind of creature had those kids found and brought to him?

When Hacky had gone outside and left Erik alone in front of the glass reptile tank, he'd taken a while to summon his courage. Erik was a brave man, sometimes insanely courageous when forced into a tight situation. He feared nobody. There had been times in his long and eventful life when he'd stood and fought opponents twice his size, or had a go when he'd been outnumbered and backed into a corner. He never ran; never turned his back on a fight. It simply wasn't in his nature to back down and walk away. But in that lock-up garage, crouching there in the shadows and staring into the glass tank, he'd never felt so much like running.

Erik was miles outside of his comfort zone on this one; his fighting distance had narrowed to almost nothing. He had no frame of reference whatsoever for the thing that had been waiting inside that tank. It was alien, from outside his realm of knowledge. He had no idea how he should even react to its existence.

There was a sound from the cat box; a low, trembling exhalation. He tried to tell himself that it was an animal noise – a mewling or a snuffling, something like that. But it wasn't. He knew it wasn't. The sound was... well, it was much too human to be labelled in such a way. The sound, he admitted to himself, was a voice.

"*Hungry*."

It had been saying the same thing since he'd brought it back here, over and over again.

"*Hungry*."

Erik stood and walked across the room. He waited at the low coffee table upon which he'd placed the battered cat box. Something moved again inside. He heard the sound of tiny nails – fingernails – scratching against the plastic walls of the box.

"Monty?" Even as he said the name of his friend, he had trouble connecting it to the thing in the cat box. He didn't want to admit this, even to himself, but he knew what was inside that box. "Is it you, mate?" This couldn't be real; none of it was happening.

But it *was* happening. He was here, enduring it. This was not a dream. It was reality – or at least what passed for it in these uncertain days.

He waited to hear the same response he'd been getting for the past half an hour.

"*Hungry*."

He dipped into a low crouch, his hamstrings complaining as he lowered himself towards the floor. He peered at the slats in the box, glimpsing slow movement between them.

"Fucking hell, Monty..."

He reached out and flipped open the cat box. The lid was on top, so he had to come up out of his crouch to look inside.

The thing... Monty... Monty Bright... that's what it was, who it was: it was his old sparring partner.

It was lying on its back looking up at the ceiling; the smooth skin of its small, shiny face caught the light. He remembered Monty as a big man, a hard man. He'd taken all kinds of shit to pump up his muscles, and worked out manically at his own gym, lifting weights and doing a lot of heavy bag work. He'd been short but huge; his wide build had been that of a battler.

Now he was small and vulnerable, like a baby, a damaged – or deformed – infant.

Monty's face was more or less the same as he remembered. It was recognisable, at least, and that was something he could hang on to. Same eyes; same blunt nose; same round head with the hair shaved off. The eyes, in fact, were identical to the way they always had been: clear and intelligent, the eyes of a thinker rather than a brawler.

The rest of Monty was unrecognisable.

The fire at Monty's gym had been bad, and everyone assumed that the owner had died in the blaze. But surely fire couldn't do this to a person? Fire blackened and burned; it charred and cooked the meat on the bones. It didn't... it didn't *shrivel* a victim down to a tiny, mutated replica of themselves.

The thing's body looked as if it had been compressed somehow, crushed and shortened and reduced by the application of phenomenal pressure. Erik remembered how, as a child, he'd put plastic crisp packets in the oven and within minutes of enduring the intense heat, they'd come out shrunk to a fraction of their original size. The same thing had happened to his old friend: the man's physique had more or less kept its natural proportions, but they'd been reduced by something like a factor of twenty.

Certain physical changes had also occurred.

The naked little body, a solid chunk of muscle, had grown several additional appendages. Monty had developed extra limbs, but ones that didn't look human. There were what Erik could only describe as tentacles sticking out of his sides, sprouting from the area directly under the armpits and forming a row down the sides of his ribcage. A clawed hand had erupted from his navel, and even as Erik watched it grasped weakly, clutching at the air, the knuckles popping and cracking. There were two toothless mouths in place of nipples; blinking eyes were clustered across his stomach below the ribcage.

This was Monty represented as a monster. He'd become what so many people had thought he was anyway: ugly, monstrous, a vision from a nightmare. The vile thoughts he'd kept locked up inside, the deeds he'd committed, had all manifested upon his flesh, chewing it up, destroying it and remoulding it into another shape entirely. Monty had become the sum of his evils, he had transformed into a manifestation of his deeds.

"*Hungry.*"

Erik looked at Monty Bright's small, pink babyish face. The mouth was open. A small, dark tongue darted between the lips, licked the top one, and then was sucked back inside. The lips smacked together, making a repellent sound.

"What... what can I get you? What the hell do you eat?"

What happened to you? What made you like this?

Maybe if he fed Monty, and built up his strength, Monty would tell him what had happened to make him transform into such a strange being. Perhaps he'd start saying something other than that one damned word.

And so he did:

"*Blood.*"

Of course: there it was. Because monsters didn't eat tinned tuna, or fish and chips, did they? They didn't sit down to a nice plate of mince and tatties. They drank blood, like ghouls or vampires.

Erik paused for a moment to appreciate the fact that he was taking all of this in his stride. He should be raving; his mind should have snapped. But he'd seen enough strange things in the Grove during his lifetime to realise that what he saw, what he felt, what he experienced with his normal, everyday senses, was not everything. There were other sights, other experiences, that lay hidden; and sometimes, when the time was right, they popped up into the light and made themselves visible. These things lived inside the black hole, and sometimes they managed to climb out.

This was one of those times.

"*Blood,*" said Monty again.

"Yeah... yeah, I know. It would be, wouldn't it?"

Erik had killed two men in his life. The first time had been in the service of his country, when he slit an enemy soldier's throat during a night-time assault on Goose Green, during the Falklands conflict. He had not been a young man, even then: he was older and wiser than most of his fellow soldiers by several years. It was near the end of his time in the armed forces, and he always thought of it as his final battle.

He'd loved the sound of the knife sliding through meat, hitting the more solid matter of the larynx, followed by the scraping sound as the metal clipped the edge of the hyoid bone. The soft spurt of blood, like a wordless whisper; the gentle sigh of a last breath escaping through the slit he'd made in the man's body. Silence... beautiful, blissful silence.

The second time had been during an organised fight in a warehouse in Gateshead, when a drug dealer had been trying to muscle in on Erik's turf. Erik had never liked drugs, but he did like to control how much came into and out of the area. He allowed people like Monty Bright to buy and sell. He didn't allow no-mark arseholes from across the water to come here and set up their own supply chains.

So he'd seen to it that the chav – who went by the name of Clancy Beevers – got to hear about a challenge. They'd met at three o'clock in the morning, shirtless, no weapons: old school. Erik had beaten the other man to death in less than five minutes. They'd chopped up the body and fed it to pigs owned by a man who'd always claimed to be Erik's second cousin, despite a lack of familial evidence. This man had proved useful on many occasions, so Erik never disputed the claims to kinship. He'd felt an almost erotic charge as he watched three sturdy porkers fighting over the remains of the man's head.

So, yes, he'd killed before. He'd killed before, and if he was honest, he'd have to say he liked it.

But surely that was something he should only do if everything else failed? Once a man got into the habit of killing, little else would fill the gap that appeared inside him. He'd seen it happen before, with soldiers mostly, but also a couple of times in civilian life. Murder carved holes in the soul, and the only thing that would close them – although temporarily – was more murder.

He shook his head, closed his eyes. His thoughts felt strange, as if they were being massaged, guided. They were *his* thoughts, of course, but they were much more intense than they should be.

His head swam. His brain twitched. Or that's how it felt: like the grey matter was flinching away from something, a stark reality that he couldn't face.

He walked into the kitchen and found the cat sitting near the back door, washing its paws. Its name was Cecil. He'd never liked the cat, and had inherited the thing from an ex-girlfriend who had stolen it from one of her old boyfriends as part of some oddball revenge plot. The animal had hung around when the woman left. Erik fed it and didn't mind that it slept somewhere around the house, but he never gave it any attention. It was as if he'd been keeping the animal for a situation like this one.

He bent over and picked up the cat by the loose flesh at the back of its neck. He slammed it into the large farmhouse sink, stunning the thing as its head smacked against the edge of the draining board.

He twisted the cat's neck, snapping the bones. It was a humane death.

He lifted the cat's body level with his face and stared into its flat, dead eyes. He felt nothing. His heart rate had not even increased.

He slid out a butcher knife from the wooden knife block on the worktop next to the cooker and returned to the living room. He set down the knife and the corpse and then went back to the kitchen, looking for a suitably large stainless steel bowl. When he found one, he carried it through and set it down on the floor. After a moment's pause, he went through into the hall and opened the cupboard at the bottom of the stairs, where he kept assorted odds and ends. He raked through the contents and found a box full of old folded plastic sheets, which he'd used to cover his furniture the last time he painted the living room walls. He selected one of the sheets and took it through into the living room, where he laid it out on the floor.

He picked up the corpse and the knife. Kneeling, he held the dead cat over the stainless steel bowl and drew the blade across its soft, furry throat. He held the corpse upside down over the bowl and watched the blood at first pour, and then slow down to a drip, as it filled the receptacle. It took a long time, because the heart wasn't pumping.

When he had enough blood he carried the bowl over to the coffee table.

"How the fuck do I do this?"

He took the bowl back to the sheet and then returned to the cat box. Gritting his teeth, he picked up Monty Bright and carried him over to the bowl. His skin was thick, like rubber, yet it was also strangely smooth. It felt like a diving suit.

"*Blood, blood, blood...*"

"Don't worry. It's coming." He cradled Monty like a baby and managed to manoeuvre him so that his face was near the blood in the bowl. He kept a tight grip on the squirming little body and pushed the face down towards the thick red fluid.

Monty lapped at the blood, his thick tongue making a wet sound as it flicked in and out of the liquid.

"That's good... that's better."

Then Monty began to struggle. He was lifting his head away from the blood and making an odd wailing sound, exactly like a testy baby refusing its food.

"What the fuck's wrong? It's blood..."

"*Blood, blood, blood...*"

Erik set down Monty on the plastic sheet. His chin was thick with cat blood, and he was spitting out whatever meagre amount he'd managed to take into his mouth.

Erik realised his mistake instantly. "It's the wrong kind of blood, isn't it?"

Without giving too much thought to what he was doing, Erik reached for the knife, wiped it on the plastic sheet, rested the blade against the palm of his left hand, and slashed lightly. He stared at the cut, wondering how it had got there. He'd felt nothing. He was empty, nothing but a puppet, a plaything for monsters.

Monty stopped struggling. His intelligent eyes widened.

Erik pressed the wound to Monty's mouth and let him drink.

He realised then that he would be required to kill a third human being. The act itself held no terror for him, but the motivation behind the deed was horrific. He watched as Monty lapped at his hand, and when he pulled away the meal, Monty tried to lift his head towards the dripping blood. His mouth opened and closed like that of a baby bird. He had no teeth. The gums were purple and swollen. The suckered limbs along his sides writhed, a sordid octopus-like motion.

Erik got up and grabbed a tea towel from the kitchen, which he wrapped around his hand to staunch the blood flow. The cut wasn't deep; it would heal quickly.

When he returned to the lounge, Monty was face down on the plastic sheet. His arms and legs, the tentacles and other appendages, were flailing, making rustling sounds against the sheet. He was licking up the spilled drops of blood and laughing, gurgling, expressing undiluted pleasure.

Erik knelt down and turned Monty over onto his back. The mouths on his chest were open and stained red. He stared at Monty's face. It looked fuller, the cheeks fatter than before. The skin looked less pale, as if his natural colour was returning. He was smiling.

"Okay," said Erik. "I get it now."

His head felt as if it were filled with foam; something was burrowing inside.

Monty cocked his head to one side. "Erik?" The voice sounded stronger, less childlike, and more recognisable as that of the real Monty Bright. Awareness dawned in his eyes.

"Yes, Monty, it's Erik."

"I need more." His eyes flickered shut. He was exhausted. The act of feeding had worn him out.

Erik closed his eyes for a second, and then picked up Monty and returned him to the cat box. "I know you do," he said, as he closed the lid. "And I know exactly where to get it."

He went upstairs to his office and sat at his desk. He stared at the screen saver on his computer – a black and white photo of Nigel Benn and Chris Eubank squaring up in the ring. He'd sparred with Benn before the man was famous. Erik had once knocked him flat out in the first round. It was a good memory, one that helped get him through some tough times when he began to doubt his own strength. Times like now, like this.

He picked up the phone and dialled a number, waited for the call to be answered. It didn't take long. Whatever he'd felt inside his head was fainter now, but it was still there, waiting.

"Erik."

"I need to see you, Hacky." He stared at the picture of the two proud fighters in the ring, doing exactly what was required to get the job done. No messing around. "Come out to the old country house tonight, at eight o'clock. You know the place. Don't tell any fucker where you're going or who you're seeing. If you do, and I find out, you won't get paid. You will get hurt, though."

"Paid?"

"Yeah. I have an important job for you. We're talking big money, son. More than you've ever seen before." He raised his eyes to the wall, examined the framed painting of a young Cassius Clay. "Consider this a test. If you do well, I'll push you up the ranks, and give you a proper role in my organisation."

"You can trust me, Erik. Always."

"I know I can, marra. That's why I called you, and not one of the others." He knew from experience that Hacky would keep his mouth shut. The kid was too afraid to disobey a direct order, and he liked money too much to even risk the chance of losing out. These scumbag estate kids were all the same: they'd do anything for cash, sell their own mother to climb up the criminal ladder and catch a glimpse of the big bucks.

"Meet me at the Barn. I'll be waiting inside for you."

"Is it... is it about the monster? That thing we found?"

"Sort of, marra. I'll tell you what you need to know tonight. Until then, lay low and don't speak to anyone. Make excuses; tell your mates you're ill and won't be seeing them for a few days. Give your girlfriend the elbow. Whatever. Just make yourself available to me, and only me. We have a job to do."

"Okay. That's easy. Am I going away, then?"

"In a manner of speaking, yes you are. Just for a little while. I'll see you at eight, marra." An idea occurred to him. "Bring a bag packed for a few nights. You won't need much where you're going; just the basic essentials." It wasn't a great plan, but it might fool people into thinking Hacky had gone on a journey.

He hung up the phone, feeling nothing. Nothing at all.

Back downstairs. Monty was sleeping inside the cat box. His eyes were closed, his chest rose and fell, rose and fell. Erik felt the same stirring inside his skull. Monty was doing something to him – or rather, the proximity to Monty was making something happen. It was like being in the presence of an electrical current.

His skin tingled. His mind flexed, like a muscle that hadn't been used for a long time.

Calmly, he sat down on the floor, cross-legged, and watched Monty sleep.

CHAPTER FIFTEEN

When Vince Rose unlocked and then opened the old, unpainted door to the first attic room, Marc expected to hear at least the whine of a rusty hinge, or the sound of boards shifting underfoot. But there was nothing; the door opened smoothly and without a sound.

"So you've never been up here before, I take it?" Rose spoke without turning around. He reached out and flicked a light switch. The room brightened. Marc wouldn't call it light, not exactly: that would be too kind a description for the weak, watery illumination. The room beyond the threshold simply became less dark.

"No," he said, following the old man inside. "To be honest, I didn't even know these rooms existed."

"Behold," said Rose. "My brother's library..."

The room was small but it seemed much more spacious because there was little furniture inside. Just a small tub chair pushed up against a bookcase. The walls were lined with books. Marc could not see an inch of wallpaper because there were so many ceiling-high bookshelves fitted along the walls, and volumes of differing sizes took up every inch of them. There were also books and dusty old box files lined up on the floor, along the skirting boards.

"Wow... this is quite a collection." He walked around the room, examining the spines. There were books on religion and philosophy, aviation, birds and wildlife. Shakespeare rubbed shoulders with Orwell and Stephen King. Biographies were stacked next to fiction. There was no recognisable order – no apparent system – to any of it. The majority of the volumes seemed to focus on Fortean subjects – real life ghosts and hauntings, sightings of monsters in lakes, murders, abductions, disappearances, UFOs, cryptos and tulpas. "He was really into this stuff, wasn't he?"

"So it seems." Rose went to the roof-mounted Velux window and opened the tilted venetian blind, allowing a little natural light into the musty room. "He was always interested in strange stuff, and I remember he started collecting books on these subjects when he was a child. I didn't realise he'd kept it up."

Marc's eyes roved over magazine collections: *The Fortean Times*, *The Unexplained*, *I Want to Believe, National Geographic, The New Scientist*... full sets, probably worth a small fortune on eBay.

One entire shelf differed from the rest in the fact that it was dedicated to a single subject. Marc had heard the name Roanoake before, but couldn't quite remember where or when. He selected a book at random from that particular shelf – *The Roanoake Colony: An American Mystery*. He flicked through the pages, skimming a few lines here and there, not taking much of it in until something snagged in his memory.

"Ah, yes..." He remembered it now: an infamous case. He'd read an article about it, seen a documentary on TV. A bunch of 16th Century English settlers had vanished mysteriously from an island off the coast of North Carolina. Carved into the trunk of a nearby tree, not far from the deserted camp, was the word

Croatoan. There were a lot of theories on why the one-hundred and eighteen people had apparently fallen off the edge of the world, leaving behind only this vague, slightly creepy message – local Indians, cannibalism, alien abduction – and the books on this shelf seemed to examine each and every one of them in great detail.

At the end of the row of books, tucked away slightly because it was so slender a volume, Marc spotted something potentially interesting. A school exercise book with a tattered blue cover, its edges dog-eared. He replaced the book he was looking at and selected this other one, sliding it out of its place on the shelf.

On the cover was handwritten the title *Croatoan and Loculus: a Study in Vanishment*.

"What is it?" Rose drew close, peering at the book in Marc's hands.

"I'm not sure. But it looks like your brother was working on something here – writing a book of his own, maybe, or at least an essay. Maybe he wanted to be published in one of those magazines he seemed to like so much."

He began to leaf through the exercise book. Written neatly on the pages was what appeared to be a series of rough notes, fractured jottings probably penned in great haste judging by the state of the handwriting. The text was unfinished; first draft material. This was clearly something Harry Rose had been planning to develop further but his demise had brought his plans to an abrupt end.

Marc read out a section at random:

"Carved into another tree nearby – an oak tree, which isn't indigenous to that area – was the word

'Loculus'. None of the books mention this. It has been expunged from history. Why?"

He turned the pages and read some more:

"The ruby-throated hummingbird is a native of North Carolina. Why have these birds been seen in the Grove throughout history, particularly around the area where the Needle was built? Did they come through from Roanoake?"

He looked up from the page. The room darkened incrementally and when he glanced up at the roof and out of the tiny window, he saw that dark clouds were massing, like harbingers of a storm.

He cleared his throat and read some more:

"The name Terryn Mowbray was recorded on the shipping manifest (but oddly not on the actual passenger list – was he classed as luggage? Stored in a coffin, perhaps, like Stoker's Dracula on the *Demeter*?), but this information can be found nowhere in any written account of the case."

He flicked through the text on the remaining pages. At the back of the book, a photocopied page had been stapled to the inside cover. He opened it and stared at the image. It was a child's pencil drawing. The lines were ragged, uneven, and the shading didn't stay inside the lines. The sketch matched the other one in his possession: it showed a man wearing a wide-brimmed black hat and a long black cape, holding a short, pointed stick. His face was white, with large black goggle-like eyeglasses perched above an oversized beak. It was a familiar image, of course – a medieval plague doctor. But the familiarity made it no less disturbing, especially as it had seemingly been sketched by a young child.

captain clikcety, said the words beneath the sketch, *drawed by Jack Pollack aged* 6

"Why the hell didn't he ever tell me about this?" He closed the book again and held on to it, not wanting to put it down but afraid to touch the volume for too long in case something infected him. It was a crazy thought, but nevertheless it caught hold inside his mind, barbed and dangerous. This information was unclean, it was tainted. Exposure to it might cause him damage.

"What is it?" Rose placed a hand on his arm. "You look... shaken."

"Whatever Harry was working on here, it has something to do with the case I was researching. The Northumberland Poltergeist. The Pollack twins. The ghost they called Captain Clickety. Even the Hummingbirds. These were all part of my own notes... Harry was keeping this stuff from me, deliberately it seems. For some reason, he was holding it back."

"I see. Maybe he was planning to tell you, but didn't get the chance?"

Marc licked his lips. "Or maybe there was something he didn't want me to find out..." He sighed. "But you're probably right. There's no reason he would have kept this information from me. He was a great help – why would he do that and then keep something this important back? It doesn't make sense."

"None of this makes sense, son. I'm starting to believe that my brother had mental health problems – far bigger ones than I ever imagined. I mean, does any of this strike you as abnormal? I don't mean to cast aspersions on the man's interests, but all this... well, it's slightly over the top, don't you think?"

Marc turned to face Rose. The man's face was pale in the gathering gloom. His eyes were moist, as if he were about to cry. Was he looking for denial or affirmation? "I suppose so, yes. It does come across as a bit obsessive."

"Just wait till you see what's in the room next door. That's the kicker." Rose turned and walked out of the room. He stood on the other side of the small landing and used another key to unlock the door opposite. "If you thought the library was weird, just wait until you get a load of this." He pushed open the door, switched on the light, and went inside.

Standing in the doorway of the library, Marc once again began to have the intense feeling that somebody was standing behind him. He knew that it was impossible, that he was alone inside the room, but the sensation of someone standing there silently in the corner grew and grew, becoming something that he could not ignore. He thought that it might be Harry, either urging him on or warning him not to pursue this any further.

Then, softly at first, he heard a steady, repetitive clicking sound. The sound grew in volume, but remained at a level that ensured no one outside the room could have heard it. The clicking remained at an even tone, droning on and on. Then, like a Geiger counter picking up levels of radiation in the air, it began to wax and wane, creating a hideous song.

Air trapped in the radiator? Old water pipes under the floorboards, making a racket?

The clicking decreased in volume and by the time he was facing the part of the room where it was coming from, it had ceased. The corner was empty. There was nobody there, watching him. Yet he felt as if there was yet another figure hiding just out of sight, perhaps drawn into a fold of darkness.

Marc backed out of the room, taking the exercise book with him. When he finally shut the door, he struggled to let go of the handle. He wanted to keep his hand there, gripping it tightly, effectively trapping whatever was inside that room for as long as he could. Like the fabled little boy with his finger stuck in the dyke, he was holding back the flood – but this was not a flood of water, it was a surging wave of darkness and desolation, the terrible precursor to an ocean of nightmare that would drown all who stood in its path.

"Are you coming?"

He turned his head at Rose's voice, which was coming from beyond the other open door. He pulled free his hand, backing away from the library, and allowed his body to turn around, too. He was beginning to feel hemmed in. Claustrophobia had never been something that had bothered Marc, but right now he felt trapped.

He stepped into the other room. The window blind was closed but Rose had turned on a small table lamp that was positioned on the floor in the far corner. It cast dim light across the room, creating a creepy atmosphere that wasn't helped by what was waiting at the centre of the room.

On a large plinth or table, and taking up most of the room, there was a scale model of the Concrete Grove estate. Marc stood and stared at it, hardly able to believe what he saw. He remembered a boyhood friend whose father had been obsessed with model railways. The man had created a system of tracks and fields, and even a small village, in the basement of their house. As a boy, Marc had been fascinated by the sight; as he grew older, he began to think it was all a bit sad and obsessive.

This reminded him of that guy and his model railway. A similar level of detail was displayed here, but possibly to an even greater degree of ambition. He recalled Harry's milk-bottle-top replica of the Needle. Had it been a practice model, a warm-up or a template he'd completed before tackling the real thing?

He moved towards the model, unsure of what to do in the presence of such a thing.

"Impressive, isn't it?"

He glanced at Rose, nodded. "Yes... and it's a bit scary, too. He must've spent hours in here, working away at this thing. It's *too* lifelike... know what I mean?"

"Yes, I do. It's creepy. Nothing like this should exist. It's... It's unhealthy."

Marc leaned across the table and reached out towards the replica of the Needle, the ugly tower block that stood at the centre of the estate. This one was not constructed from foil bottle tops.

"I think it's made out of cement, or maybe even proper concrete. He must've cast it himself, mixing the materials, constructing a little mould..."

Marc's hand had paused in mid air. He moved it forward, brushing his fingertips against the side of the tower. It was hard and rough, unpleasant to the touch.

Rose sounded troubled. "Cardboard I could understand. Even balsa wood. Perhaps some MDF off-cuts from a DIY store. But cement? That's going a bit too far."

Marc remained silent as he inspected the model. He didn't know what to say.

The estate was designed to form a series of concentric circles, each street wrapping around the one before. The plan view, looked at in this way, was weird. It looked like a magic circle, or a form of pentagram. Marc knew this was nonsense, but his gut instinct suggested otherwise. Why build the estate in such a specific layout? What was the purpose behind the circular pattern?

There was no furniture in the room; no shelves on the walls; no carpet on the floor. Just bare plaster and varnished boards. The model took centre stage. It was the reason this room existed. Nobody but Harry Rose had ever been in here until it had been discovered by his brother – Marc could sense it. The man had worked on his model every night, adding and subtracting tiny elements, making repairs and replicating alterations carried out in the real world by builders or council workmen. It was an ongoing project; his life's work. He must not have told anyone about the model. It was his secret. He had kept it all for himself.

But now that Harry Rose was dead, the seal had been broken: eyes other than his had taken in this small-scale urban wonder.

Some of the houses were made from the salvaged parts of plastic model kits. The vehicles on the streets were almost certainly bastardised toys and model kits; the tiny people were plastic toy soldiers that had been moulded and altered by the application of heat and a sharp craft knife, then dressed in perfect little clothes that Harry had fashioned from scraps of material.

The grass, when he touched it, felt like pieces of Astroturf. White lines had been painted by hand onto the road surfaces; drainage gullies and gutters had been fitted into the kerbs. No detail had been missed. Marc had no doubt that Harry's model matched the real thing down to the tiniest detail. He could tell by the painstaking work the man had put in that there was little margin for error. It was obvious how much love, dedication, and sheer hard work had been carried out in this room.

Then he noticed the flags.

They looked like minuscule versions of the kind of flags found on a golf course, the ones used to mark the holes. Or football corner flags. A cocktail stick topped off with a triangular cutting from a sheet of cotton had been used for each pole. As he looked closer, he saw that each of the flags had a name and a number written onto the material.

Connie 7
Alice 8
Fiona 9
Tessa 10

He knew what these were immediately. They were the names and ages of the Gone Away Girls, and each flag was positioned in the place from which they'd vanished. He made a mental note to look up the information, just to collaborate his hunch, but he knew he was correct.

Connie's flag was stuck in the grass at the sorry excuse for a children's playground the locals called Seer Green.

Alice's flag was in the car park of the small supermarket to the east of Grove Lane.

Fiona's flag had fallen over and lay flat inside the skateboarding park.

Tessa's flag stood forlorn and lopsided on the pavement outside a sweet shop near Grove Corner.

"What does this mean?" Marc turned and looked at Rose.

"I'm not sure. I think I'm too scared to even think about it."

"You noticed the names?"

Rose nodded.

"Do you know what they are? Do you know who those flags are meant to represent?"

"I do. It's those poor little girls, the ones that went missing."

Marc licked his lips. He didn't even want to think about this too deeply, but he needed to ask the question. "Do you think... do you really think that Harry could have been involved in their disappearances? Is there any way that he could have been responsible, or at least that he might have known who was?"

Rose didn't speak for a few seconds. He stared at Marc, then looked quickly away and examined the model. When he looked at Marc again, his eyes were moist. "In all honestly, I don't really know."

* * *

Back downstairs, in the small, neat kitchen, they drank coffee and stared at each other across the table.

"Here." Rose reached into his jacket pocket and took out a key. He placed it on the table in front of him, alongside the keys to the attic rooms. "It's for the front door. Use this place as you please. I have a feeling all that stuff upstairs might help you with your book, and if you can shine any light at all on Harry's possible involvement with those kids, I'd be grateful. I can't stay here – can't even come here. It feels... wrong."

Marc nodded and sipped his coffee. He reached out and took the keys, making a fist around them. "Thanks. I'm not sure what your brother was into, but I'll be honest – my muse is sitting up and begging for more."

"Just keep me posted. Let me know what you find out. I... I can't stay here. It's too much for me. I'm not a young man. I need to get out and breathe."

Marc nodded. "I understand. And I appreciate this, I really do." He opened his hand and looked at the keys. "I'll find out what I can and keep in touch."

Rose didn't take his eyes off Marc's face. "Let's just hope you find out that Harry wasn't involved."

"What do we do if... well, if he *was* involved? How the hell do we tackle that situation?"

Rose set down his cup. He placed his hands, palms down, on either side and made them into fists. "I don't know. Let's just see what you dig up first, eh? We'll face that problem if it *is* a problem."

"Okay. We'll see where the wind blows us on this. I'm pretty sure Harry wasn't doing anything bad. I think I knew him well enough that I'd be able to recognise something... you know, if he was a bad man." He paused. "And you were his brother: you'd at least have a slight inkling if he was some kind of child abductor. I doubt we're going to find any bodies buried under the cellar floor." He tried to smile but it was a struggle. "Worst case scenario: he knew a lot more than he ever let on, and something scared him enough that he kept quiet for all these years."

"That's what I'm hoping."

Marc nodded. "Yeah. Me, too."

LATER, BACK DOWNSTAIRS, MARC STOOD at the front window of Harry Rose's lounge, watching the sky grow dull and leaden. Like time lapse photography, the clouds moved quickly across the heavens, darkening the area, cutting it off from the sun. It was an unusual effect; he had never seen anything quite like it before. When he'd been up in the attic rooms with Rose, he'd glimpsed similar dark clouds out of the attic window, but these were much more expansive. He'd thought of those earlier clouds as harbingers of a storm, and still the idea felt right. But the oncoming storm was not one caused by atmospheric conditions; it was more of a spiritual upheaval.

Marc was not a religious man. Depending on what day he was asked, he would tell people that he was either an atheist or agnostic. He certainly didn't believe in the God his parents had prayed to. Look what that had achieved for them... nothing; nothing at all. Just a slow, painful, drawn-out death in front of their son.

He watched the darkening sky, his skin prickling as if tiny ghost fingers were pitter-pattering across every inch of his body. He felt cold. The hair on his arms and on the back of his neck was bristling. It was a sensation he'd only ever read about in books, but now that it was happening to him he realised that the physical experience – like most clichés – was based in reality.

"*Jesus...*" He reached out and closed the window blinds, then turned to face the room. He didn't feel comfortable here. Not on the estate or in this house. Everything seemed vaguely hostile, as if his presence was unwelcome.

When Rose had left, Marc had gone straight back up to the attic. After studying the model of the estate for a little while, he'd crossed the landing to the library. Ignoring the sensation that there was still someone in there, standing in the corner and watching him, he'd browsed again through the volumes. On a shelf near the door, he found another notebook. He'd failed to notice it the first time, but this time it was as if his eyes had come to rest immediately upon it, deliberately seeking it out. He refused to believe that it had not been there the first time, and someone had placed it on the shelf for him to find when Rose wasn't around.

The two notebooks were now on the coffee table. He crossed the room, sat down, and picked up the second one again. It was old, the cover creased and stained, yet unmarked by any kind of writing.

There wasn't much content inside this one, but on the first page was stapled a faded copy of an old-fashioned print or woodcut of a plague doctor. The name Terryn Mowbray was written underneath in Harry's neat, small script.

"Terryn Mowbray is Captain Clickety..." Even as he said the words, he appreciated their inevitability.

He turned the page and read the words over, trying to understand them more fully this time. There were scribbled footnotes at the bottom of the page, and Marc could at least see the shape and structure that Harry had been attempting to impose upon the writing.

In 1349, during the Black Death, a plague doctor was summoned to the village of Groven[1] in the northeast of England. King Edward III himself was said to have given the man his orders. Groven, it was said, had managed to avoid all signs and marks of the Plague. The Black Death had not crossed its borders; the people who lived there were fit and healthy and oblivious to the darkness that had fallen over the rest of Europe[2].

The plague doctor, Terryn Mowbray, was around thirty years old. There is no record of his existence prior to his mention here, and even this was difficult to piece together from various unreliable sources. He apparently arrived in Groven sometime in May. What he found there (here?) enraged him. The people of the village had embraced ancient rites and rituals and even created new ones of their own – normal pagan beliefs had been supplanted by something stranger, like a mutated, nameless religion. They prayed to unnamed deities and Mowbray claimed that they offered up children – twins were thought to be the most prized – as a sacrifice. The children were stabbed to death at the centre of a grove of oak trees, their blood left to soak into the earth. A path of black leaves is said to have led the way from the village to the grove[3].

---

[1]Groven – Grove – the Concrete Grove.

[2]Edward Plantagenet clearly hoped that some great and hidden knowledge would be revealed to him if he discovered why the village of Groven remained Plague free.

[3]Surely a metaphor?

Mowbray apparently noted many strange sights[4]: visions of a tall, grey structure at the centre of the grove of trees, birds that hummed and flew backwards, a young girl with multicoloured wings, and animals that he could not name – a horse with a single truncated horn, like a mutilated unicorn, dogs with the faces of humans, a large, bloated snake that smelled of offal and was drawn to the site of the bloodshed. He called this giant serpent the Underthing[5].

Mowbray was enraged. He ordered the village cleansed. People were hung, burnt in bonfires, and quartered by his men. After the massacre[6], he and his men slept one more night in the village.

The rest is sketchy[7] at best. Some say that a great number of ghostly twins appeared in the village, and others say that it was a pack of ravenous human-faced dogs. I was even told by one drunken old-timer that it was giant hummingbirds.

However it happened, Mowbray's men were killed, their skinned bodies hung from the branches of the oaks. Only he was left alive. An envoy sent by the King arrived a few days later and found Mowbray, starving and filthy and jabbering, sitting at the centre of the grove of oaks, surrounded by the rotting, flyblown remains of his men's bodies. He spoke about other worlds, and gateways,

---

[4]I could find no trace of these notes. I assume they went with him, wherever he vanished to.

[5]I have no idea what this means. Could it represent the nameless forces the villagers worshipped?

[6]There's no record of how many victims there might have been.

[7]I got some of this story from obscure Fortean literature, and the rest has been told in the back rooms of certain pubs for decades, changing, like a game of Chinese Whispers, with each telling.

and secrets that should never have been disturbed. He whispered the words *Croatoan* and *Loculus*. Upon his face and body, beneath the mask and the cloak, were the buboes and postulant sores of the Plague. He had brought it here, to the place that had previously remained untouched. His spirit had polluted the sanctity of Groven, first with the sin of his banal evil, second with the blood of the villagers, and then finally with Black Death itself...

The only whisper I heard about what happened next makes little sense out of context. Apparently Terryn Mowbray stood, bowed, and started turning in a slow circle upon the ground. He disappeared as if he were sinking into the earth, corkscrewing away into infinity, chanting a single word over and over again: *Loculus*[8]. All that was left in his place was a small mound of blackened leaves[9].

The King's envoy was imprisoned, a gibbering idiot after what he'd found. The King said he was a liar and a heretic. The man killed himself in his cell three years later.

Marc set the notebook down next to him on the sofa. He leaned back and tilted his face up towards the ceiling, closed his eyes. It was madness. None of this could be true – it was all myth and hearsay, local legend given the kind of attention that it surely did not deserve. He opened his eyes and stared up at the ceiling. There was a large cobweb in one corner; he could see the fat black body of a spider, motionless against the white plaster ceiling. The spider seemed to be watching him. Or perhaps it was dead.

---

[8]Again, this word. This place. Where is it? Is it here, in the Concrete Grove? How does one find it, and how to gain access? Was this the secret knowledge King Edward, through Terryn Mowbray, was seeking?

[9]What's with the black leaves again?

"Why the hell didn't you get yourself a computer, Harry?"

Harry's system was difficult to follow. The books in the library were kept in some kind of highly personal and esoteric order, and he had found no more of the slender notebooks on the shelves. There wasn't much written down. It must all be in Harry's head, burned to ashes along with his body.

"What else did you know?" The spider moved; it was alive after all. The web shuddered. The spider was no longer there. But something was... and not just in the corner of the ceiling. Marc became convinced that it was everywhere, inside and outside the house; all around him, trying to get inside him. Something was coming.

"What is it that you were keeping from me, and are you trying to tell me now that you're dead?"

He thought about the Pollack twins, and the Northumberland Poltergeist. He'd always known there was more to the story than a simple urban haunting, but who the hell would believe any of this? His publisher would laugh at him; they'd send him away without an advance. It was fantastic, improbable... more than that: it was fucking insane.

Other worlds, demonic plague doctors, links to a famous case of vanishing New World settlers, a monster called the Underthing... the more he dug, the more incredible all this seemed.

He closed his eyes and tried to pin down the facts. But facts were thin on the ground here; all he had to cling to was a bunch of ghosts and stories within stories.

Only one thing was certain. Doors were opening, or being opened.

Something was on its way.

Something was coming.

mummy went out to pub and daisy like a flower a sleep. sumbody else in the house wi me. i here him breething. captain clickety comign for me. he see me all the time even when he not here. he everwhear not just in the house. he all over the estate like grass and roads and houses. he lives in the needle but he can see through walls. he wants me and daisy like a flower because we look the same. two things the same make him stronga. two things the same fill him up like food. this time he bring others with him. they clothes are funny like old style in the museum or wot scarycrows have on. they smiling. some have blood on them clothes and faces. they hungry. I be food for them. me and daisy like a flower. a humingbird fly in the room. i go to play with it. keep it away from baby.

– From the diary of Jack Pollack, April 1974

PART THREE

Scarecrow Culture

"I heard its fucking heart beating."

– DS Craig Royle

CHAPTER SIXTEEN

Royle usually went over to Vanessa's place once a fortnight for dinner. He wasn't sure why they did this, or what she got out of the experience, but it meant that they could at least maintain regular face-to-face contact. It was part of the unspoken terms of their separation. Even though they were no longer officially together, neither of them could stand the thought of being apart, so they went through this stylised charade on a regular basis.

It had been her decision to temporarily separate – most of the major decisions in their lives were down to her – and although he'd never wanted it to happen, he could see the logic in her proposal. A bit of space; some time to contemplate what it was they both wanted; the distance he needed to pull himself together. His main fear – his *only* fear – regarding the situation was that she'd discover she didn't want him back and that would be the end of them.

Vanessa still lived in the house they'd pushed their budget to the limit to buy, while he slept in that cramped little flat above the shops. He didn't mind the arrangement, but he missed going home to her after a long, hard shift, missed pressing his body against hers in their double bed. But she'd never understood his anxiety as manifested in the Crawl, and his lasting obsession with the Gone Away Girls.

His obsession with every case he'd ever worked on, if he was honest... it was this precise intensity that he failed to bring to their marriage, and it hurt her that he reserved it only for his work.

The car engine made a soft burring noise as he drove out into the Northumberland countryside, heading towards the small village where they'd set down roots. Royle had always been a city boy but Vanessa preferred to be out in the sticks, surrounded by trees and green fields and spaces that weren't filled with the stench of motor vehicles and the sounds of a hemmed-in, overstimulated population.

It was dark now; the stars were out. The sky looked like a perforated black sheet backlit by a weak bulb. His hands ached as they gripped the steering wheel and his mind was filled with images whose collective meaning he found hard to define: a scarecrow with a missing girl's face, a small crawling thing that remained out of sight, the mortally wounded body of a young man lying in a pool of blood.

These, among others, were the pictures he was forced to carry around with him, like unwanted family portraits of people he'd rather not be related to. He lived with these images; they were part of him now, central to who he was and what he had become. He wished that things were different, that he could have been a bus driver or a shopkeeper, or an internet millionaire... but he was a copper, and he always would be. Some things, it seemed, never changed, no matter how hard you wished they would.

When he pulled up outside the small detached house, he sat there for a little while, staring at the lighted windows and trying to define a shape beyond the glass. The Crawl was far behind him now; he could almost pretend that it didn't exist, that it was something he'd once read about or seen in a film. This was real: the small, neat house in the country, his pregnant wife, the baby they'd made together, the untapped potential they had cherished before the darkness had come between them, driving a wedge between their feelings for one another.

Then, out of habit more than any sense of perceived menace, he glanced in the rear-view mirror to see what was behind him. Darkness bulged along the street, like food caught in a giant throat. Something flickered; a sense of quick, nervous movement. Even here he wasn't safe.

None of us are, he thought. *Not ever*.

The skin of his back and shoulders started to prickle; then it spread along his arms, reaching round to his chest, almost hugging him. The Crawl – it was here, even here, where he had mistakenly thought there might be safety. Somehow it had reached out, following him from the Grove, and managed to grasp hold of the rest of his life, tainting everything, polluting his thoughts and even his dreams.

He opened the door and got out of the car. A gust of wind blew along the street, buffeting him, almost knocking him off his feet. Then, a second later, the air was calm and still; there was not a trace of the wind he'd felt. Royle stared back along the street, in the direction he'd come. The darkness twisted, corkscrewing. He half expected to hear disembodied laughter.

Something's coming, he thought, but he had no idea where the thought had come from or specifically what it meant. *It's on its way*.

Someone crossed the street, turning their head to glance in his direction. It was a small girl. She was wearing a dress but no coat. It was much too late for children to be out, unless they were up to no good – and this one didn't look like the kind of kid who hung out on street corners, smoking fags and drinking cider with her mates. She was too sensibly dressed, and there was a sense of innocence about her that he could make out even from this distance.

The girl stopped in the middle of the road and stared at him. She lifted her arms as if she were about to take flight. Darkness webbed in the space between her arms and her body; black gossamer wings unfolding. Royle took a step forward, and the girl's image seemed to waver, like a faulty piece of film.

He shook his head, closed his eyes. Opened them again.

The girl was no longer there. Wind gusted but he could not feel it. A soft clicking sound, like someone running a stick along metal railings, moved away from him along the dark street, fading into the distance. It was a sound he'd heard before, but he couldn't remember where or when. He never could; it was like some kind of primal echo, a memory from a time that was lost to him.

Royle turned away and headed towards the house, the lights, his wife and unborn child. He opened the gate and walked up the path, flanked on either side by tiny lawns, flower beds Vanessa kept looking neat and tidy, even during the winter months. He took a few panicked breaths, trying to calm down, and then knocked sharply on the front door. Waiting, he gazed through the glass panel in the door and saw a wide, blurred figure approaching along the hallway.

The door opened and she stood there, an engorged angel, on the threshold.

"Hi Craig." She smiled.

"Hi." He stared at her narrow, pretty face, the bright maternity dress, the bulge she was massaging softly with both hands.

"Come on in." She turned and walked into the house; he followed her, close to tears, tottering on the edge of absurdity.

The house smelled of beef casserole and Vanessa's coconut body lotion. He glanced up the tight staircase as they passed alongside it, wishing that he could stay the night, sleep in their bed, hold on tightly to the woman he loved, had always loved, would never stop loving. Like a shadow of the past (or the future?), he saw a faint image of himself walking across the upper landing, heading for the bedroom they'd once shared.

"How are you today?"

She sat on the sofa as he entered the living room, stretching out her legs and resting her feet on the leather pouffe. "I'm achy." She smiled. Her face was drawn and pale, her eyes were heavy-lidded, but still she was beautiful. "Had a few cramps, several hard kicks or punches in the stomach. I think this one's going to be a kick-boxer."

Royle sat down in the armchair opposite, leaning forward with his elbows resting on his knees. "Anything I can do for you, or get you?"

She shook her head.

He tried not to look at the framed photographs on the mantelpiece, the pictures on the walls, the magazines in the rack. Each ornament reminded him that he no longer lived here; every new knick-knack on a shelf was another barb in his heart because she'd bought it alone, without him.

"What about you? What kind of day have you had?"

"Weird," he said, without thinking.

"Oh, yeah? How so?"

He shook his head, scratched his right knee with his index finger. "Somebody's playing silly games on the Grove estate, leaving scarecrows in people's gardens. Nothing major, just stupid stuff. Some kind of wind-up."

"I see," she said, leaning back on the sofa, her interest having dried up and blown away. "I'll serve up dinner shortly. It's beef casserole... your favourite dish." She narrowed her eyes when she said it, as if to make clear that she meant nothing by the gesture. It was just a meal, nothing more.

"That sounds good. Really good actually. I'm starving." He couldn't remember when he'd last eaten, or even what he'd eaten. Probably some kind of junk food: a burger, a TV dinner warmed up in the microwave. Had he even taken breakfast this morning? But why the hell was he thinking about food when he should be down on his knees begging Vanessa to take him back, to give it another go? It was an indication of how his life was unravelling. Nothing was straightforward, every road had too many bends and he always got caught up watching the scenery.

Vanessa stood and waddled across the room to the kitchen door.

"Need any help?" He began to follow, but she turned around.

"No, I'm fine. I can still serve a meal. You just sit down and I'll call you in when it's ready. I'd offer you a drink... but..."

He smiled. "I'll be happy with a glass of water with the meal."

She nodded. "I'm pleased to see you're making an effort." Before he could add anything more, she vanished into the kitchen.

Royle was too restless to sit, so he walked to the window, glancing out at the street. The old stone wall opposite the house held back a line of trees whose branches flapped and twitched in the breeze. The sky was black and distant. No traffic passed by; the road had always been quiet, hardly ever used except by the people of the village. He stared at the swaying tree branches, their leaves gone; they resembled spiny fingers grasping at the air, trying to gain purchase in the world. Some of those leaves had fallen to the ground, and they looked black in the darkness.

"Okay, you can come through now."

He reached out and shut the window blind, then turned away from the window. He walked across the room and opened the kitchen door. Vanessa was already sitting at the big dining table, pouring water from a clear glass jug into two glasses. Large bowls of casserole sat steaming on the table.

"Looks good," he said, sitting down opposite her.

"Thanks. You always say that."

They started to eat and said nothing. There was a strange tension between them, as if they barely knew each other. Perhaps they didn't; maybe that was the problem. They'd never known each other, not properly, and now the cracks were starting to show.

"So you're keeping off the drink?"

Her question took him by surprise but not enough to faze him. "Yes," he lied. "Well, as best I can, anyway."

She stopped eating, put down her spoon. "What does that mean?" Her eyes were wide. In their depths, he saw everything: the life they'd had, the way things had been cut short because of his behaviour, the possible future they had together if only they could work things out. Behind this, pulsing in the darkness, were so many questions that had so far remained unasked.

"I keep slipping, a bit. I'll go for days without even thinking of drink, but then I'll suddenly find myself in a bar, or sitting at home with a glass in my hand. It's nothing major. Not like it used to be..." He reached for his glass, gulped down the water, and refilled it. "Need a top-up?"

"No thanks." Her eyes didn't leave his face.

"I really am trying my best, you know. I want you back... I want us back together, with the baby. It's the only life I see ahead of me, the only viable option. If I don't have that, I have nothing."

Her eyes gleamed beneath the kitchen lights. He wasn't sure if she was crying or if the bulbs were too bright.

"I am trying." It seemed pathetic that this was all he had: a promise, one that was only partially true. Words, empty reassurances, like pleading for forgiveness. He felt the Crawl upon his flesh, making him shudder. His skin prickled, his shoulders began to tense. He thought of those black leaves on the ground outside, a charred pathway to oblivion.

"Eat up," she said, picking up her spoon. "It'll go cold."

Royle couldn't help reading too much into her statement. Did she simply mean the casserole, or her love for him? Might that also go cold if he couldn't pull himself together in time? Was she trying to say that there was a finite time span on this separation, and if they couldn't get past these current obstacles he would lose her forever? Her and the baby...

He ate his casserole, but it was tasteless now.

After dinner he washed the dishes and she dried and put them away. They stood side by side at the sink, their hips occasionally touching, their hands moving in some kind of pattern designed to achieve a common goal.

"We could have used the dishwasher, you know."

He glanced sideways, catching her profile. She was smiling.

"This is better," he said. "This is much better."

"Yes," she said. "Yes, it is."

When the dishes had been put away, they went back into the living room and sat together on the sofa. He had a glass of orange juice and she was drinking herbal tea. The television was on; they stared at the screen without watching what was playing. Some old film: Paul Newman and Natalie Wood.

Royle wanted to reach out his hand and place it on her thigh, but it was too soon for such an intimate gesture. Instead he tried to be content with the minimal contact: thighs touching, breath mingling, feet resting side by side on the same low footstool.

"Oh..."

He turned, putting down his glass. "What's wrong?"

Her face looked shiny, as if she were sweating. Her eyes were huge, glowing. "I think... I think baby's kicking." She grinned.

"You said it had been restless all day."

"Yes, I did. Maybe excited about you coming..." She was still smiling, but he could tell that she was in pain.

"What can I do?" He swivelled his body on the sofa, ready to get up and fetch whatever it was she needed.

"Give me your hand."

He wasn't expecting that; he needed an errand to run, a task to perform. He always worked better if he had a specific job to do, a problem to solve.

"Come on." She reached out and opened her fingers.

He slipped his hand into hers, shaking, feeling as if this was a pivotal moment, that it meant something in a way that no other moment in his life ever had.

"Gently..." She slowly pulled his hand towards her body. She placed the tips of his fingers against her belly. "Don't be scared." She'd never done this before. Here was progress, at last. She was warming to him again, forgetting about the pain he'd caused, remembering that they'd created this life together, out of the raw material of love.

He opened his hand and pressed the palm flat against her belly. Even through the thin cotton of the maternity dress, her body was hot, as if a fire burned somewhere under her skin. He waited for some movement, holding his breath, perched on the edge of a miracle.

The baby kicked. It happened once, a sharp little prod, as if it was trying to hit his hand.

"Did you feel it?"

He was unable to speak. He nodded, feeling the heat of his tears as they rolled down his cheeks.

"This is what you're fighting for. Keep it up, stay off the drink, forget about the job and the stress... fight for us, Craig. For *us*: all three of us. We're a family, and that's how I want it to stay."

"Can I... can I listen?"

She nodded. "Yes, if you like."

He slid off the sofa and got down on his knees in front of her, a supplicant before this goddess, this carrier of immense power and promise. When she clasped his head in her hands and drew him in towards her, he remembered all the times she'd carried out the same movement before, but for a different reason. He tasted a ghost of the tang of her sex on his tongue, smelled the musk of her juices. He ached for her; every part of him, each single cell, wanted to be with this woman.

He placed the side of his head against her swollen belly, his hands going up, and his arms slipping around her widened waist. He closed his eyes and he listened; he listened for the heartbeat of his saviour, the answer to his pathetic secular prayers. At first he could hear nothing, and then he began to detect her heartbeat... and beneath that, or alongside it, he swore that he could hear a second frail rhythm. It was the heartbeat of his son or daughter; the only sound in the world that really mattered.

Then, he heard something else.

It began softly at first, and he thought it might be the droning of a distant motorbike disturbing the moment as it raced along the empty village streets. Then he realised that the sound was coming from inside Vanessa. It was originating from the same place as those two heartbeats.

A faint clicking sound, like castanets muffled by a pillow. It grew slightly louder, clearer, and then began to wane. The sound didn't last long – just a couple of seconds – but as he listened, the Crawl seemed to answer its song. His entire body went cold; gooseflesh rose on his skin; he started to shake, to tremble like a frightened child.

He pulled away from Vanessa, stumbling across the floor and falling onto his backside.

"What's wrong?" Her face went slack. Her eyes narrowed. He didn't want to see the distrust in her face, not again, not now.

"Nothing." He stood, running a hand through his hair. "I just… it was the emotion. I was overwhelmed. That was a heartbeat. I heard its fucking heart beating."

Vanessa relaxed, reaching out to pat the sofa beside her. "Come and sit by me, Craig."

He moved to the sofa and sat down. He was cold. He tried not to shiver.

She clasped his hand, squeezing his fingers. Her skin was warm; it took away the chill.

"I'd like you to stay the night," she said.

He turned to face her but she wasn't looking at him. She was staring at the television, her face serious. Paul Newman was standing in the street, looking up at the sky.

"I don't want you to go, not tonight."

"I…"

"No, wait. Just hear me out." Finally she looked at him, and her eyes were hard, like chips of ice. "I've had this feeling all day… a feeling that something's on its way and it won't be good for you. For us. I'm scared. It's probably just hormones, but the fact is... the fact is, I'm scared. I want you to stay. I want you to sleep beside me, in our bed. I don't know what this means in terms of us, but I think it says a lot that I want you close to me, I want you holding me in the night."

His lips were dry, but he was no longer cold.

"You can say something now." A flicker of humour crossed her face.

"Of course I'll stay. There's nothing I'd like better."

She looked down at her knees. "Thank you." Her voice was quiet, not much more than a whisper.

She squeezed his hand. He squeezed back, desperate not to break the fragile connection.

They stayed that way for a little while longer, holding on to each other yet still maintaining a short distance between their questioning bodies; intimate strangers waiting for some kind of sign or signal. Then, when the film ended, they went wordlessly upstairs to bed and fell asleep in each other's arms.

CHAPTER SEVENTEEN

This time Abby is aware of sitting up in bed and turning to face the door. The room is dark; the shapes of the furniture are somehow threatening, as if they are poised to pounce. She feels as if she might be in danger, but she isn't sure what form it will take.

She walks across the room, shedding her nightgown. She is hot; her skin is covered in a thin layer of sweat. She opens the bedroom door and steps out onto the landing. The door to her daughter's room is already open and light spills out across the carpet. Shadows caper across the walls. Abby is holding her breath. If she lets it out, she might disturb whoever is in there.

She moves slowly towards the room, her arms hanging down by her sides, hands open. Her skin prickles, excitement makes her blood run faster.

She enters the room and there is no one there. The homemade totem, the stack of Tessa's things, looks larger, taller; its tip is now almost touching the ceiling. She cannot remember adding anything new to the pile. She has not touched it for quite some time, as if some residue of fear has kept her away.

She walks across the room and stands before the conical mound of her daughter's belongings. Things have been rearranged. The photo of Tessa's face is no longer there, and toys she does not recognise have been added to the construction.

She kneels down and closes her eyes.

"*Tessa, Tessa, Tessa... bless her, bless her, bless her... come back to me.*" She recites the familiar prayer without even thinking about it. She does not hear the words as they pass her lips.

She hears the creaking, rustling sound of the totem shifting. She does not open her eyes. If she sees what is happening, it might break the spell. Something touches her face, brushing softly across her cheek. It feels like a tiny hand, but one that is not fully formed. The fingers are fused together and the skin feels soft and inchoate.

Whatever it is pulls away, making a louder rustling sound this time as it is sucked back into the mass of the totem.

Abby opens her eyes.

She is no longer inside the room, or even in the house.

She is kneeling at the centre of a grove of oak trees. It is dark. The sky is black and starless. There is no moon. The ground is covered with leaves.

Figures are hiding in the undergrowth, standing silently, watching her. The figures are small, slight, like malnourished children.

"Hello..."

The figures do not move. Their eyes sparkle behind a screen of foliage. White teeth are bared in either smiles or snarls. There are three of them, and slowly she begins to realise that they are waiting for her. In unison, they raise their hands above their heads, open their fists, and each of them drops a handful of black leaves onto the ground.

She stands and walks towards a clear spot between two trees, where the overhanging bushes have been forced apart to form an archway. She passes through the archway, feeling leaves brush eagerly against her skin, and makes her way along a narrow, ill-defined pathway. The trees and bushes on either side of her sway, as if dancing. Her bare feet sink into the soft loamy ground.

Before she has time to be afraid, she emerges from the grove and is standing in a clearing. The figures are standing up ahead, at the top of a slight rise. She can see them clearly now, despite the lack of natural light – still there is neither moon nor stars to light her way. There are, as she suspected, three of them, and they are little girls. The girls are wearing tattered clothing – torn coats and dresses, shoes that are falling apart on their small feet. Their bodies are painfully thin, which makes their heads look oversized. They look half starved, as if they have not eaten in months. Abby is put in mind of video footage from African trouble spots: big eyes, dark, sunken cheeks, pot bellies filled with air not sustenance.

As one, the three girls turn away and start to walk down the opposite side of the hill, black leaves falling from their palms to scatter on the earth. Abby follows them, unconcerned at her nakedness, just desperate to make sure that she does not lose sight of the children.

The grass stretches on for as far as she can see, broken here and there by solitary stands of trees, ruined stone buildings, flapping tent-like hides or dwellings inside which small fires burn. Smoke rises from holes in the roofs of these flimsy structures, grey against the black, starless sky.

She can see the dark leafy path they are following, make out small animals running alongside her as she trails the girls. She knows exactly who they are, these three children: they are the Gone Away Girls, all but one; all but her daughter, Tessa.

They're taking me to see her...

But she has no idea if this is the truth. For all she knows, they could be leading her to certain death, or straight off the edge of a cliff. If they were leading her into the mouth of some hideous monster, she would have no clue until she got there, and stared directly into its fiery eyes.

But at least I'll know... at least I'll know what happened to her.

And isn't that what's been killing her all along, the lack of knowledge? Long ago, she told herself that knowing Tessa was dead would be at least better than not knowing anything at all. Her life has been on hold, her soul has withered; she is barely even human. The loss stalled her in time, made it so that she ceased to develop as a person. All she was, all she is, is a thing that waits.

She follows the small, thin forms of the three girls, watching their dark backs, terrified that they might bolt or – even worse – simply fade into the darkness, leaving her there alone on the pathway of black leaves. She is walking quickly to keep up but she does not feel out of breath. It is as if she is standing in one place and the landscape itself is moving, rolling past her like a set dressing on castors.

Hills loom out of the darkness up ahead. They form the foothills of a high rock face. There are caves: dark, jagged holes cut into the hillside. The girls pause, look back, wave. Then they bend over and enter one of the caves.

Abby increases her pace. She feels a light chill against the side of her face, and it is pleasant, keeping her cool. When she reaches the cave, she looks up at the sky – wishing that she could see some stars – and then follows them inside.

Darkness swallows her up. She feels like turning back, following the black leaves to the safety of the grove of trees, but realises that she has no choice but to carry on into this uncertain darkness. She hears water dripping down the cave walls; the hard ground is cold and wet underfoot. She can see nothing, only blackness. She holds out her hands, feeling her way deeper inside, and even though she expects to come up against granite walls, she feels nothing... she might be walking a path with a sheer drop on each side.

But that's okay. She doesn't fear death, not now. She has not been afraid of dying for a long time. In fact, she's often flirted with death, taking too many drugs and sleeping with strange men in the hope that they might be killers. But nothing bad ever happened. She has led a charmed life since her daughter went missing, as if the forces of the universe have conspired to keep her alive, as a form of punishment for losing the only person she ever loved, the only human being who ever loved her as much as she never deserved.

Vague light up ahead.

She moves towards it, quickening her pace. Soon the backs of the heads of the girls resolve out of the darkness. She is closer than she thought; only a few feet behind them. She has the feeling that they have deliberately slowed their pace.

Tiny electric bulbs – like fairy lights – hang from wires along the cave walls. The light they shed is meagre, barely illuminating the space, but it is so much better than darkness.

Abby begins to glimpse markings on the cave walls: crude paintings of animals, buildings and people. She pauses before a representation of a grove of trees, and then, farther along the tunnel through which she is passing, she sees the ragged outline of what looks like the tower block at the centre of the Concrete Grove, the Needle.

But how can this be? These drawings are primitive, like the ones she's seen on documentaries on television. Primitive Man, using inks made out of berries, would decorate the walls of his cave with illustrations much like these.

She stands and stares, unable to take it all in. How could shambling cavemen, dressed in the hides of wild beasts, even know about a place that has yet to exist – a housing estate tens of thousands of years in their future? None of this makes sense. She fights against the sight, trying to force it out of her mind.

She looks up ahead, along the tunnel, and sees the girls watching her. Their eyes glow in the weak light, but there is nothing behind them. In unison, they beckon to her. Then she hears the noise – a soft, slow humming sound. She tilts her head and stares over the girls' shoulders, trying to catch sight of what is busy behind them. The darkness moves as if composed of a million smaller parts, each one spinning and twirling and making a pattern in the air.

"Tessa?"

No... it isn't Tessa. It is not her daughter.

The girls steps aside, allowing her access to the back of the cave. Beyond them, the tunnel opens up into yet another cave, and then there is only darkness. She steps forward, moving past the girls, and is only dimly aware of the girls blending into the rock walls, becoming part of the cold, damp stone. There are no electric bulbs here, just the cold air, the constant dripping, and a strange, barely perceptible luminescence which emanates from the rock itself.

She walks across the uneven ground, over a small, natural walkway that spans an underground stream. She looks down, into the rushing water, and sees faces staring up at her through the churning white foam. She does not recognise any of the features, but she feels a connection to their pain. They are trapped here, in the endlessly running stream, but they are not unhappy. Their pain has brought them here, just as her own pain has allowed her to access this strange, desolate place. It is a pain that has no place in the real world, the world she's left behind; but here, underground, and even in the greater world beyond, through which she's passed, it is welcomed.

Those faces belong to dreamers, and they are dreaming of themselves.

At the end of the walkway is a low stone plinth, a pedestal carved out of the solid rock. As she draws closer, Abby sees that there are two tiny hummingbirds hovering above this plinth, facing each other. When she reaches them, she goes down on her knees. It feels right to show respect to the wonder before her. It isn't prayer, exactly, but it is a subtle form of worship, a willing act of subjugation.

One of the birds is black, the other is white. No other colours mar their purity. Their wings move in a blur; the beating of those wings equal, the sound they make a single endless note. Not one of the two birds is stronger than the other. It is unclear whether they are mates or enemies. They simply hover there, balancing what at first she thinks is a diamond between the tips of their beaks.

She shuffles forward, not caring that the skin of her knees is torn by the rough stone. Bending forward, she inspects the scene more closely. The black hummingbird is pure black. The effect of looking at it is hallucinatory. She feels as if she is staring at a hummingbird-shaped hole in reality, and glimpsing the utter blackness beneath. The white hummingbird is so bright that it almost blinds her to stare directly at it, so she is forced to look askew. Yet, curiously, it sheds no actual light. These are not colours: they are an absence of colour. And they are locked into a battle that can never have a victor.

The thing she initially thought was a diamond is shaped like a teardrop. It is tiny, but it draws her gaze, growing massive at the centre of her vision, like a black hole sucking towards it all of time and space.

"It is a teardrop. It's a frozen tear..."

She has no idea who has shed the tear, whose sorrow has given birth to such a magical thing, but there is no doubt in her mind that it is here, underground, in this dark cave, protected by – or perhaps imprisoned between – the twin hummingbirds, one black, the other white. Everything is focused on this scenario; this is the pivot around which everything else turns, and she's been given a glimpse of the mechanics behind the universe.

Behind her, the three girls giggle softly.

She stares deep into the frozen teardrop and sees it all: tectonic plates shift, carving up the planet; icebergs collide; caverns fill with seething magma; above the surface, dinosaurs roam, then die, take flight to live in the trees; monkeys come down out of trees and begin to dream the dreams of humanity; and this place is born, it comes into being on the strength of those first fleeting dreams; the first tear that is shed in this place is encapsulated, frozen into a solid gemstone, and it becomes the centre. Balance is achieved; eternal, everlasting, a fulcrum upon which nothing will ever turn, because the energy will never tip one way or the other.

"Is this place the dream the world has when it's sleeping, or was the world dreamt into being by that grove of trees out there?" She is talking to herself and doesn't expect an answer.

The teardrop shimmers; the opposing hummingbirds are unchanging, infinite.

The girls giggle again. The sound is eerie yet strangely comforting. It reminds her of her daughter.

When she turns around to confront the girls, to chastise them for sullying the purity of this subterranean grotto, she is back inside her daughter's room. Shards of fractured moonlight shine through the window, their brightness making her wince. The sky is overcrowded with silly stars, each one of them a dead world, a place where life will never be possible.

* * *

Abby stood and walked out of the room, pausing outside the door. Her cheeks were wet with tears.

The three girls giggled again... but, no, this time it was only one.

She turned back and entered the room.

"Tessa, is that you?"

She felt the beating of her heart like a tiny fist within her chest. The tears rolled freely down her face, dripping off her chin, smearing against her naked throat and chest.

The top of the shrine had slipped, toppled at an odd angle. The point of the cone, so carefully modelled, had sheared away. She walked over to the mound and was forced to struggle onto her tiptoes to inspect the damage. She peered inside the gap, straining to see down inside the pyramidal mound.

There was someone inside there, crouched low, arms up and wrapped around their head. It was a small figure, barely formed, yet recognisably human. Like a new-born child, it looked wet, slimy.

"Tessa?"

The arms moved, snaking downwards across the slick, bald scalp. They made a sound like liquefied flesh sliding off bone – or at least how Abby imagined that might sound. The figure was breathing. She could hear the gentle, regular rhythm of its inhalations and exhalations. Its shoulders rose and fell fractionally. More movement: small, silver branches erupting from the slick head, reaching upwards, towards the top of the totem, quivering as they climbed.

Abby fell backwards, stumbling across the floor until her back hit the wall. She raised her hands, but had no idea what to do with them. She lowered her hands, feeling foolish.

The pointed tip of a silver branch emerged from the hole, waved around for a second, and then vanished back inside, dislodging a doll's arm from the pile.

What was it, human or flora? When she'd been looking down inside the totem, she could have sworn that she'd seen arms cradling the top of a head... but now there was only a knot of branches, like those of a budding sapling.

Mind racing, blood pumping, heartbeat doing double time, she did the only thing that seemed sensible in her distressed state. She went into the bathroom to get some water for her new plant.

CHAPTER EIGHTEEN

THE CAT BOX was resting on the back seat as Erik drove out to the old country house. He hadn't wanted to put it in the front, beside him, didn't feel comfortable having it in such close proximity. He knew this was unreasonable, but it didn't make him change his mind.

He kept his eyes on the road, not wanting to have an accident or draw attention to his presence from any passing police vehicles, but he was acutely aware of what had become of Monty Bright curled up in the box behind him. He'd realised, of course, that there was far more different about Monty than just his appearance. The twisted remnant of the man was somehow reaching inside Erik's mind, grabbing hold of his will, and gently coercing him. It felt like soft waves of energy, caressing his brain, massaging the lobes and releasing chemicals that softened all the hard edges.

Erik wasn't exactly doing things that were out of character, or that he wouldn't have done anyway. No, it was more down to the fact that he was doing them without thinking, and not even questioning his motives. He was like Erik Best turned up to eleven; a rock n' roll version of himself with no holds barred and lacking an off switch.

He realised that he was on his way to meet a man he was planning to kill – he wasn't befogged enough to blank out that particular piece of information. But somehow it didn't matter. He felt... well, he felt nothing. That was the thing. His emotional responses were empty, as if the emotions themselves had been drained away, leaving behind only a faint residue, an echo.

It was like rushing on strong drugs, but better: easier to relinquish control.

The big old house reared over the horizon to his right, a familiar face with dark eyes and a tightly shut mouth. The Barn – a separate building on the same plot of land – looked dark and foreboding, as if it had sloped quietly away from the side of the house, up to no good. He'd never before noticed that the Barn was this spooky, not until he'd shut it up after the bout that had ended in Marty's stabbing. There would be fights there again, one day, but he was in no hurry to organise anything, not even a dog fight. He'd gone off the kind of people those events attracted. He liked their money, and had always ignored the bloodlust because of it, but something inside him had changed. He could no longer stomach being around people who were so cowardly that they would rather pay to watch two men fight on a roped-off section of dirt until only one was left standing than face their own battles.

He pulled up at the side of the narrow road, the wheels spitting gravel. There were no streetlights out here. He glanced up at the sky and could see few stars. The moon was a ghost; its outline was barely visible against the blackness, as if it were afraid to take a good look at what was going on below.

Erik opened the gate to his property and got back inside the car. He drove in slowly, leaving the gate open so that Hacky could enter freely, and continued slowly towards the Barn. He parked behind the old wooden structure, so that his vehicle wasn't visible from the road. There was no reason to get out yet, so he sat there, behind the wheel, and listened to the night.

He wound down the window to let in some air. Night birds sang; it was an eerie, mournful sound. It made him feel lonely, bereft of things he didn't even realise he'd lost. He thought about his missing daughter, and how everything had started to go wrong around that time. When Tessa vanished, the rest of his world had begun to crumble, bit by bit: his relationship with Abby, the business ventures, even his uneasy partnership with Monty Bright. His hold on the world had loosened, and even then he'd realised that he either had to tighten his grip or let go for good.

He looked behind him, at the cat box. Its occupant was silent. There was no movement.

"What the fuck am I getting into here?"

There was no reply. He wasn't expecting one, anyway, and was glad that none was forthcoming. The inhabitant of the box had shut up after being fed. It had not uttered a word since, other than inside Erik's head.

He turned back to the front, stared through the windscreen. Saw headlights on the road as a small, battered Ford Corsa made its way along the fence line towards the gate.

Hacky.

Erik climbed out of the car, opened the back door, and carried the cat box to the Barn. He unlocked the main double doors, opened one of them with his foot, and slipped inside, closing the door behind him. He set down the cat box on the ground and opened the flap. Monty rolled out, his appendages scrabbling like rat's claws in the dirt. The small, damaged figure didn't look strong, but it moved fast now that it had fed. He watched in silence as it scurried over the ground to wait in the dense, syrupy shadows at the rear of the Barn.

He switched on an electric light that hung from a loop of wire nearby, but it flickered and barely illuminated the space around him.

Erik sighed and walked over to the old ring, where the fights had taken place. The ground inside the roped-off quadrant was scuffed, disturbed by combatants' footprints. So many men had bled and screamed on that hard patch of earth; and how many men had suffered trauma that would then go on to ruin their lives? He didn't know; didn't care. The only time he had cared was when his friend Marty had been stabbed by a pissed-off Polish corner man. Erik had never told Marty, but at one time he'd loved him like a son. He'd let the younger man off the hook so many times, allowed him to get away with things that would have ensured anyone else had their legs broken.

But he'd not once told Marty how he felt. He wasn't the kind of man to show his feelings, to allow anyone to sneak inside his guard. He didn't regret the omission. There was still time – even though he hadn't had a proper, in-depth conversation with Marty for a while. He had his number. When all this was over – whatever the hell *this* was – he could always ring him and confess how he felt.

"Erik?"

He turned to face the doors. One of them was open and Hacky stood there, trapped in the frame. He looked tiny, vulnerable... so damned easy to kill.

"Did you shut the gate?"

"Yeah. No worries."

"Where's your car?"

"I parked it next to yours, well out of sight."

Erik nodded. "Good lad. You catch on quick – did I ever tell you that? A hell of a lot quicker than the rest of those stupid twats."

Hacky smiled. He was so fucking easy to please. "No... not ever. I didn't even think you'd noticed me."

"Come on inside, marra. Shut the door behind you. We have things to discuss."

The scruffy, wide-shouldered kid made his way across the Barn. He had his hands stuffed into the pockets of his tracksuit bottoms. He was wearing his usual baseball cap – the one with the badge on the front: Scooby Doo, smoking a spliff.

Why did that seem so important right now, after he'd been thinking of Marty? It set off vague sparks at the back of his head, but Monty's grip was too tight. He couldn't quite place the thoughts.

Erik didn't know anything right now; he couldn't think. Monty's fingers were crawling around inside his head, prodding the soft spots and burrowing into the exposed matter. All he could think of was to wonder how he was going to do this. It wasn't quite clear yet, but he trusted that he'd know when the time came, when the opportunity for slaughter presented itself. Only then would Monty relax his grip and let Erik do what he needed to do...

"What's all this about, then, Erik? You mentioned... you mentioned a job. Are you moving me up?" Under the circumstances, the combination of hope and expectation on the kid's face was obscene. He'd do anything Erik asked; he might even kill someone he loved, if it meant worming his way into the boss's favour.

Despite the grim situation, Erik almost laughed at the thought.

"First I have a few more questions." He stood over the boy, his physique dwarfing Hacky's slighter build to make him resemble a small child in the gloom.

"Yeah. Cool." He took out a cigarette, lit it, and waited, his posture loose, resting most of his weight on one leg.

"That thing you found. You definitely didn't tell anyone about it, even after you left me?" Erik moved into a fighting stance. He didn't even have to think; it was an instinctive physical response whenever he stood this close to another man.

Hacky shook his head. "We told nobody. We ain't stupid, man." He grinned. His teeth were yellowed.

"What about tonight? Does anyone know you're here? Lie to me and I'll find out... and then I'll have to hurt you to make an example."

The grin dropped. He licked his lips. "No. Didn't tell anyone. Everyone thinks I'm off shagging some bird, innit."

"Good." He moved closer and put one arm around the kid's shoulder, turning them both so that they faced the rear of the Barn. "This place has seen a lot of bloodshed. So much combat that the violence has been absorbed into the wooden beams and uprights." He walked towards the rear of the building, moving slowly, not wanting to spook Hacky, to put him on his guard.

He was aware of Monty's presence inside his mind. Not pushing... not controlling. Simply guiding.

"I know."

"Men have fought, men have fallen, and men have bled out into the dirt. I've learned a lot of lessons in my time, and above all else I've come to know that we all must look after ourselves. You can't trust your friends, women come and go, and money gets spent all too quickly. All we have is these." He held out both hands and made them into fists. "These are my gods, marra. I worship them, I make them offerings. These beauties will never let me down. I've tested them, to the limit." He stared at his scarred knuckles, feeling a sense of awe. He was confused to discover that he had an erection.

There was a subtle movement in the shadows up ahead. Hacky didn't notice; he was still staring at Erik's fists, wide-eyed and hopeful. But Erik heard clearly the slithering sound of something moving briskly towards them, like a snake moving through tall grass.

"Listen to me." He grabbed Hacky's shoulders and spun him around so that his back was facing the rear wall. "I've been watching you for a while now, and what I've seen has pleased me." He stared over Hacky's shoulder. The darkness near the ground was shifting.

He closed his eyes.

"I have something for you. I have a role for you to play, and I think it's very important. I don't know why yet, or how, but I'm sure it's vital to the outcome of some game none of us can see. Like moving a chess piece, sacrificing a pawn." He lifted his hands, pulled them swiftly apart, and then slammed them together, with Hacky's neck caught between them.

Hacky's knees buckled immediately.

Erik pulled back his right arm and slammed it straight right into the kid's face. He felt the bones break, the warmth of the blood as it splashed his hands. Hacky went down like a dead weight. He had no fight in him; he was weak, a puny specimen. Erik grabbed him by the collar with one hand and hit him again with the other... again, and again, and again. His cheekbones turned to chalk; his right eye bulged obscenely from its socket; a few of those yellowish teeth, stained red now, spilled amid a thick wash of bloody saliva from his mouth and onto the ground. He twitched a few times, and then was still. Erik laid him gently on the ground at his feet and stepped away.

Monty came darting out of the shadows and clamped onto the side of Hacky's face, suckling. The kid opened his mouth and tried to scream, but a long, fat appendage slipped between his shattered teeth, filling his ruptured throat, and choking him. Hacky thrashed around on the ground, but Monty gripped tight, eating away at his face, demolishing the already ruined flesh. The baseball cap fell to the ground and rolled a foot or so away. Erik bent down and picked it up, stuffed it into his back pocket; a small memento of this strange night.

Then he took a few more steps back, away from the scene. He didn't want to see this. The further he moved away, the looser Monty's grip on his mind became and he began to forget the details of what he'd done. There was blood on his hands. He wiped it off on his jacket. The sounds Hacky made as the life was choked out of him were difficult to ignore, but he turned his head and stared at the old, makeshift boxing ring.

After several minutes, the struggling sounds ceased. They were replaced by sucking, slurping, smacking noises: all the sounds of feeding.

Erik tried to feel something but it wouldn't come. The more he was exposed to whatever forces had warped Monty Bright's body into this small, stunted monster, the less human he became. He knew it was happening, and this knowledge somehow made things worse. But still he could not experience any kind of genuine emotion.

It's like watching a film, he thought. *Or reading a book. I'm here... but I'm not here. I'm standing off to the side, not really part of what's going on.*

He turned around and made for the doors, shutting them behind him as he left the Barn. The night air was warm; in the sky, clouds were gathering, forming little clumps and clusters. The moon had finally reappeared, a partial face in the darkness, and the stars were coming out to see the show.

Better late than never...

The thought, when it came, felt like so much more than it meant on the surface. Things were shifting, breaking free. Somewhere, doors were opening – or had already been open for some time – and something was trying to come through, from another place entirely. He stared out over the landscape, the familiar fields and the dark hills beyond, and was sure that there were trees he'd not noticed before. Their branches moved, clutching like hands. They were black silhouettes huddled against the blacker sky, strange growths that had shot up while he'd been inside the Barn, allowing himself to be used as a weapon.

To Erik, standing alone there under a weird, vivid night sky, this felt like the end of something he'd not even realised had begun. For years now, he'd been blind. He had orbited this great black hole, taking from it what he could, and now the black hole was claiming everything, including him, turning it all into cosmic debris, blasting it all into black flame. If he could open up his chest, exposing his innards, he'd find bits of charcoal, a charred ruin. He was a shell; no longer a real man.

His whole existence, his perception of what it meant to be alive, had changed now that he'd met a monster.

CHAPTER NINETEEN

"Hi." He was standing on the doorstep like an unwelcome visitor – and perhaps that's exactly what he was, despite what she'd said earlier on the phone. He was beginning to get used to the fact that she always made him feel uncomfortable, and he could never be sure if he was welcome or not.

"I suppose you'd better come in." Abby stepped back, turned and walked slowly down the hallway, her bare feet soundless on the worn carpet. Her feet were dirty, as if she'd been walking in mud. He wondered what on earth she'd been up to.

Marc followed her inside, trailing her into the living room. The lamp was on but the main lights were off. The curtains were open, letting in the light from the streetlamps.

"How about a drink?"

He could see that she'd already been drinking: a wine bottle, half empty, was resting on the table.

"Yeah, cheers."

She left the room and returned with another wine glass and a new bottle, the belt on her dressing gown hanging loose, a flash of grubby thigh exposed under the flap. She topped up her own glass and then filled his, killing the first bottle. She sat down without tightening the belt.

"So how come you couldn't sleep?"

"Bad dreams."

He nodded. "I can sympathise. What about?"

"My daughter." She sipped her wine. Her face was so pale that it looked bloodless. Her long fingers seemed to lack meat; they were all bone.

"I'm sorry... it's none of my business."

"It's okay," she said, standing. "Fancy some music?" She moved over to the stereo without waiting for a response and switched it on. Classical music came through speakers that were set high up on the wall, mounted on brackets in the corners of the room.

"I wasn't expecting that." He smiled.

"We're not all hopeless fucking chavs, you know. I realise that people like you – journalists, the middle class, all you wankers – like to cast us in a set role, but a few of us have experienced culture." She sat back down, drank from her glass.

He ignored the remark about class. He didn't want to get into that now. "Shit... that's not what I meant. I just didn't realise you were into classical music."

"I like to read, too. Dickens, Emily Bronte, Mary Shelley, George Orwell... surprised, aren't you, that a fuckwit like me even knows who Orwell is?" Colour rose back into her cheeks, her eyes flared, challenging him.

He held up his hands in mock surrender. "Okay, okay, I'm a dick. I shouldn't make assumptions."

"No, you shouldn't. Just because I live on a shitty estate, drink too much and sleep around, it doesn't mean I'm stupid."

He was unable to tell now if she was rattling his chain or being serious. She was a mystery, this woman. Perhaps that was part of the reason he was so drawn to her, why he found her so damned irresistible. Why he wanted to fuck her, even when he didn't want to be near her.

"Sit down. You're cluttering up the room." She patted the sofa next to her, those long fingers twitching like the limbs of a pale mantis.

He sat down, took a mouthful of wine, wincing at a slight bitterness. She was much more animated than the last time he'd seen her, and he liked this version of her better. There was passion here, the type of which he had not even been aware of before. A fire burned deep inside her, but obviously she rarely let it out on show.

"I'm glad you called. I've been thinking about you."

She turned to face him, a smile playing at the corners of her mouth. "Don't get too cocky. Yours was the first number I could think of to call. All the other guys I know, they'd read too much into this. I was lonely. I got scared because of the nightmare. I just want some company, okay?"

"That's fine by me."

"Just don't fall in love with me. They fucking all do that, and I hate it."

He stared at her profile, once again wondering what on earth it was that he saw in this hard-faced bitch. "Don't worry. That's the last thing on my mind right now. Company sounds good to me... just the right deal. I promise not to get too clingy."

She shook her head, her mood softening. "So what kept you up late tonight?"

"I was going through some of Harry Rose's things. I'm staying there. His brother gave me the key."

"I thought you managed to get here quickly. That explains it. What kind of stuff? Like, his will?"

"No, it was nothing like that. Just some old records... books and files, notebooks he'd kept about the Northumberland Poltergeist and something called Captain Clickety."

Abby giggled. Then, softly, she began to chant a rhyme.

"Captain Clickety, he's coming your way. Captain Clickety, he'll make you pay. Once in the morning, twice in the night. Three times Clickety will give you a fright."

"What's that?"

"Just an old skipping song. We used to sing it when we were at school."

"The Pollack children called their ghost Captain Clickety."

She laughed, quietly, humourlessly. "He's like a catch-all around here, our own little bogeyman. Everything gets blamed on good old Captain Clickety."

Marc took another drink of wine, leaned his head back against the sofa. "I'm starting to think that Captain Clickety might be a lot more than some colourful local urban legend."

"What do you mean?" her hand strayed to his thigh, rested there, gripping him lightly.

"I think he really existed. In Harry's notes, I found a name. Terryn Mowbray. He was a plague doctor, back during the time of the Black Death."

"Really?" She sounded drowsy. The wine was affecting her.

"Yeah. Not a very nice man, by all accounts, and he went missing in the grove of oak trees that used to be where the Needle was built. Two hundred years later, someone by that name also turned up at a colony of settlers in America. They went missing, leaving behind strange words carved into trees. I think the trees were oaks and rowans... English trees, not native to America. The same name was mentioned, but I'm certain it wasn't the same guy... I mean, it couldn't be. That's impossible." His mind was racing again, struggling to put together a puzzle to which he only possessed a handful of pieces.

"Sounds like a fairy story to me," said Abby, stretching her spine, like a tired cat.

"Yeah. Yes, it does." He closed his eyes and saw a beak-faced man standing unmoving in the darkness behind the lids.

Abby set down her glass on the floor, turned, and lunged at him. Her dressing gown gaped, exposing her breasts. She rammed her tongue between his lips, bit at his mouth, grabbed at his cock. She smelled of loam and wood smoke: the aroma of autumn.

"Whoa," he said, pulling back. "At least let me get warmed up first."

Five minutes later they were upstairs, fucking like banshees.

Afterwards they lay side by side in bed, finishing off the wine. Abby rested her head on his chest and he stroked her dry, brittle hair. He ran his fingers along her long, smooth throat, and cupped one of her breasts.

She stirred, moaned, pulled up her head and kissed his chest. Then she turned her attention to the tattoo on his left bicep. She leaned on one elbow and traced the outline with her other hand.

"What is it?"

"A flower."

"I can see that, you idiot. What kind of flower?"

"It's a daisy, I think."

"You think?" She kissed it, the tip of her tongue flicking lightly at his flesh.

"Yes... it's a daisy."

"Does it mean anything? Anything particular, like?"

He shook his head. "No, not really. It just means I was pissed when I got it. See the weird black lines around the petals? I liked the look of it. I had it done when I was eighteen, after an all-day drinking session with a few mates. Not one of my finest moments, I'll admit. In retrospect, I wish I'd got something more profound."

"Like a British bulldog?"

"A Union Jack or a football badge... perhaps a scroll with the word 'mother' on it."

She laughed softly. Pulling away from him, she lay on her back with her breasts exposed. The nipples were standing up like bullets. Her skin was corpse-white, apart from the few faint mucky smears he'd noticed earlier.

Marc shifted his position and lay on his side, so that he could watch her reaction to his question: "That bloke, the one who came to see you the morning I was here..."

"Erik? What about him?" Her face was impassive as she stared up at the ceiling.

"He was Tessa's dad, wasn't he?"

She nodded, but didn't speak.

"He threatened me. Warned me off, told me he'd hurt me if I came around here again."

"But here you are."

It was his turn to nod. He stroked her arm and once again cupped her breast, unable to keep his hands off her.

She smiled. "Don't worry." She closed her eyes. "He does that all the time. He can't stand to see me with someone else. It's partly my fault, I suppose. I used to go with men right under his nose, rub it in his face. Just to hurt him, like."

"Why would you want to do that – hurt him?"

She sighed and opened her eyes. Her breasts rose and fell, filling and then emptying the motionless palm of his hand. "Because he's a reminder of the way things used to be, when Tessa was still here. I can't stand to even look at him because whenever I do, I think of her. I see her, standing there, holding his hand and smiling. She loved her Dad... and he loved her, in his own way. He loved us both too much, and not enough."

"I see." But he didn't; he didn't see at all. She was making little sense, but he was too tired to go into it any deeper. Let her have her rants, her furies. Just as long as they could fuck: as long as she allowed him inside her, where it was cold and harsh and compelling.

Before long he heard the sound of her snoring. It caught hold of him, that sound, and he felt himself slipping away, entering a light sleep. He was still clasping her breast in one hand. The nipple was hard, but it started to soften as she slumbered. He tried to open his eyes but it was impossible. When finally he did open them, she was gone from the bed. Time had passed but he wasn't sure how long. The bedroom door was open. There was a light on somewhere along the hall, coming from an open door.

Tessa's room.

He got out of bed and put on his clothes, feeling drowsy and disorientated. He left the room, walked along the hall, and stood outside the room, looking in. Abby was there, naked, kneeling before the pile of clothes and toys and paper. Her left hand was thrust between her legs, working furiously. There was sweat on her brow. Her shoulders were hunched, her back arched. When she came, she did so silently. Then she stood, walked past him without noticing, and returned to bed. By the time he'd followed her back into the bedroom, she was once again sleeping. He stood there, listening to her snore, wondering exactly how fucked up she might be. Wondering if she was more fucked up than he was.

HE WALKED BACK to Harry Rose's place. It wasn't far, and by now he knew the way. The night air was warm, the moon and the stars were bright, and most of the streetlights were still working. Voices carried on the air; he heard the distant sound of a revving engine; an alarm started to blare, but it was too far away to bother him. Occasionally, he glanced back over his shoulder, certain that he was being followed, but there was never anyone there. One time he thought he glimpsed a shadow – not much, just a swiftly moving dark patch. It looked like it might be a dog, but its head was much too large, lolling on a thin, stalk-like neck. He only caught sight of it for a second, and then began to doubt that he'd seen anything at all.

Back at Harry's place he locked the door and checked the ground floor windows were secure. Everything was good; he was sealed safely inside, where no one could get to him. He tried to shrug off these paranoid thoughts, but they wouldn't let go. They clung to him like strands of silk, sticking wherever they touched.

The sex and the wine had exhausted him, but not enough that he'd wanted to stay at Abby's place until morning. He'd left a note on the bedside cabinet, a hastily scribbled message telling her that he'd call her in a few days. He figured that it was enough. If she didn't want commitment, it should be plenty.

He sat down on the sofa and grabbed the remote control, switching on the television. Harry had only used the normal terrestrial channels: no cable, no satellite. There wasn't much on at this late hour, just a re-run of some old black and white American sitcom, a documentary about insects, and news programmes. He left on the documentary, staring at images of mandibles and segmented exoskeletons. Before he knew it, he was dozing again, the world growing dark and empty.

He woke to the sound of movement. At least that's what he thought. He couldn't be sure, because he had been dreaming of movement, too: massive insects, crawling across the estate, scuttling through the darkness.

He sat up and felt the muscles in his neck tighten. He rubbed at the area, trying to ease the pain. "Fuck..."

The sound came again: this time he heard it properly, something shifting upstairs, like furniture being moved. The television was off but he couldn't remember if he'd done it or not. Hadn't he gone to sleep with it still on? The room was dark, with only a chink of streetlight leaking through gap in the blinds.

Marc was no longer alone. He could feel it, just as he could feel the sofa beneath him, the cushion pressing against his back. It was not some abstract emotional sensation, but a physical realisation that he was not the only one occupying the space between these walls. There was somebody else inside the house.

He thought about leaving but he would feel cowardly if he left without checking that his suspicion was true. His mobile was somewhere near by – perhaps even in his pocket – but he didn't want to call the police. He wasn't sure how he knew this, but a burglary was not taking place. Whoever was in the house, they meant him no harm. He was afraid, but he felt in no danger. If they'd wanted to hurt him, they could have done so while he slept.

He remembered the man who'd threatened him, Erik Best. Abby's ex. What if he'd been watching the house, and then had followed Marc back from her place?

No, if it was him, he'd have hurt Marc by now, probably battered him half to death as he dozed on the sofa. This was someone else, something different.

Calmly, he stood and walked to the living room doorway. None of the lights were on in the house. He considered reaching out to switch on the stair light but that would announce his presence in the stairwell and give whoever was up there fair warning that he was going up. So he left the light out, and slowly began to climb the stairs.

Halfway up, he paused. Fear had crept softly up the stairs alongside him, and now it had reached out to grab his hand. His palms were sweating. His knees felt soft, as if they might give way.

What if it *was* Erik, the crazy ex-boyfriend? What if he was playing a game, toying with Marc, luring him upstairs so that, once he reached the top, he could push him down and pretend that his death was an accident?

He got himself under control and finished climbing the stairs. At the top, he looked around at the door which led to the attic rooms. It was open. Faint light spilled down the attic stairs. There was somebody at the top of the house. He moved slowly along the landing, and when he reached the open door he peered around the frame. He couldn't see anyone, but the door to the model room was open, and he saw shadows spill across the stair walls as someone or something moved and momentarily blocked out the lamplight. He could've sworn that he'd turned off the lamp and shut the door when he came down earlier that evening. Now the door was open, the lamp was on.

He climbed slowly, lifting his feet with great care and setting them down again as gently as possible. Boards creaked; the banister shuddered against the wall, the screws slightly loose. He couldn't believe he was doing this, approaching potential danger – whenever he saw it in a film, he always mocked the character's stupidity.

When he reached the top of the stairs he was unable to move. He was too afraid to do anything but stand there, poised for fight or flight, and stare at the door frame. He drew in a deep breath, clenched his fists and moved.

"Fuck!" He screamed the word at the top of his voice, planning to shock whoever might be in there into making an error. But the room was empty; there was nobody inside. He looked around the room, looking for signs of interference, but nothing had been moved. He walked over to the model table and stared at the miniature layout of the estate. It took him a while to see it – longer than he would have thought possible, when he thought about it later – but eventually his eyes picked up on the changes.

Someone had added certain details to the model.

Small trees had sprouted, breaking through the roads and pavements and thrusting upwards. Windows were broken, cars were overturned, and yet more trees had appeared inside some of the tiny houses. He could see their shapes through the intact windows; in other places, spindly leafless branches poked through the shattered panes.

Dotted throughout the model neighbourhood were small figures, half-bodied scarecrows dressed in rags and supported on thin wooden stakes. They lolled at angles, leant against walls, and a couple of them had fallen over and seemed to be frozen in the act of crawling along the street, dragging their supporting columns behind them like battered and exposed backbones.

The biggest change had been wrought upon the Needle. The base of the tower block was wrapped in thick, gnarled roots, as if it were in the process of transforming into a massive oak tree. Trunks and branches had penetrated the concrete walls, growing from the inside, and snaked around the building, forming a fibrous spiral along its length.

Marc's mouth was dry. His hands were shaking. Was somebody playing tricks on him, having a laugh at his expense? It might even be Abby. She was certainly psychologically damaged enough to think that something like this would be amusing.

He reached out and touched the wide, serpentine trunk that had wound itself around a portion of the Needle. It was not made out of paper or card, or even rubber and plastic. What he felt beneath his fingers was real wood. Like some kind of freakish bonsai, the small tree had taken root, sprouted, and started to grow.

Then he noticed the figures. He was sure they hadn't been there, in this position, when he'd first entered the model room. Tiny scarecrows, their upper bodies wrapped in raggedy clothing, their lower bodies consisting of nothing more than cocktail sticks pushed into the ground, anchoring the figures in place. They were standing on the Roundpath, the narrow road that circled the Needle, looking up at the central tower. Each of them was wearing a floppy hat; their arms were outstretched, in a Jesus Christ pose. Marc wasn't sure if they were caught in an act of worship or surrender. He didn't think it made much difference either way.

The lamplight began to flicker, creating a strobe effect. Between one second of light and the next, something appeared on the model table. It was a small notebook, like the ones he'd found in the attic library. A patch of darkness moved away from the table; a quick, snaking movement, like an arm being drawn back.

"Harry? Is it you, Harry?" He was too anxious to feel stupid, but somehow the very idea of talking to a ghost felt wrong, awkward. He didn't believe in ghosts... Or did he? If that were true, then why was he researching the Northumberland Poltergeist? And now that he thought about it, wasn't he holding back on that research, keeping it at arm's length? It was as if he were attached to a heavy weight by an elastic belt. Whenever he moved forward, the elastic became taut and it held him back. He could feel his feet sliding across the floor, moving backwards.

He stepped over to the model table and picked up the book. The front cover was dusty. He opened it to the first page. There wasn't much written down there, but it was enough.

He read the words and felt doors opening up inside him:

Apart from the Pollack twins, there was a third child in the flat. A baby.

He closed his eyes and things twitched back there in the reddish darkness. Those doors stood ajar; they would not open fully, but it was enough for light to leak through the gap. Shadows twirled and danced; a ballet of darkness. Marc struggled to grab hold of whatever it was that capered there, inside him, but it was too slippery to get a grip on.

There was something there but he couldn't make out what it was. Like a body under a sheet, he could discern only the outline. No details were visible.

He left the room, closing the door firmly behind him. In his hand, he gripped the notebook.

On the small landing, he stood with his back pressed up against the door, trying to convince himself that he could not hear the sounds of scrabbling from behind him, somewhere inside the room. On the table that held the model of the estate. He wasn't quite ready to accept that. Such an admission would indicate a state of mind that he wasn't prepared to face.

In fact, admitting that those sounds were real would be akin to embracing madness.

Downstairs, he sat on the sofa and began to read the rest of the notebook.

Apart from the Pollack twins, there was a third child in the flat. A baby[10].

Jack Pollack died when he was thirteen. He was found hanging from a rafter in the squat where he lived.

Daisy Pollack turned to prostitution when she was fourteen, then drugs. She was dead in a gutter by the time she was fifteen.

Nobody knows what happened to the baby[11]. There is no record of the twins having another sibling – itself a surviving twin who's brother was stillborn, if local gossips are to be believed[12]. After the events in the Needle, when it seems that some kind of spirit came through and wrecked the flat, the family disappeared –

---

[10]Should I tell him? I have no idea. But I must make a decision soon.

[11]Whose baby was it? Were the Pollacks its real parents? Did Mike take it in out of duty or pity, or for some other reason?

[12]And why not? They've been right about everything else so far.

they seem to have vanished off the face of the earth, up until the car crash that killed the parents. All the stories and rumours told on the estate make specific mention of the twins and what happened to them, but not once have I been told about a baby.

But there <u>was</u> a baby. I've seen it. The baby came to me in a waking dream. It crawled across the ceiling of my room and spoke to me, telling me that nothing ever ends and nothing ever begins, and saying that Captain Clickety will return.

The baby is already here. It's found its way out of the woods and has come to finish the story. The story is that of the baby... should I tell him?

CHAPTER TWENTY

SHE KNEW THAT she was dreaming, even though she was asleep, so when she woke up she was at first puzzled by her surroundings. The room was dim, with just a desk lamp to light it, and instead of trees and moonlight glinting between dried leaves, there were solid walls, a desk – upon which she'd been sleeping, with her head resting on her hands – and a variety of medical apparatus.

"Wha...?" She could barely speak. Her mind was fogged. She didn't even know what day it was, let along what time. She could see the night sky through the tiny basement window.

"Wanda," she said, remembering her name. *Miss Wandaful*, said a soft voice inside her head. She smiled, rubbed her short hair with her hand, then reached around and scratched the back of her neck.

She'd been working late, as usual. These days there was little to go home for, and the police station offered a solace that her tiny one-bedroom flat no longer seemed to supply. Not since Katherine had moved out, anyway.

She closed her eyes. Thought about Katherine's naked body; her smile; her dark, shining eyes; the way she'd loved to sleep with the covers pulled up over her head.

She missed having Katherine around. The truth was, she missed having anyone around. Before Katherine had arrived on the scene, Wanda had grown accustomed to being alone. She'd stopped being lonely and learned to enjoy her own company. Then Katherine had moved into the flat, hitting her life like a storm, and everything changed. She was still – even now, eight months after the relationship had ended – waiting for things to return to normal.

Then again, if DS Craig Royle decided to step up and take Katherine's place, she wouldn't need anything to go back to normal. They could go ahead and change again, and she'd be happy to wake up with him every morning instead.

It had been Royle she'd dreamt about. They'd been standing at the centre of a grove of oak trees, moonlight dappling their naked bodies. His erection had prodded her in the thigh and she'd reached out for it, grasping him. He'd either hissed or taken a sharp intake of breath, and his cock had pulsed gently in her palm, thickening.

Then she'd woken up, head down on her desk, the lamplight making her wince when she opened her eyes.

She stood and stretched, feeling the tiredness thread through her muscles. She carried out a few calf and hamstring stretches, the ones she used to cool down after a long run. Then she reached behind her head, grasping for the centre of her back, one hand after the other. Muscles relaxed, she turned to look for her bag. She didn't really have a spot where it belonged, so she tended to drop it in a different place every day. This meant that each time she left the lab, she went though the same performance of trying to find the damn thing.

"Where the hell are you...?" She peered under the desk, along the work benches, on the floor by the sink, but the rucksack wasn't there. She'd jogged into work this morning and forgotten to leave her gear out to air. She remembered bunching up her lycra leggings and T-shirt and shoving them into the bag, with the intention of taking them back out later, when she got the chance.

"Christ, my fucking memory!" Frustrated, she stalked around the office, trying to locate the bag. Because of the distraction, it took her a little time to realise that there was something different about the room.

She stopped and stared at the gurney. It was empty.

"No way," she said, turning to inspect the rest of the room. There were too many dark corners. She wished she'd switched on the main lights, but now she was clear across the other side of the room, far away from the switch. Reaching the lights would involve walking across the floor, in full view of whatever was hiding in there with her.

"Don't be stupid. There's nothing here."

Her words were answered by a short, sharp tapping sound, like the tip of a broomstick hitting the tiled floor.

"Fuck."

The sound came again, and this time she could make out where it was coming from. Behind her.

Slowly, she turned around. The lamp seemed to dim, but she knew it was just her mind creating the effect. There was nothing wrong with the lamp; the bulb was new, she'd changed it herself a couple of weeks ago. Fear was causing the illusion of increased dimness. It wasn't real.

This time the tapping sound went on for a couple of seconds – *tap-tap-tap-tap-tap-tap* – and she was reminded of the sound Long John Silver's wooden leg had made on the ship's deck in an audio version of *Treasure Island* she'd listened to as a kid. She used to love that tape. It was scary and exciting at the same time. But this situation, right now, was simply scary.

"Who's there?" The answer was another rapid succession of tapping sounds on the floor.

Wanda began to back away. She held out her hands in front of her, warding off whatever might come tap-tapping out of the shadows. The sound followed her, advancing towards her across the room, and soon she began to make out the form of her pursuer.

The scarecrow was hopping along on the tip of its wooden stake, moving in short, quick jerking motions. Its upper body twitched forward with each separate hopping motion, the hat wobbling but not falling from the wooden head. The black and white photo of little Connie Millstone was stuck firmly back in place, her drawn-on eyes staring out from the flattened sheet.

Wanda continued to move away from the scarecrow, raising her hands, opening her fingers, trying to ward off what was becoming increasingly inevitable. Where was her bag? Her phone was in there... she glanced over at the desk, where the landline was located. Too far away; she'd never make it, even if she ran. She might reach the phone, but there wouldn't be enough time to actually make a call and get someone down here to help.

She looked back at the advancing figure. It was cloaked in shadow, as if the light from the lamp was insufficient to burn away the clinging darkness. It had brought that darkness with it from wherever it had come from.

She started looking for a weapon – anything with which she could defend herself. She grabbed a Bunsen burner, and then threw it to the floor. Her grasping hand caught hold of a rack of test tubes and she threw them at the hopping nightmare, but it just flung out its arm and batted them away. The sound of breaking glass was tiny, inconsequential. She was too deep inside the building for anyone to hear. It was pointless even screaming.

The door was miles away, on the other side of the room, with the light switch on the wall nearby. She'd been moving in the wrong direction. The scarecrow knew exactly what it was doing, herding her into a corner like a trapped rat. When she felt the work bench pressing against the small of her back, she almost fell to the floor in defeat. This was it: there was nowhere left to run. She had come up against the wall at the other side of her life, and now it was all over.

She thought again of Katherine's face, and she smiled. Then she thought about how she'd never get the chance to tell Craig Royle how she felt about him. But that was probably a good thing. He wanted to get back with his wife. The last thing he needed was another complication, some lonely woman claiming that she was in love with him.

But she was, wasn't she? She hadn't been in love with Katherine – that had been a combination of lust and availability. Or was that all love really was, anyway?

She'd never know.

It was too late. It was all too late to matter...

The scarecrow's wooden support scraped on the tiled floor, making a squeaking noise that broke up the horrible tap-tap-tapping.

Wanda was only aware that she was crying because she felt the moisture on her cheeks. She wiped it away with one hand, puzzled. She'd never been a particularly emotional woman, so it seemed odd that she should weep at the prospect of her own demise.

She reached behind her, trying to find something on the work bench that might help. A sharp blade sliced her fingers, and she closed them around the scalpel. She brought round her arm and brandished the tiny blade, almost driven to laughter because of how pathetic it looked in the face of the hopping figure.

The scarecrow halted a foot in front of her. It was immobile, as if it had never moved at all. The photograph rippled. But there was no breeze, no wind to cause the fluttering motion.

Wanda looked back at the blade, and then at her wrist. No, that would be too slow. And she didn't have the will power to cut her own throat.

"Come and get me, then, fucker." She waved the scalpel slowly in the air, tracing a pattern that she hoped would act as a magic charm. "Come on." She was whispering now. Nobody could hear anyway, so why waste her breath on loud threats or screams? Better to saveit for the fight to come.

The scarecrow began to silently shake, as if it were rapidly shrugging its shoulders. It took a second for Wanda to realise that the damned thing was laughing at her.

there monks down the stairs like in that filum i saw. they singin. hear them now wen I rite this. like prayering on a sunday school. i want my mummy and daddy. daisy like a flower not hear. she gon somewr els an I don now were. want sing to stop. scared. don wan go down the stairs. mite get me. mite kill me. clickey comin now. i hear him comin. clickety-clickety-click. mummy. mummy. daddy. i scared mummy. but mummy sing aswel. i can hear her sings louder than the rest of the sings. my i scared mummy.

mummy i scared of mummy.

of mummy and daddy.

– From the diary of Jack Pollack, April 1974

PART FOUR

Growth

"Armed sieges, hostage situations... flavour of the fucking month."

– Detective Superintendent Sillitoe

CHAPTER TWENTY-ONE

ERIK SAT IN his car outside Abby's place and watched the sun as it started to rise. Faint, blood-red smears stained the grey wash, transforming it into a thing of savage beauty. He raised his hands and scrubbed at his face, trying to clear his head.

On the back seat, Monty Bright was silent, wrapped up in his blankets like a new-born baby. And wasn't that an apt description? He'd been born anew into this world, passing through from some other place – a place he'd been searching for his entire life and had finally found. But the place had rejected him; it had sent him back here, where he no longer belonged.

Erik had watched that smug little writer bastard leave Abby's place while it was still dark. Maybe he should have done something then, but he'd been unable to move, as if his rage had immobilised him. In the past, he would have got out, smacked the guy, and then dragged him into the car and taken him somewhere to teach him a lesson. But now he felt different. He couldn't act; his limbs were tired, his brain refused to work in the same way. So he'd stayed here and watched the house, waiting for things to become clear.

Like the sky above him, he was caught up in the process of transformation. The only problem was, he couldn't be certain regarding what he had been or what he was about to become.

No, he would let someone else sort out the bastard who was fucking his Abby. He wouldn't get his own hands dirty on a secondary character in the tragic story of his life, not this time. There were more important tasks to deal with. He took out his phone and dialled the number of a kid whose particular skill set he'd used before, and who'd been primed to expect a call. This kid ran a tight little crew who knew how to swing baseball bats and exactly what to do with them when they did. It would cost him a couple of hundred quid, but the job would get done properly. There would be no mistakes. The pathway to Abby would be clear.

He made the call, feeling nothing at all: no doubt, no shame, and no sense of wrongdoing. When he hung up the phone he felt lighter, as if he'd shed several layers of skin.

After a short pause, he put away his phone, reached down under the passenger seat, and took out the plastic Tesco carrier bag he'd stashed there. He placed the bag on the seat between his knees and carefully opened the package. He took out the gun. It was a small-calibre handgun, something he'd confiscated from a drug-dealing chav a couple of months ago. Instead of disposing of the weapon, he'd kept it. At the time, he hadn't known why he'd done so. Now he realised that he'd been hurtling towards this moment for a long time.

This moment; this place: *Loculus...*

The voice that spoke the word in his head belonged to Monty. Since he'd killed Hacky, the bond between them had strengthened, and they could communicate clearly like this: snatches of dialogue, words and phrases rolling around in his head.

We can go back there, together. Once you've tidied up your business.

He nodded, stroked the gun. The metal was cold. The plastic handle felt brittle, as if it might break under pressure. He was only going to scare her, and this would do the trick. For once, he'd wring some true emotion out of the hard-nosed bitch...

Erik got out of the car, stuffed the gun down the belt of his jeans, and walked across the road to Abby's house. He was smiling. The sun was still rising. There was nobody out on the street but him. The world felt like it belonged only to Erik, and he could do whatever he wanted without risk of being seen.

He still had a key to the house. Abby didn't know, but he'd taken a copy before returning the original to her when they'd split up. He didn't use it often, just a few times a year, to sneak in and rummage around in her underwear drawer while she was out, or to lie on her unmade bed and masturbate. It wasn't something he was proud of, but it helped to ease his pain.

Glancing around to check that he couldn't be seen, he took out the key and unlocked the door. He stepped inside the house and shut the door behind him, feeling light-headed. His limbs were floppy but his core was solid, as if a thread of steel rope ran through his centre. His blood ran hot and cold. He didn't know if he was about to laugh or cry, or even scream.

Slowly, he climbed the stairs and stood outside Abby's bedroom door. The floorboards groaned quietly under his weight. He could hear a faint chanting noise, but was unsure in which room it originated. He pushed open the bedroom door and looked inside. As usual, the bed was unmade; the sheets were in a state that could only be caused by two people fucking. He wanted to close his eyes but he didn't. Instead he walked into the room, approached the bed, and sat down. He ran his hands over the mattress. It was still warm. He bent over and smelled the sheets. The aroma of sex filled his nostrils: stale perfume, sweat and semen.

He stood and left the room. He followed the landing to what had once been Tessa's room. The chanting was coming from behind the closed door. There was a sing-song quality to the chanting, like a nursery rhyme.

"*Tessa, Tessa, Tessa... bless her, bless her, bless her... come back to me.*"

The voice belonged to Abby. He would have recognised it anywhere.

He reached out and placed the palm of his hand against the door. It was trembling. But, no: his hand was trembling, not the door. He was afraid, but he could not identify the source of that fear.

Erik grabbed the handle, turned it, and opened the door.

Abby was naked and kneeling before a large pile of what he realised must be Tessa's things – clothes, drawings, toys, photographs: all piled up into a conical mass, like a stunted tower of mourning.

"Abby... what is this? What are you doing?"

Loculus, said a voice in his head. He thought of Monty on the back seat of the car, and wondered if he should have brought him inside.

Abby ignored him. She acted as if he wasn't there. She was rocking backwards and forwards, as if she'd lost her mind. Her skin was streaked with dirty sweat, there was mud and leaves in her hair. Her face was smeared with dirt, like primitive camouflage paint.

She continued to chant the rhyme:

"*Tessa, Tessa, Tessa... bless her, bless her, bless her... come back to me.*"

Erik walked over and grabbed her arm. She was limp, like a sack of flesh without bones. "Abby!" He pulled hard on her arm, turning her around. Her eyes were rolled up into her head: all he could see was the whites. He raised his free hand and slapped her across the face.

She didn't respond.

He slapped her again, leaving a red mark on her cheek, and then tugged her, dragging her limp body across the carpet towards the door. Still she chanted; she hadn't even paused for breath. She just kept saying those same words, over and over, a prayer to whatever dark urban gods she thought might be listening.

Erik felt power flood through him. It wasn't rage, nor was it hatred. This was a purer force, and it came from somewhere outside his body. Like an alien sun shining down on him, the energy warmed his body, cleansing him like a balm.

"This is it," he whispered. "This is where it all ends." He tugged the gun out of his belt and clenched his right hand into a fist around the handle. He brought it down, hard, on the top of her head. The sound it made when the base of the grip struck her skull was like a hammer blow. He hit her again, this time with the barrel on the side of the face. He felt her cheekbone crack. Her skin split and blood spattered, splashing the carpet and even the weird tower she'd made at the centre of the room.

He only wanted to scare her...

Erik was blind. He could see nothing beyond the violence.

He hit her again and again, shredding the skin of her face, shattering the bones of her skull, and yet still she continued to chant those words, through mashed, bloodied lips, and even when her broken teeth began to fall from her mouth.

...to scare her into loving him again.

When Erik stopped she was lying on the floor, curled up like a baby. There was blood everywhere. Still she chanted the rhyme, taunting him.

He was breathing heavily, as if he'd just done a tough workout. His gun hand ached, the knuckles were swollen. He raised his face to the ceiling and let out a wordless wail, an animal sound of pain and self-hatred. Then he returned his attention to the room, and what was in it.

Abby continued to mumble from the floor. She'd stopped chanting and was now trying to speak, but he couldn't make out the words.

"Look what you've done," said Erik. "This is your fault – you did this. I only wanted to scare you. You've made me into something that I despise." He raised the gun and stared into the barrel. It would be so easy to end it all now: one bullet for her, one for him. Maybe that's what had been coming all along. Neat and tidy: a smooth little suburban death. He pressed the end of the barrel to his cheek, and then moved it across to his temple. After a second, he pointed the gun at Abby, his finger tightening on the trigger.

"Please..." Her voice was weak. She was speaking through a mouthful of blood and shattered teeth. "Don't kill me..."

"No, I'm not going to kill you. I love you... all I've ever done is love you. Can't you see? Don't you understand? I've loved you ever since I first met you, and when we lost our baby I would have kept on loving you, but you wouldn't let me. Instead you went with other men and told me about it. You rubbed my nose in it, like a fucking dog that's puked up on the carpet."

"Sorry... hurting... everything hurts." Her voice was unrecognisable.

For a moment he was acutely aware of the selfishness of his actions, the intensity of his feelings, but then he shoved that insight aside, ignoring it. Why the hell shouldn't he be selfish? There was no one else to look out for him, to protect his interests. Ever since he was a kid, he'd been forced to look after himself. That made a man hard; it toughened him to the point that nothing could penetrate the armour he had worked so hard to put in place.

"You bitch... look what you did. Look what you did to us. We could've been happy. We were a family... a proper family..."

He could no longer bear to look at her, so he raised his eyes and stared across her collapsed body.

Behind her, there was movement. Thin silver branches, leafless and grasping, were slowly emerging from between the gaps in the conical mound of Tessa's belongings. Like long, thin arms, the branches slid out, swaying in the air; gnarled twig-hands reaching for something that wasn't there.

Erik tightened his grip on the gun. He approached the mound. The branches appeared to sense him and twitched towards him, turning from silver to brown. He raised the gun and took aim. His hand was shaking so he used the other one to steady the gun, just like he'd seen in the movies.

"No..."

Abby, still on the floor, was speaking to him. He turned around.

"Don't kill it... our baby... our Tessa... she's come back..." She spat out blood. There were gaps where a couple of teeth had been.

He swivelled and watched the branches. There were now patches of skin on them, like pale pink bark. As he watched, the patches grew, the skin, spreading like a stain to cover the rest of the branches. The branches became thin arms; the spindly twigs at the ends turned into small hands. Pieces of the construction fell away from Abby's sculpture – jumpers, paintings, a My Little Pony duvet cover – and parts of a body were visible beneath. The sapling child was quickly transforming into flesh and blood, as if the process were speeding up because he was watching it happen. Like a low-rent Pinocchio, the lifeless simulacrum was gaining sentience.

His finger twitched on the trigger – a reaction that he was unable to control – and the gun went off. He managed to twist his wrist so the shot went wide, punching a hole in the wall near the window.

"Tessa?"

Her face formed quickly, like reversed footage of plastic melting, and he began to make out her lovely features beneath the mess of creation. What at first looked like a long, beaklike snout shortened to form her delicate little nose. The eyes opened, trailing strings like pizza cheese between the upper and lower lids. The eyeballs pushed outwards, and then settled back into the sockets. The eyelids blinked.

Erik dropped the gun. He fell to his knees and clasped his hands together as if in prayer.

The Tessa-thing stepped from out of the hollow cone, parts of her makeshift sarcophagus breaking away, the whole structure tumbling and falling to the floor. She walked towards her father and embraced him, enveloping him in her warm, damp flesh.

"Baby... my baby..." He was weeping now. He could hold back the tears no longer.

Abby had crawled across the floor and now lay at his side, reaching out towards them both. He felt her hands grabbing at his legs, and angled his body so that she could be included in the embrace.

The three of them, together again, reunited at last, right at the centre of the black hole.

The family unit was coming back together, reforming. The damage had been repaired. He had no idea what kind of magic this was, but he didn't want to question it too deeply. In his experience, those kinds of questions usually led to trouble, and he didn't want to wreck what had been made here, in a dim bedroom in a council house at the back end of nowhere.

This was not the kind of place where wonders were meant to happen. But here it was: here was wonder. Here was awe.

Then, weary and aching, he became slowly aware of a faint clicking sound.

He moved back, pushing Tessa away to create a gap between them, and what he saw made him question everything else he'd been thinking. The thing that resembled his daughter stood there, naked and genderless – with just a bare patch of skin between her legs and no navel or nipples –wearing a strange white mask in place of her pretty face. The front of the mask jutted out to form a hideous beak, and its eyes were hidden behind small black shades.

She raised her arms to the ceiling, spreading her legs and bending her knees to brace herself against the floorboards. Black leaves that fused together to become a long black cape or overcoat cascaded downwards, seeming to flow from her open hands, to cover her body, flapping at first like wings before moulding itself to her shape.

In one hand she was holding a short pointed cane.

It was only when she looked back down, staring directly into his eyes, that he realised the clicking sound was coming from Tessa. And then it occurred to him that this half-formed creature was not Tessa at all, but something that was using her image in an attempt to gain entry into this world.

He turned away from the image, unable to fully comprehend what he was seeing.

"Put on some clothes," he said to Abby, trying to cling to anything that might represent normality.

CHAPTER TWENTY-TWO

ROYLE RUSHED ACROSS the hospital car park, thinking the worst.

He'd received the call twenty minutes ago and had wasted no time in getting here. His car was parked at an angle, taking up two spaces, but he didn't care. As far as he was concerned, he was lucky to have made it here without running someone down. He could remember none of the journey; he'd completed it on auto-pilot.

He barged through the main doors and headed towards the maternity wing. The hospital was quiet; people were pushing trolleys laden with breakfast into side rooms, a few patients wandered the halls in their dressing gowns, doctors and nurses with weary eyes and soft morning faces talking in low voices.

At the reception desk, Royle told a small, frail woman with thick spectacles who he was and why he was here.

"And we called you?"

"Yes," he said. "I got a call not long ago to tell me that she was here."

The woman checked her computer for the second time, the light from the screen reflecting in the lenses of her glasses. "What was the name again?"

"Mine?"

"No, the patient's."

"Vanessa Royle."

Her eyes darted across the screen. "I'm sorry, but she isn't on here… when exactly was she brought in?"

"She came in last night, with pregnancy complications, or so I was told. Listen…" He paused, trying to rein in his temper, and something occurred to him. "Oh, hang on. She might be down under her maiden name." He shrugged when the woman glanced up at him, her face filled with tired pity. "Vanessa Mantel."

"Mantel… ah, yes. Here she is. Ward Ten. Just go down the corridor there and turn right at the end." A smile crossed her face, briefly but brightly, and then she dismissed him by peering over his shoulder at the other people milling about near her desk.

He walked through the doorway the woman had indicated and passed a couple of empty rooms, several closed doors, and a ward containing a group of pregnant women. When he finally reached the ward where Vanessa was staying, he paused and tried to gather his thoughts.

They hadn't told him much over the phone, just that he needed to get down here because his wife had been brought in with complications. They told him not to worry, but to get here as quickly as he could. Not to worry… such stupid advice, especially when it came from someone at the hospital where your pregnant wife had been rushed in the early hours of the morning.

He remembered the sound he'd heard – or thought he'd heard – coming from her belly the last time he'd seen her. Hadn't she also said that the baby had been kicking hard? Surely that was a sign that the baby was okay, that it was developing well. A dead baby couldn't kick.

He closed his eyes, trying to banish such thoughts. But it was no good. This was his biggest fear, the terror that gripped him every night, part of the reason he reached for the bottle: that the baby would die, and it would kill his marriage when it did so. All he wanted, everything he needed, was in this building. He couldn't face the idea of leaving it here, in a medical waste bag headed for the incinerator.

Fuck, why did he always have to think such negative thoughts... why was he so damned dark? Sometimes he blamed the job, but then he thought that he was probably drawn to become a police officer in the first place because of that darkness, which had always been at his centre: a hard little kernel of night. And wasn't the alcohol just another way of trying to drown that seed, to render it powerless? Or was it just a way of watering it and helping it to grow?

He ran a hand through his hair, straightened his shirt collar, and pushed open the door.

He saw Vanessa immediately. She was in the bed nearest the door. Her face was so pale that she looked like a ghost of herself. She didn't see him at first, so when he approached the bed she twitched in shock when he spoke.

"How are you?"

She smiled. "Okay. It's good to see you."

He felt like crying. He wanted to start punching and kicking the walls, tearing apart the place. "What happened?"

"Have you spoken to the doctor?"

He shook his head. "Not yet. I came straight up here, to the ward."

A nurse walked over from her station. "Mr Royle?"

"DS Royle," he said, not understanding why it was important to state his rank to this civilian. That wouldn't help here. Death would not be scared off by official seniority.

"DS Royle... yes. The doctor asked me to let him know once you arrived. He'd like to talk to you, if that's okay."

He reached out and Vanessa's hand found his. He squeezed it, looked down at her.

"It's okay," she said. "Go and see the doctor. I'll be fine." She squeezed him back.

He followed the nurse back out into the corridor, where she led him to a small, cramped room. The door was open and a middle-aged doctor sat behind a desk, squinting at a computer screen.

"Doctor Gable," said the nurse. "Mr... sorry, DS Royle is here."

The doctor looked up. He had a large, open face and a grey goatee beard. He blinked several times, smiled, and nodded. "Thanks, nurse. Please, DS Royle... won't you come in?"

The nurse hurried away. Royle stood in the doorway for a couple of seconds, unsure of what to do, and then he stepped inside, leaving the door open behind him.

"Sit down, please." The doctor leaned back in his chair. He had a big belly and thin arms. His medical coat was ill-fitting, as if they hadn't quite been able to accommodate his odd shape.

"What's wrong with my wife?"

The doctor grabbed a pen off the desk and rolled it between his palms. "As you know, she was brought in here a few hours ago. She called an ambulance complaining of pains and they wasted no time in getting her here. A woman of her age... well, we can't afford to take any risks."

Royle nodded. "Go on."

"We did an ultrasound and found something unusual." He paused.

Royle waited for him to continue.

"There's a growth, DS Royle. It's attached to the wall of her womb. At first we thought it might be an underdeveloped twin. That happens sometimes, one twin is stronger than the other and the weaker one expires."

"Twins?"

"No. Not twins. That's just what we thought at first. I'm afraid your wife has a tumour. We can't tell if it's benign or malignant at this stage, but one thing's for certain – it needs to come out. We have to operate, and we have to do it quickly."

Royle stared at the window behind the doctor's head. The sun was almost full up; the sky was lightening by degrees, the clouds parting. "How soon can you do it?"

"You have private health care. That means we can bump her up the list and do it almost immediately – certainly in the next twenty-four hours, here at the hospital. We need to monitor the situation first, get the results of a biopsy. We're not sure how serious this is, but I need to warn you both that it might be very serious indeed. If the tumour is malignant... well, I'm sure you understand what that might mean." The doctor stopped playing with the pen. He placed it on the desk, then touched it a couple of times with the tip of his finger, rolling it a few inches back and forth across the surface. "I'm sorry," he said, almost as an afterthought. "We'll do everything we can."

Royle stood and backed away from the desk. "Yeah. Thanks." He needed to get out of there, to get away from the hideous little man and his distracted demeanour. He couldn't take it all in; the world was coming apart at the seams, letting in impurities from whatever lay beyond the veil. The dark seed at his centre was starting to flower.

He stumbled out of the room and back along the corridor, falling against the wall, dragging his feet along the tiled floor. He entered the ward and went straight to Vanessa's bed, where he held her hand and stared into her eyes.

"I love you," she said, simply and honestly.

"This is it," he said. "This is the moment. This is what it all comes down to: you and me, in a hospital room, praying for the life of our unborn baby. Everything else is bullshit. The past cases, the crimes I could never solve, the drink, the stupid fights and arguments... none of it matters. Just this. This moment."

She nodded, closed her eyes. "I'm sleepy, baby... take care of things while I have a little rest."

He squeezed her hand. He knew exactly what she meant. For the first time in his life, he understood her completely. They were back together, just like he'd wanted. Every other problem in their relationship slipped away into the darkness, dwarfed by the immensity of this current situation.

Take care of things while I have a little rest...

He'd do that. He'd sort everything out; make it so that the world was ready for the arrival of their baby. Nothing else mattered.

Just then his mobile phone started to ring. He stood, glancing towards the nurse's station, and fumbled it out of his trouser pocket. The nurse he'd spoken to earlier gave him a dark look. He shrugged, mouthed the word "sorry" and headed out of the ward, raising the phone to his ear.

"Where are you?"

It was Detective Superintendent Sillitoe, from the station.

"Sorry, sir, I'm at the hospital. It's my wife... she's been brought in. It's an emergency."

"Is she okay?"

"I don't know, sir, but everything's in hand. I'm just on my way back to the station."

"Don't bother. Stay where you are. They're bringing her in."

"Who?"

"Ah, yes, you don't know... it's Wanda."

"Miss Wandaful?"

"Yeah. She should be there any minute. She was found on Grove Road early this morning by a jogger, in a bad way. I don't want to say much over the phone, because you'll need to see this one to believe it... but she's in a really bad state."

"Okay, I'll head down to Casualty now. That's where they'll take her."

"If she's talking, get what you can and report back here. There's some weird shit going down, and I have a feeling this might just be the start of it. Remember that scarecrow?"

"Yes, of course."

"Well, it's gone missing. And just to cap it off, this morning there was an identical one in the garden of each of the houses where the parents of two of those other missing girls lives... two of them: Jacobs and Warren. Royle, each of them has one of those fucked-up photographs taped to its face. It's like some kind of twisted message. Like someone's playing a game."

"I'm on it, sir."

"Let me know as soon as you know anything. It's all kicking off at the Concrete Grove. We now have reports of gunshots on the estate. What is it with these fucking people?"

The phone went dead before Royle could respond.

Weird shit... what exactly did Sillitoe mean by that? He thought about the scarecrows and what they might actually mean. The first one could be passed off as a silly, tasteless joke, but all of them together could only be a message. Was the person who'd taken the Gone Away Girls back in town? Did he want to resume his work, and was taunting the police in the process? And what about those gunshots? Who the hell was firing rounds in the Grove, and why?

The separate pieces of some huge plot were slowly moving together, shifting slowly, like tectonic plates. Royle suspected that he would never be able to see the full picture, only these separate sections. But hopefully that would be enough to take care of things, to rearrange into the correct order those parts of his life that were currently misaligned.

He rushed to the fire exit and down the stairs, heading for the Casualty Department. Just as he arrived there, on the ground floor at the rear of the hospital building, there was a lot of commotion. Two white-coated men were pushing a sheet-covered gurney through the reception area, followed by a nurse shouting orders. He followed them, pulling out his ID.

"Police! Who do you have there?"

The nurse turned towards him, her face slick with sweat and her lips pressed together in a thin line. She was breathing heavily. "She's one of yours... from the lab at the station. There's severe trauma to the lower abdomen and limbs. You really don't want to know..."

"I'm afraid I have to know. Is she conscious?"

"Unbelievably, yes... She should be dead, but she's managed to hang on. Fading fast, though, so if you don't mind we need to get her prepped for immediate surgery."

He jogged after them through the building, and waited outside when they entered an examination room. Shortly, a young doctor joined him. The man was Asian, with short hair and bushy eyebrows.

"Can you tell me anything, doctor?"

The man sighed. "She's in a bad way. She's lost a lot of blood and the mutilations are... well, I've not seen anything like this before. It's sick."

Royle took a step closer to the man. "What do you mean? Nobody's told me anything. I have no idea what you're talking about."

"Shit." The doctor wiped his brow with the back of his hand. "She's had the lower part of her body removed, everything severed from the waist down, and the wound cauterized by massive heat."

Royle couldn't understand what he was being told. He glanced at a clock on the wall but failed to register the time. Movement caught his eye over the doctor's shoulder: a door swung open, someone scurried along the corridor clutching a bloody sheet or towel draped over some kind of container, perhaps a small bucket.

"I'm not sure what to tell you, here. This is... unbelievable. In crude terms, someone's torn off her legs at the waist and stuffed a broom handle into the wound, making her into some kind of doll. She was found crawling along the street, dragging her shattered spine and the broom handle behind her. She should be dead, but somehow she's still alive."

The doctor wouldn't meet his gaze. "Can you save her?"

The doctor looked away, staring at the wall. "I'm not sure. We're doing all we can in there, believe me. She should be..."

"Yes, I know. She should be dead. But she isn't."

An hour later he was allowed into a side room, where Wanda had been put in a single bed under the window. She was wearing an oxygen mask, IV tubes were sticking out of her arms like skinned veins, and a heart rate monitor beeped by the side of the bed. Her body was covered with sheets, and there was some kind of raised chicken-wire structure encasing the lower half of her body – more specifically, the part where her legs should be.

Royle went to her and sat down in the chair at the side of the bed. He groped for her hand. She grabbed his fingers, squeezing lightly, with all the strength that she had.

"What happened to you?"

The heart rate monitor increased in volume, the beat becoming more erratic. Wanda let go of his hand. She reached up, to her face, and removed the oxygen mask.

"No, don't..." He tried to replace the mask, but she turned her head on the pillow. Her face was white. Not pale, but white.

"*Royle...*" Her voice was barely much more than a whisper. He could hear her pain; he knew how difficult it must be for her to speak. "*Go back... go to the Grove... something... coming... stop it... stop it and save your baby... the last... Gone Away girl... go to her family...*"

Her body went limp, her mouth hung open. She was dead. She'd hung on for as long as she could, until she could see him and pass on this oblique message. He was meant to go back to the Concrete Grove, to witness whatever the hell was going on there and somehow prevent events that he could not understand.

He had no idea why this all seemed to revolve around the Gone Away Girls, but it almost made sense. In terms of his failure to solve the case, it made a lot of sense. But still it was difficult to believe that his personal obsession should make such a tangible impact on the world. There was something larger than his own despair going on here, but he was only being allowed glimpses: tiny snatches, like weak light through a broken window.

Somehow he needed to suspend his disbelief and find some faith in himself, because if Wanda was right, the life of his baby depended on what he did next.

Royle closed Wanda's eyes with a gentle stroke of his hand across her face. "Thank you," he said, and left the room to try and take care of things – just as his wife had asked.

CHAPTER TWENTY-THREE

THE FIRST POLICE car arrived about fifteen minutes after the shot had been fired. Then, pretty quickly, the street outside Abby's house was cordoned off and several more vehicles arrived on the scene – three more police cars, a Black Maria van and an ambulance.

Erik watched from the bedroom window as the TV news crew set up their cameras. Some pretty blonde woman in an expensive suit delivered a to-camera update. She kept turning to indicate the house, lifting her head, tossing her hair, and Erik started to realise that he was about to be famous.

"Don't fucking move." He stood before Abby, grinning. She couldn't move, of course; he'd tied her to the radiator with packing tape after he'd watched her get dressed. Then he'd gone down to the car to fetch Monty. He hadn't made a very good job of the bindings, because he'd been in a rush, but they had held her long enough for him to get back here.

He turned and left the room, ignoring for now the ruined shrine and the motionless bastardised figure that was standing in the corner, watching in silence. He went downstairs and checked the front door again. He didn't want anyone coming in; didn't even want them walking up the path to the doorstep. He knelt down, lifted the letterbox, and shouted to the gathered crowd: "Anyone comes near this door and she's dead.

I'll shoot her in the fucking face." He wasn't sure if he meant it, but the proximity of Monty's mutated remains made it difficult to focus. Everything was fuzzy, as if he'd been on a day-long alcohol binge and somehow managed to drink himself almost sober.

As one of the police officers outside started speaking through a bullhorn, Erik let the flap of the letterbox drop back into place and retreated further inside the house. He went into the living room and stared at Monty, who was curled up like an ugly house pet on the sofa in front of the television. Images of Erik's face flashed across the screen. The text beneath the photographs described him as a 'local gangster', a 'psychopath' and a 'danger to society'. Perhaps he was all of those things; perhaps he was none of them. It didn't matter now, because events had begun to take on a momentum of their own, and nothing he did would matter.

"Is this what you wanted, Monty?"

It'll do...

"What do we do next?"

Monty slithered off the sofa and across the floor, like a snake with a human face. *We wait... that thing upstairs; it's my way back to Loculus. We need to wait until it's fully formed, and I can hitch a ride back there.*

Even now, Erik wasn't certain that he was actually hearing the voice in his head. He seemed to sense the words, to feel them, more than hear them. It was a strange experience, and not at all unpleasant. The voice was like a huge, warm hand stroking the rear of his brain. He could just sit back and let it tell him what to do.

He looked at the gun in his hand and wondered how it had got there. Not the physical act of picking it up, but the progression of events that had led him here, to this juncture, where he stood armed and dangerous with a police siege taking place outside the house.

Had it started with his friend Marty's stabbing, all those months ago? Certainly things had changed soon after that. Marty had subsequently gone to London to help raise another man's child, leaving behind him that same man's corpse with a knife wound in its belly. Or had the catalyst been much earlier than that, when he'd gone into business with Monty Bright, a lost, damaged man who always seemed to be looking for something that didn't exist, not in this world anyway?

So many different roads had brought him here, and he could have avoided none of them. Everything was sucked into the orbit of this big black hole. People, thoughts and memories, ideas... inexorably, it all ended up here, in the Concrete Grove, where it would be devoured by whatever monsters lived behind the scenes.

"Can't I stop now?" He fell to his knees, cradling the gun like a baby.

No, it's gone too far. You were never in charge, anyway. You were simply used, as we all were. Great forces have been wrestling over this site for centuries. Men and woman have tried to gain access to another world, a place where hummingbirds act as messengers, where trees are alive, and where ancient races of creatures once lived. Now it's just a wasteland, a place of diminishing power... but whoever can harness what's left of that power might be able to salvage something from it. That's all I ever wanted... power, real power.

This was the longest the voice had spoken, and it made the inside of Erik's head itch. It felt like there were insects in there, crawling around on the surface of his brain. He sensed the black hole at the centre of things flexing, opening up like a cosmic vagina to either ejaculate energy or suck it deep inside. He was no longer sure of which event would occur. But whatever happened, it would be a form of birth... of creation.

A phrase came to him, unbidden: *the Concrete Grove is the doorway to Creation.*

Where had he come across those words? Was it something he'd read, or something that had been said to him, long ago, like an old nursery rhyme whose meaning has been forgotten? The words resonated, vibrating along the channels of his being, turning to glass and shattering at his core.

He stood, holding on tightly to the gun. That's what this was all about: creation. Not destruction. That would be too obvious, too easy. The true test of a man was his power to create, not his willingness to destroy.

Erik looked at the pathetic remnant of his friend and he made a decision.

"I don't know what's happening here, but it all has to end."

Go back upstairs. Kill the woman. Let the other thing grow...

"No."

He raised the gun, trying not to think about anything beyond the moment. All he had was his instincts. Let other men puzzle over what happened here after it was done. He would simply act as his gut told him.

No. This is wrong...

He pointed the gun at Monty; the small, twisted shape began to writhe on the carpet, its appendages flailing, grasping at nothing but empty air. The bond was broken – he could no longer influence Erik's actions. Because Erik wouldn't let it happen. In the depths of this darkness, he had finally found himself... and he knew exactly what was required of him.

No.

"Yes." He pulled the trigger.

Monty's tiny upturned face disintegrated into a cloud of red powder. The body bucked and writhed, the limbs and tentacles clenching, clutching, and then going limp. The small, compressed body began to change, flesh becoming fluid, changing into a succession of faces that screamed silently as everything withered, becoming as dust.

Erik knew that these were the faces of every person Monty Bright had ever trapped when he was still in business as a loan shark; they were his debtors, the people he had controlled and finally absorbed, making them a part of his monstrous whole. They were free now; their debts were finally paid. Their recession of the spirit was over.

He walked across the room and peeked through the gap in the curtains. Nothing had changed; they were all still waiting for him out there, wanting him to come out. They were demanding blood, and they would not rest until they had it. His blood, primarily, but the blood of a hostage would suffice. It would give them a good story for the evening news.

He turned away and went back upstairs. Abby was sitting against the radiator, shivering. She'd managed to scrape away most of the tape, releasing her hands. She rubbed silently at her reddened wrists.

"We're trapped," he said.

She looked up at him, into his eyes. Her face was battered; dried blood was smeared across her cheeks; the area around her left eye was swollen. "You did this... you trapped us."

"I know. I had no choice. I'm weak... a weak man. All my life I've pretended to be strong, but I'm not. Never was. My father used to beat me and masturbate over my shaking body. My mother would sit in the chair, drinking brown ale, and laugh about it. My brothers were all maniacs, and I followed them down that path. Nobody here gets out alive. This place – all the places just like it – is toxic, a waste dump for humanity. All of our dreams, our hopes, are rotted away. This is the end of the line and none of us asked to be here..." He faded, unsure of what he was trying to say. "This is all there is. Beyond here... there's nothing. Even the place Monty wanted to get back to, it's just shit: another world of shit that exists inside this one."

"Let me go, Erik. Finish untying me, and I'll take our daughter downstairs. We'll get you some help. I'll tell the police that you lost your mind for a little while, but you're better now. You'll get therapy. They'll mend you. We can be together again."

He sank to his knees and placed the gun between his thighs. "I wish I could believe you. That would be nice. But you're lying, I know you are. I can smell the lies on your breath." He shook his head. "You don't understand. We're all monsters. None of us chose this route, we didn't do it deliberately, but the world turned on us and changed us into beasts. Nobody out there gives a flying fuck about any of us. They demonise us in the news and in TV shows. They call us names and give us hoods to wear. And we accept the role they force upon us – we adapt and we take it on, sucking it all down, because we don't have anything else. All we have is their disdain, their hatred, and we fucking lap it up like beaten dogs."

His breath was coming in short little hitches, like that of an asthmatic. He could barely speak, so he stopped talking. He bowed his head and looked at his hands. They were cupping the gun, feeling its dread weight. The barrel of the gun was a tiny, endless black hole, sucking him down: a reflection of the black hole around which they all orbited.

"What are you going to do now?" She shifted against the radiator, loosening the tape around her ankles.

Erik remained silent. There was nothing left to say.

CHAPTER TWENTY-FOUR

He should have come here earlier, right at the start. This was where it all began, at least for the Pollack family. It was where they had lived with their ghost, and where they had finally given in to the pressure it had brought them.

This was where he'd been raised... perhaps even where he'd been born.

He'd tried to get to Abby's house first, to ask her if she'd come along with him to the Needle. But the road had been blocked: police tape and official vehicles, TV news vans and spectators. There was something going on, and it looked to him as if Abby might be in trouble. It didn't take a genius to realise that her ex was involved – that fucking gangster Erik Best. He hoped that Abby got out of it in one piece. The last thing he wanted was to go to her funeral.

He stood outside the main entrance to the tower, looking up at the building. It loomed above the construction hoardings, a battered monument to man's failures. The sky was dark around its apex, as if storm clouds were concentrated there, drawn to it by strange energies. Small birds hovered outside the upper floor windows, making dark patterns against the charcoal sky.

"I'm here," he whispered. "I'm home."

Home...

He knew the truth now. He had always known it, deep down inside, where he could never quite reach the information. Marc was the baby that he'd read about in Harry Rose's notebook. He'd come here looking for a story to write up, and had instead found his own lost plot strands, the loose threads of his existence.

He was the baby; the third Pollack child, the only one to have survived the unknown horrors the family had endured here, inside the Needle.

There were no memories of ever having lived here, just a large blank spot, as if someone had wiped that part of his brain clean. His earliest childhood memories were of the car crash that had killed his parents, and then of Uncle Mike.

He'd left Uncle Mike as soon as he was old enough to look after himself, gone to University to study journalism, blotting out his fractured childhood, fabricating new memories to smother the ones that didn't exist anyway. He'd been successful, until now. Harry Rose's notebook had opened up a crack in his mind, allowing images to seep out: a bare room with a crib, an uncarpeted floor, two dirty-faced young children, a man with a beak for a face... and there was nothing more, just the grubby taste of fear at the back of his throat.

"It's me," he said, confirming the fact, trying to make it stick. "I'm the baby... I was there, in the flat. I was haunted." And in many ways, he still was: haunted by the past that he could not remember, and by the screams of the siblings he had never known. Little Jack and Daisy-like-a-flower; the twin sibling who had never lived: he detected a trace memory of fondness for his brother and sister – much in the same way that he loved the characters in all the best books he'd read as a child.

Of his parents, if indeed that's what they had been, there was no clue.

Then, as the cracks opened slightly wider, he had a glimpse of something else: a man and a woman, dressed in dark robes, kneeling beside a television set draped with a black cloth. Lying on the cloth was what looked like a hen or a chicken, but it was covered in blood. The man and the woman were chanting, rocking back and forth, and the shadows around them looked alive, not like shadows at all...

There was nothing more, just that single snapshot, like an isolated scene from a film.

They tried to give me to Captain Clickety.

The thought was like a knife through his heart. It could not be denied. It came with the image; a nice little package, all wrapped up in despair. He knew it was true – he felt it. His parents had tried to sacrifice him, as part of a deal to protect the twins. But something had gone wrong. Instead of him being taken, and the man and the woman rewarded with whatever it was they sought, the entire deal had fallen through. The ghost had left them... but it had taken with it something vital that he and the twins were unable to live without. Their souls, their life-force... whatever it was that made them who they were.

He didn't think he'd ever find out what had soured the sacrifice, but none of that mattered now. His book would never be written, because he was a vital component in the plot. There was no way that he could write a story that was still happening, with no real ending in sight. He was a reporter, not a novelist; he dealt in cold, hard facts, not blood-hot fiction.

There was a section of hoarding that had either blown down in a wind or been vandalised. Marc made his way over to the area, keeping an eye out to make sure that he wasn't seen. He had no idea who might be hanging around out here, but he didn't want to be disturbed.

The fallen section was easy to climb over. He grabbed hold of a timber upright, hauled himself on top of the fence-like structure, and leapt nimbly over to the other side. As he did so, a strange sensation passed through him: it was like a cold breeze stirring up his insides, creating a chill at the pit of his stomach.

Don't be so stupid, he thought, brushing down his trousers and walking towards the main entrance.

The double doors were open. He was expected. He paused outside, wondering if this wasn't such a good idea after all. Who the hell had opened up the place, and why had they done so? Was this some kind of trap, or were there perhaps villains waiting inside, ready to mug him and give him a beating? Perhaps there was nothing at all supernatural about this situation, and he was simply walking into an empty building where a group of drugged-up maniacs would hurt him.

Why had he been so quick to believe that there was more to this situation than reality? He'd never believed in ghosts. He even questioned the motivation behind his quest for the truth about the Northumberland Poltergeist... a quest that, if he was honest, he'd never taken too seriously. For instance, this was the first time he'd been to see the building where it all happened. He'd had no idea about the baby–

(*I'm the baby*)

–until the spirit of Harry Rose had been forced to stick the notebook in front of his eyes.

He was an idiot; he had no clue what he was doing. He never had done.

But still he pushed wide the doors and stepped inside, crossing over the threshold from one story to another; one reality to the next. His skin seemed to quiver on the bone. His head was filled with the sound of humming.

The foyer was filled with hummingbirds, but the sound was inside his skull, not out here in the real world. The birds were motionless. There were hundreds of them, hovering silently in the air, perched on windowsills and standing on the floor. They all watched him with their tiny beady eyes. They were like windup toys; there was a strange, innocent beauty to them that both scared him and calmed his nerves.

"I'm coming in," he whispered. The birds gave no response. They didn't move.

Carefully, he made his way across the foyer, watching where he placed his feet in case he stood on one of the small birds. He thought about that old Hitchcock film: the final scene, with Rod Taylor and Tippi Hedren making their way through a crowd of similarly silent and watchful avian antagonists. It was eerie. There was a sense of calm, but beneath that there was the suggestion of frantic movement, almost panic.

He moved slowly towards the stairwell and out of the foyer. At the bottom of the stairs, he stopped and took a moment to catch his breath. He'd not been breathing that entire time as he crossed the foyer, walking among the hummingbirds. His mouth was dry; his throat ached.

After a short while, he continued up the staircase, holding on to the handrail as he climbed. The steps were filthy; the stairwell smelled of old piss mingled with the coppery hint of blood. He didn't want to be here but he was unable to turn around and leave. He had to follow wherever the story – *his* story, now – led him. There was no other option.

The flat was on the top floor. He remembered, even though he had no memories of ever having been there. He climbed slowly, reluctantly, but with a sense of purpose. It didn't take him long to get there, but during the short climb it seemed that the seasons had changed; the world had turned, everything had altered subtly. When he stood on the top floor, bathed in sweat, it was as if he'd stepped into another place, perhaps a country whose borders messily intersected his own version of reality.

"I'm here. I'm home."

The building was silent. The rooms were empty. There was nobody else here, just him... him and the birds.

Every door but one on the top floor was shut. The only one that was open belonged to the flat where the haunting had taken place. Again, he knew this instinctively, as if there was hidden knowledge stored inside him and only his emotions could read it. He listened for sounds of movement, but none came. He truly was alone here, inside his own lost past. There was no one else to help him, to hold his hand.

His brother and sister were dead and he had no idea what might have happened to his real parents.

He was alone, and that made him happy.

He stepped softly across the landing, towards the open door. There was no light in there; it was pitch-dark, like the entrance to a cave. Sunlight lay across the walls and the floor out here, on the landing, but inside the room was only darkness. It was fitting somehow; he would not have expected anything else.

He stopped immediately outside the door, his breath coming in short, sharp jags. Sweat poured down over his forehead and into his eyes. He wiped it away with the back of his hand, but still his vision began to blur.

"Home."

He took a step forward, and then another, and entered the place where it had all started.

Darkness swallowed him. Then it receded, and he finally saw what had happened all those years ago. The final chapter of his story – which was also the prologue – unfurled before his eyes.

There's a couple on the living room floor, dressed in long black robes with nothing underneath. They have strange symbols painted on their hands and faces. They've turned the television into some kind of altar: a black piece of cloth is draped over the set, covering the screen, and there's a dead chicken or hen or rooster with its throat cut so deeply that its head hangs at an angle. Its feathers are black.

No blood.

No knife.

Just the dead fowl.

The man and the woman are singing or chanting. They've clearly rehearsed the words many times, and their faces betray not a hint of emotion. There is no music, just their voices, and neither of them can hold a tune.

At the woman's side, wrapped up in blankets, there is a small baby. The baby is silent; it does not cry. Its eyes are only half open; its mouth is twisted into an odd shape, the lips limp. The baby might be drugged.

The man nods as he chants. Tears begin to well up from his eyes and then spill down his cheeks. The woman reaches out clumsily and grabs his hand. The man shakes his head, vigorously; it is the woman's turn to nod.

The woman lets go of the man's hand, turns her body, and picks up the tiny baby.

They both continue to chant. The man's voice is quiet but the woman's is loud, as if she has something to prove.

Then, abruptly, the chant changes, one word, repeated over and over again: Loculus.

The woman holds up the baby by its throat. The blankets drop to the floor. The baby remains still, its sedated form motionless as they woman closes her eyes and starts to squeeze.

The man looks down, at the floor. Behind him, something stirs. Darkness rushes in, like a thick fog, coiling at floor level and then rising, forming a tube, before it takes on the shape of a man. A white-beaked face leans forward, eager.

The man opens his eyes. He reaches out and grabs the baby. The woman does not resist. It is over, just like that: the moment has gone. The spell is broken.

The beaked figure fades to blackness, flapping its arms and thrashing its head from side to side. Then, after a few seconds of this violent activity, it is gone.

The man and the woman stare at each other, reaching some kind of unspoken agreement. They reach out and hold hands, the baby clasped between them.

The sacrifice has failed. They could not go through with it. They could not kill the baby, even to save the other children.

Marc's parents – his real parents, who loved him after all – have backed out of whatever deal they had made.

That is the reason for the subsequent haunting. That is why Captain Clickety tried to get to the twins. Because the life he was offered, the one he would have accepted without pain or pity, was revoked. The one he'd been told about all that time ago when he'd first encountered the village of Groven: the Witness.

So instead he went after all the others – the Pollack twins and all the rest: the ones he took and the ones that got away. The Pollack twins, the three boys he lured inside the Needle, the Gone Away Girls... but none of them was ever the right one. Because that one escaped, he was snatched away.

But now he'd come back.

CHAPTER TWENTY-FIVE

Royle parked in the next street and made his way on foot to Abby Hansen's house. He'd already been briefed on the two-way radio, so he knew what was going on. Erik Best – a man he'd met and spoken with on several occasions – had gone crazy with a handgun and there was a full-on armed siege taking place in the Concrete Grove.

As he approached the property, flashing his ID at uniformed officers as he made his way through the police cordon, he saw members of the Armed Response Unit getting into position. A man with a high-powered rifle was visible on the roof of the house opposite; the rest of the team was dotted about at various points close to the house, their weapons trained on the front door and windows. There'd be at least a couple of officers at the back of the house, doing the same thing. It was all locked down tight; Erik Best was going nowhere apart from down.

Detective Superintendent Sillitoe himself came walking over when he saw Royle, raising a hand in greeting. The tall, thin man looked anxious. He never had been good with television crews, and there were a lot of cameras on the scene today.

"Sir," he said, nodding.

"Glad you could make it, Royle. We have a... well, a situation here."

"I've been briefed, sir. I know what's going on."

Sillitoe glanced towards the house and then back again, his eyes narrow and focused. "You know this man, Best?"

"I do, sir. I've dealt with him on a few occasions. He's a local gangster – did time for GBH and assault, but we could never pin anything else on him. It's a known fact that he runs bare-knuckle boxing bouts but not from anywhere around here. We think he has links to the drug fraternity, but again there's no hard evidence. He's Teflon, sir. The bastard always manages to stay out of our sights."

"Okay, anything else?"

Royle paused, tried to remain calm. "The Gone Away Girls, sir."

Sillitoe tensed, seeming to grow in height. "What about them, Royle. Don't start all that shit again, please. Not here, not now." His eyes opened wider, flashed.

"No, sir, you don't understand. The last girl taken, before it all stopped... it was Best's daughter, Tessa Hansen."

"And the mother's in there with him..."

"So I believe, sir."

"Fuck. That's all we need, to revisit another old mess." He paused, looked again at the house. When he turned back to Royle, his features had softened. "Can I rely on you, Royle?"

"You know you can, sir."

Sillitoe smiled. "Good... that's good. Let's try to keep any mention of the Gone Away – of *that* case – to ourselves." His lips curled, as if he'd tasted something unpleasant. "The press are all over this to begin with.

Armed sieges, hostage situations... flavour of the fucking month, especially after that Moat business last year over in Rothbury. The bastards can't seem to get enough of this 'mad gunman' shit."

"Yes, sir. I know." He stared at Sillitoe's face, trying to read the man's thoughts. But that was impossible; nobody could read Detective Superintendent Sillitoe. That was what made him so good at police force politics, why he'd risen so far and so quickly through the ranks, despite being such a piss-poor detective.

Royle was about to add something more when he heard the gunshot.

The sound was followed by a commotion: bystanders hit the deck, police officers ran around trying to look as if they had some kind of control over the situation, members of the Armed Response Unit hunched over their weapons, awaiting the order to fire at will.

Sillitoe moved quickly behind the nearest vehicle, protecting himself. Royle moved away, taking the opportunity to give his superior officer the slip. He'd been told to come here, he was meant to be on site, right in the middle of the action. He didn't need any distractions. He just wanted to get to the heart of the matter and rip it out, still beating if necessary.

"Royle!" The voice came from an upper storey window.

He stopped walking, turned, and looked up at the front of the house. He could see a figure partially obscured by a bedroom curtain.

Looking around, he saw an officer cowering nearby with a bullhorn in his hand. He jogged over there and grabbed it, hitting the switch and causing a whine of feedback. He put the apparatus to hips lips, took a breath, and spoke:

"Best? Yes, it's me, DS Royle. You remember me, don't you?"

A pause... nobody on the street dared to speak.

"Yeah, I know you. I'll speak to you... only you." Another pause; the man was thinking things through, examining his options. "Get up here now, or I'll kill the woman and the kid."

Royle stopped himself from responding immediately. This didn't make sense.

"The kid?" His voice echoed. "Let me get this straight. There's a child up there with you, Best?"

"Yeah, a fucking kid... or so it wants us to believe. Come up now or they're both dead. I'm not fucking around. The time for all that's gone. This is serious. This is where it all ends, Royle."

Royle did not wait for confirmation from his superior officer, nor did he look at anyone as he stalked across the street and pushed open the gate. He walked up to the door, waited, and listened. He heard someone coming down the stairs, heavy-footed, and moving along the hallway. He couldn't make out details through the stippled glass panel in the door, but it didn't look like Erik Best.

There was the rattle of a bolt in its slot. The door opened an inch; the security chain tautened, made a faintly musical noise. A woman's battered face peered through the gap.

"Miss Hansen?"

She nodded.

"Miss Hansen... Abby, are you okay?"

The more he saw of her face the more worried he became. She was cut and bruised, with what looked to be a broken nose and a shattered cheekbone. Both of her eyes were swollen almost shut.

"He hurt me... he's got a gun." Her voice was dull; she struggled to make the words clear through her beaten face. "He's halfway up the stairs... if I try to run, he said he'll shoot me in the back."

Royle nodded. The decision was made.

"Let me in."

She shut the door. He heard her pawing at the security chain, trying to release it from its catch. Then the door opened again, wider this time; just enough for him to step inside. She moved to the side, and once he was through the doorway, she slammed the door and replaced the chain, slid the bolt back into place. She was shaking. The unfocused look in her eyes made it seem like she'd just woken up from a long sleep and was still only half awake, still caught up in the wild webbing of dreams.

"This way," said a voice from further along the hall. "Come here, where I can see you. And keep your hands away from your body."

"I'm unarmed," said Royle, moving slowly forward. "I'm not a firearms officer, anyway. I would probably shoot myself in the foot if I started waving a gun around. How about you?"

"Don't worry about me. I know how to use this thing."

Royle could not see the bottom few stairs of the main flight. As he drew closer, he saw a pair of feet, then legs, and finally a torso.

"Keep coming," said Erik Best. He held the gun out, away from his body. The tip of the barrel was angled slightly downwards, but it was pointed vaguely in Royle's direction. "No quick moves."

Royle was aware of Abby Hansen standing with her back to the wall. She slid along the hallway cautiously, focusing all of her attention on the man who was standing halfway up the stairs.

"Okay, start climbing. We can talk up here, on the first floor, so we're well out of the way of your mates out there."

Royle nodded. "That's fine, Erik. I'm here for you... all for you. We can talk about whatever you want." He kept his hands held out, away from his body, the palms turned towards the man with the gun. "I want to find a peaceful conclusion to this. I don't want to see anyone get hurt – and that means you, too. Let's see if we can get everyone here out alive, yeah?"

Best shook his head slowly, a grim smile on his face. "We're all already dead, marra. Don't you see? This is a hell, and we're all trapped here, in this hell. Like demons or ghosts... we can't ever leave again. We're haunting this place... haunting it..."

He's insane, thought Royle as he started to climb the stairs. *He's lost his fucking mind*. He moved slowly, carefully. He didn't reach out to grab hold of the banister, preferring instead to keep his hands up at waist level, showing that they were empty. He could hear Abby Hansen mounting the bottom step behind him. Her breathing was heavy. She whimpered quietly, but just the once and for only a second or two.

"It's okay," he whispered, keeping his gaze fixed dead ahead and hoping that only she could hear him. "Stay calm."

"Shut the fuck up and get your copper arse up here." The gun barrel twitched, pointing directly at him. "She doesn't need to hear you. She doesn't need to hear anything."

"Okay, okay... hold your horses. I'm coming. Like I said, I'm here for you. We can sit and talk, you and I, and see what we can organise."

Slowly, Best moved backwards up the stairs, taking one riser at a time. He placed his feet carefully as he went, so there was no danger of him stumbling and falling no matter how hard Royle wished for it to happen. The man might, indeed, have lost his mind, but he was aware of his surroundings and seemed intent on having his way.

When he reached the top of the stairs, Royle followed Best along the landing to an open door. Best stood to the side, flicking the gun as if he were chasing off flies. "Get in there."

Royle nodded. "No problem." He entered the room. At first it wasn't clear what he was looking at, and then he realised that there was a pile of what looked like a child's belongings in the middle of the room, as if they'd been arranged into a heap and then spread out messily. There were clothes and toys, pages from magazines, and even photographs in the pile. He realised then that these things had once belonged to Erik and Abby's daughter. These were her things; they'd been placed here deliberately.

Then he saw the thing that was standing in the corner.

He stopped, feeling the urge to turn around and run, to just get the hell out of there and not look back, not once, not ever. Just keep on running until he was out of sight and far away from the Crawl.

The figure was small – child-sized. It was dressed in a floppy-brimmed black hat, a long black cloak, and had some kind of weird bird mask covering its face. Placed over the mask where the eyes should have been, incongruous and lending a further surreal touch to the already eerie figure, was a strange-looking pair of black goggles. The figure did not move. It just stood there, with its back to the wall, staring into the room.

Royle had overcome the urge to flee. "Hello," he said, disappointed at the fear in his voice.

"Shut the fuck up," said Best, entering behind him. "It doesn't talk."

Royle didn't want to turn around and take his eyes off the figure. If he stopped looking, it might move; and if it moved, he was fucked. He wasn't sure how he knew this, but it felt right. The last thing that needed to happen here was for that thing to start moving. Or crawling.

Abby Hansen walked past him on the right, moving towards the small figure. She stood near it, but not too close. She didn't seem to know what to do – should she go to it, or stay out of reach? Her fingers flexed at her sides, her lips trembled, and she swayed on her heels for a moment, as if she were about to fall. Then, after a second or two where things looked fragile, she recovered and straightened her spine, lifting her chin in defiance.

Royle smiled at her, but Abby stared right through him. She was probably in shock. Or maybe she'd simply retreated inside herself, where it was safer.

Finally, Royle managed to look away from the figure in black. "Okay, Erik," he said, turning reluctantly to face the gunman. "So I'm here. Now, what shall we talk about?"

Best used the gun to point at the bed. "Sit down. I don't trust you on your feet. I don't trust any of you fuckers."

Royle stayed where he was. "So why did you ask me in here, Erik? I mean, if you don't trust me, why am I here?" He gestured with his hands, shrugging slightly.

"Don't get fucking clever. You're only here because you tried to help when our Tessa went missing. You were the only fucker who cared. Nobody else did. They just turned their backs and walked away, probably thinking I had something to do with it." He licked his lips. His gaze wouldn't settle on one thing; his eyes moved around the room, looking at everything, doubting everything. "Now, sit down on the fucking bed before I put a hole in you." Finally his gaze settled on Royle, and there was a blank spot behind those eyes that Royle wished he'd not had turned upon him.

Royle did as he was told and sat down on the small single bed. The soft mattress bowed beneath him, making him feel like a giant, or a man sitting on a toy bed. "Okay… just be cool, Erik. Tell me the problem."

The other man laughed. "Fucking hell, man. Are you blind? This…" He gestured with the hand that wasn't holding the gun. "This is the problem. All of it."

"This house?" Royle was acting dumb, pretending that he was slow on the uptake. Anything that might buy him some time.

"Jesus..." Erik Best shook his head. "Not the house... not just the house. Everything else, too. This place, this estate – this fucking life." He walked across the room and stood by the window. The curtains were closed. The beaked figure did not move as he approached, and he barely even looked at it. "I'm right at the centre of the black hole, Royle. I can't move, can't breathe. Nothing I do makes any sense." He turned towards the small figure. "Look at this... this thing."

"What is it, Erik? I can see it, too. Where did it come from?"

Best turned away from the window. He dropped the gun hand down by his side. "It came from the black hole. Right over there." He nodded towards the pile of items at the centre of the room.

Royle wasn't certain, but it looked like there was a hole in the carpet right at the middle of the untidy heap. The hole looked like it might even penetrate the wooden floorboards beneath.

"That thing... I think... I think it's my daughter. Or at least a small part of her."

That was Abby Hansen's cue to move. She seemed to snap out of whatever fugue state she'd entered, and moved sideways, towards the figure. It stood there like a statue, tense and immobile. Even when Abby put one arm around its narrow shoulders, the thing did not move.

"Get away... you get away from it." Best raised the gun.

"Listen, Erik. Let's just stay calm."

"Get the fuck... *away*." His finger tightened on the trigger. It was a subtle movement, but Royle was looking at exactly the right place to see it happen. He was ignoring the man's face. He was more interested in that hand, and the gun it grasped so tightly. Without thinking, he stood and made a single quick movement towards the gunman.

Erik Best's finger twitched on the trigger. The gun went off: a single shot, but in the small room the sound was deafening.

Royle reached him too late. Abby was already bending over and clutching her abdomen by the time he grabbed the gun hand, twisting it to release the weapon. By this time, Best had gone limp. He let go of the gun without a struggle and sank to his knees, his head going down and his shoulders hitching in a silent sob.

That was when the figure by the window started making a noise.

It raised one small, thin arm, pointing at the wounded woman, and let out a sound like a broken motorcycle engine. The din was unearthly... that was the exact word that came to Royle's mind, even at the time. The sound was not of this world. A long, high-pitched clicking sound, like nothing he'd ever heard before.

Other than raising its hand, the figure did not move. It just kept on clicking: a single endless ratcheting note, with not even a pause for breath.

Royle went to Abby Hansen. She was down on her knees. Blood had turned her legs red; she was clutching at the wound, trying to stem the flow. She started crawling on her knees, making her way over to the pile of items on the floor – all the things she'd kept when her daughter went missing. When Royle tried to help her, she brushed away his hands. She kept on moving, staggering on her knees, until she came to the hole in the floor.

Royle could hardly believe what he was seeing.

The hole had enlarged; the edges were burnt, as if an intense heat had seared the floorboards and the carpet. There were black leaves clinging to the lip of the hole. It was a perfect black circle – a black hole, just like Best had said. He felt his hand open and the gun dropped to the floor. He made no effort to keep hold of it. His muscles were limp, lifeless.

He sensed movement before he saw it, and by the time he'd turned around Erik Best had already picked up the gun. He was holding it with the barrel in his mouth, his eyes wide and his teeth chattering against the steel barrel. He smiled around the barrel, and then he pulled the trigger. The back of his head detonated in a confusion of red, like something from a dream. It didn't look real; it was a special effect, one that would play out on the screen behind his eyes for the rest of his life.

Royle watched as the man crumpled to the floor, blood pouring from his open, slack mouth as the gun slipped away. Then, when he turned back to Abby Hansen, she was crouching by that hole in the floor, shivering. The beaked figure had somehow made its way across to her, and they were embracing tightly, as if one were absorbing the other. The small figure in the black cloak looked vague, insubstantial, like a rag doll that was no longer held together by the glue of its parents' grief.

Abby Hansen smiled.

Then both figures fell into the hole and vanished.

CHAPTER TWENTY-SIX

She's back there, inside. She's in the grove inside the Grove; the place that exists just out of sight, out of step, beneath and off to one side: the place that is sometimes known as Loculus. This time she knows where she's going; she is no longer a tourist. This place has begun to feel more like home than her real home, back in the world that she can barely bring herself to think of as real.

She walks quickly, her bare feet whispering across the soft ground and the black leaves. She does not hurt her feet. It is as if they know exactly where to tread so that they can miss the stones and roots that might cause them harm.

She glances down at her belly, where she was shot. There's still blood there, but the wound is already healing. Leaves cling to it, fusing the flesh, repairing the damage.

Before long, she is once again at the mouth of the cave, which stands among others just like it at the foot of the high cliffs. It all looks different this time, darker, deeper, and more menacing. She pauses at the threshold, uncertain. Why is she here? What happened to the thing that might have been her daughter or might just have been something else trying to impersonate Tessa?

She is beyond doubting any of this. She knows that it is as real as that other place – the one where Erik

Best took his own life, and where that policeman is still standing, covered in Erik's blood and wondering what to do next.

Both places are real. The only place where that reality is thin is the joint between the two worlds, where she crossed over. The first time she came here, it felt like a dream within a dream. But now it feels like she is wide awake. Before, she thought that her spirit was walking here, treading on ground that would be unable to take the weight of her body, but now she realises that her corporeal self is here, standing outside the cave.

This means, of course, that she might be in danger. Anything that happens to her here will have repercussions in the other world. If she dies here, she dies there, too. There is a connection, a bond, as if one world feeds the other. She wonders briefly what came first, which grove sired the other. Then she realises that it doesn't matter.

She stares up the cliff face, making out small hand and footholds. What's up there, at the top? What kind of view would she be rewarded with if she made it to the summit of those cliffs?

A sound draws her attention: something slithers inside the cave. She isn't afraid, but she feels as if she has been noticed.

As she watches the cave mouth, a small figure emerges and takes shape. She feels her breath catch in her throat, but then as the figure is revealed she is saddened to see that it isn't Tessa. It's a small girl, but not the one she'd hoped for. The girl walks towards her, the hem of her dirty white shift dress swaying around her knees. She is smiling, but her mouth is black: no teeth are visible. Her lips are thin and pale. Her eyes are heavy-lidded, as if she has just woken from a deep sleep.

The girl beckons with one hand, a tired come-hither gesture.

"Who are you? Tell me your name, honey."

The girl shakes her head. In that moment, Abby recognises her from the news reports and the footage on television. This is the first one; the original Gone Away Girl. It's Little Connie Millstone... but a different version to the one that went away. She looks older, as if the soul of an ancient crone has been trapped inside the body of a child. Abby can tell by the eyes: they are far too deep inside their sockets, and look much too old for such a young girl. She wonders what those eyes have seen, what horrors have passed before them, playing out as awful and inappropriate as an adult film in a nursery.

The girl turns away and disappears into the entrance of the cave.

Abby does not know what to do, so she follows. The darkness closes around her like a fist, dragging her inside.

The fairy lights from before have been taken down. She cannot see the cave paintings. Everything is dark: black upon black. She feels her way, trusting that the girl will not lead her astray. She has no choice now. To turn back would be foolish. She can only ever move forward now, if she wants to survive.

Suddenly she is able to see. Up ahead, there is a familiar sight, but this time it is distressing. Subtle changes have taken place, and what was once a picture of beauty has become a sketch of terror.

The stone plinth is broken; jagged cracks mar its surface, a black oil-like substance has leaked out from the cracks. The hummingbirds are bedraggled, covered in grime. Their feathers are no longer the distinctive black and white that she can remember: now they are grey, all grey, covered in a light coating of dust or ashes. One of the birds has a broken beak. The other has lost an eye. As she moves closer, she realises that the dusty layer is mixed with fresh blood. Either the birds have been fighting or something has attacked them... but still, despite all this damage, they somehow manage to balance the frozen tear between them.

"Oh, no... what happened?"

Connie Millstone appears at her side, kneeling as if in prayer. Abby does the same, sinking down to her knees as she stares at the torn and bloodied hummingbirds.

"Something came. The pollution... the Underthing We thought it was gone – we thought it had gone away forever. But it came back."

There is a loud rending noise and the cracks in the plinth open wider, forming great fissures. The blur of the hummingbirds' wings stutters, making the shape of each wing visible, but then they speed up again. The birds dip in the air for an instant before returning to their usual level.

"Look... that's it. The pollution. The Underthing. It's trying to come back, to return to the surface."

She shuffles forward on her knees and peers into the fissure, acutely aware of the activity of the hummingbirds' wings above her. The fissure is deep; it seems to go on forever. All she can see is the sides of the rock, small stones and dusty gravel particles falling away. Then, for a split second, she catches sight of something else: like a river of filth, or an underground lake of sewage, something thick and brown and hideous slithers past. Then it is gone.

"The Underthing," says the girl. "That's where it lives, where it's trapped. Underneath. But it wants to get back up on top."

Strip away the weight of allegory and metaphor, rip off the layers of pretension, and those words are the purest warning she has ever heard. They mean so much; they mean so little. They mean everything and nothing simultaneously. She struggles to reach the deeper meaning of whatever it is she is being told, but it's out of sight.

"I'm sorry," she says, turning to the girl.

But the girl is merely an outline, a patch of dusty darkness at her side.

She reaches out and grabs hold of something that might be a hand, but it slips through her fingers. The Gone Away Girl is gone again. Perhaps she was never really here.

Abby gets to her feet and stands before the hummingbirds, witnessing their titanic, eternal struggle. That's when she realises what is required of her: she is a witness, albeit a temporary one. But that's all they need, these beautiful creatures; just someone to watch, to see what they are doing, to make it mean something again.

"I'm watching," she says, crying. "I can see you." But she isn't the one: she isn't the witness they were promised.

The sound of their wings is like an ancient prayer, the rigidity of their bodies is a truth that cannot be denied. They are here; they are real; they are the only thing that stands between humanity and the gaping void (the Underthing?). As long as there is someone to bear witness – not all the time, just once in a while, to remind the great consciousness of the human race that this is still here, still happening – their strength will be renewed and the fight will go on. Whatever is underneath will stay there, banished from the upper reaches. Everything will be synchronised; forces will remain in balance. Twin energies will be aligned.

Her face is hot. She lifts her hand to dab at her cheek, and her fingers come away wet. Glancing down at her fingertips, she sees red... she is bleeding. This time she raises both hands to feel her skin, and she is aware of a lot of fluid. She traces the lines of blood up to her forehead, where the skin is broken in several places. There are small wounds, lacerations; the type of tears and gouges that could possibly be caused by the beaks of tiny birds.

She glances up, above her head, and sees them circling near the ceiling. There are a lot of them, small, silent hummingbirds. Her gaze follows a trail of them across the ceiling and into the dark cave mouth behind the shattered plinth.

Then the noise starts.

It sounds like distant helicopters, but she knows exactly what it is: it is the sound of a million hummingbird wings. They fly out of the hole in the cave wall as a single mass, a solid blur of motion. Her eyes struggle to cope with the sight and she reels backwards, falling to the ground.

The hummingbirds pass directly over her head, only inches from her moist upturned face. An endless flock, they are not interested in Abby; they are heading elsewhere, summoned by a silent song, answering a call that she is unable to hear. She lies on her back and watches them, praying to a god in whom she has never believed, hoping against hope that amid this feast of miracles she might just get the one she's always wished for: she might just get to see her daughter again.

She waits for the thunder to pass. It takes a long time. This storm has been brewing for millennia, and now that it has broken there will be no stopping what destruction shall be wrought.

CHAPTER TWENTY-SEVEN

NURSE BENNETT STOOD over the bed, looking down at the policeman's wife. There was something strange about the woman, and he couldn't quite place what it was. He'd been nursing for fifteen years, and in all that time he'd never had a patient quite like her. The way she lay there, so quiet and calm and unconcerned, as if she knew something that the rest of them didn't. The angle of her body, the way she tilted her head to the side, as if staring at the plain white wall... it was weird, but it was also oddly comforting.

Yes, that was it: she was a comfort. The ward had never been this quiet, not for as long as he'd worked here. The other patients seemed to take some kind of strength from her presence, too. He'd even caught a few of them casting sly glances her, as if she were something special.

As he stood there, pondering these things, the ward went dark. The lights remained off, not set to come on until later that evening, and he glanced at the window. The sky beyond was filled with squirming black clouds; they seemed alive, writhing over themselves like a nest of snakes.

The patients started to sit up and ask questions. Chatter buzzed around the room. But the patient below him – the calm, comforting policeman's wife – did not move. The sky outside continued to darken, turning to black. There'd been no freak weather conditions mentioned on the radio, so he had no idea what was going on.

He strained his eyes to make out what was happening up there, and slowly began to realise that the shapes in the sky were not clouds. They were birds. Millions upon millions of birds had come together to form a canopy over the hospital, and over the area beyond. The streets outside were cast into darkness. No lights came on; the false night was vast and threatening. Car alarms went off, wailing in the blackness. Figures hurried indoors, trying to get to safety.

The canopy of birds blotted out all daylight. They were coming from the direction of that shit-hole estate – the Concrete Grove.

There was a sound behind him, a noise other than the rising panic of the patients and the running feet of the other hospital staff: a loud, harsh rustling, like that made by stiff plastic sheets shifting across a tiled floor.

He turned and saw that the policeman's wife was sitting up, her knees raised and her legs open. Shadows were streaming from between her legs and scuttling across the floor, heading towards the door. For the moment, no one else could see what was happening. They were all caught up in the excitement of this unnatural nightfall.

Nurse Bennett did not know what to do. Was the woman actually giving birth to the tumours they'd detected inside her?

The woman's eyes were closed. She didn't seem aware of what she was doing.

Nurse Bennett took a single step forward and then stopped, entranced by what he saw. The shadows were solid; they were corporeal. When he turned his head slightly to one side, he made out small, skittering creatures, made of dust and darkness and empty spaces held together by strings of atrophied matter. When he looked directly at them, they were shadow; if he used his peripheral vision, they became much clearer...

These were not tumours. They were something else... something incredible.

"What are you?"

"*The Slitten*," he said, answering his own question in an unfamiliar whisper. He had no idea where the word had come from; it just appeared in his head. But he knew, beyond all doubt, that it was the name of these things. He also knew, somehow, that they were not to be feared – they had been summoned for a purpose, and it had something to do with that sky full of birds.

The Slitten.

He knew what they were called, and that they had come to help. What he didn't know, was where they had come from.

Then, as the woman who'd birthed them settled back against the mattress to sleep, they were gone.

Tom Stains was drunk again. He was always drunk, but that was okay. Being drunk was how he handled the world; or, rather, how he liked to keep it at bay. Ever since his disabled Helen had killed herself he'd been aware of the world – of stinking humanity – reaching out to try and grab him by the throat. Helen had somehow managed to drag herself out of bed and throw herself down the stairs, snapping her neck. Some days – especially when he began to doubt his own memories of the incident – he wished that he had the guts to emulate her.

So, drunk and shambling around the first floor of his house on Grove Road, he at first thought the sight of all those birds blocking out the daylight was another one of his whisky-fuelled delusions. He closed his eyes, opened them again, and was forced to admit that this was real. None of this was inside his head. Not this time.

He reached out and tried to turn on the light, but the bedroom remained in darkness. He stumbled out onto the landing, and then into the back bedroom. The sky at the back of the house was the same: it was filled with birds, forming a screen of black against the sunlight, cutting it off, trapping him down here, in the pitiless dark.

He glanced down, at his tiny rear garden, and saw a figure standing outside the gate. But there was something wrong with the figure... It had no legs. No, that wasn't quite right: it had one leg, a very thin one, upon which it was balanced.

He pressed his fingertips against the window glass. He rested his forehead against the cool pane. Downstairs, more figures joined the first one, hopping along on those thin, rigid appendages.

"Scarecrows," he muttered, hardly even believing what he saw. "Fucking scarycrows."

He watched in stunned awe as they headed off along the street, in the direction of the Needle.

He ran for the stairs, taking them two at a time as he headed down to the kitchen. On the kitchen work bench, there was a bottle of whisky, only half full. He snatched it up and took a large swig, then another... before he was done, the bottle was almost empty. He thought about poor dead Helen; the Sea Cow, that's what he'd called her when she was alive. He missed her sometimes. Not all the time, because to think about her too often brought strange memories to the surface... memories he'd managed to block out for a long time. Something about a woman and a girl and the things they'd done together.

He'd always known this day would arrive. Deep down inside, he'd been waiting for the monsters to come. They'd been here before, many times, and they would come again. They never stopped... but now everyone else would see them, and not just him.

There was a loud noise from outside, like thunder... like an earthquake. Tom moved through the ground floor rooms, watching as his trinkets and knick-knacks rattled on the shelves. He pulled open the front door, too drunk to even think about his own safety, and looked on as the surface of the street rippled and writhed, curling around and breaking, snapping as it was torn to pieces and the ground beneath surged and swelled, as if something were approaching from below.

He imagined a monstrous sea cow smashing through and rising above him...

The first tree broke the surface and shot up out of the road, its branches clenched like a fist, and then opening, spreading, coming to life. This tree was followed by others, springing up like crazy film-set props, as if they were on springs. Geysers of water erupted from shattered pipes, soaking the fronts of buildings and flooding the gutters. Car and house and distant shop alarms bleated, creating a deafening cacophony. And the trees kept growing; they rose from the ground almost comically fast, smashing through the man-made skin of society and churning up the earth.

Tom smiled. He backed away, leaving the door wide open. He stumbled, fell, and watched in silent awe as the uppermost branches of a mighty oak tree shattered the pavement right outside his house and the gnarled trunk began to rise, rise, rise, like the long, straight arm of a god reaching up towards that darkened sky, fingers unfurling to grab at whatever it could catch.

He smiled. This was it. They were here. Nothing would ever be the same again.

CHAPTER TWENTY-EIGHT

His mind buckling under the force of the revelation, Marc knelt on the floor in the grubby room and breathed deeply, as if he were underwater. One hand rested palm-down on the floor by his feet; the other gripped his side, where a stitch had developed. He opened his eyes and stared at the peeling walls, dotted here and there with obscene graffiti, the boarded window, the floor upon which tatters of carpet still clung like stubborn scabs. Someone had painted the word *Flange* on a wide skirting board; six-inch-high letters, bright red against the scabbed white paintwork. The floorboards in one corner were curled up, like a row of tongues.

"I'm the baby," he said, breathing normally again. "I was there... I was here... I'm the baby."

This explained his reticence to really commit to the book he was writing, and the fact that he found it so easy to create excuses not to write, not to research too deeply. Harry Rose had been a distraction. That was the truth. Rather than being drawn to the man because of the information he had (which turned out to be a lot more than he'd ever hinted at), Marc had used the old man to divert his attention from the actual work of writing his account of the Northumberland Poltergeist.

His parents had not died in an accident. They'd driven off the road deliberately, to end whatever nightmare they had started when they refused to offer baby Marc as a sacrifice. That was why the memory of the crash had always seemed so unreal: he'd filled in the blanks himself, giving a context that was false. They were holding hands when his mother swerved the car off the road. They were in it together; it was a suicide pact.

He stood, shaky and exhausted. His body felt bruised, the result of a massive force rocking him to the core. He stood at the centre of the room and wondered what the hell he was supposed to do with this new-found knowledge. He had an entire history of which he'd previously been unaware; a whole new aspect of his life had opened up like a dark flower.

He stared at the walls, at the flaps of wallpaper. He recognised the pattern on a strip that hung down like a window blind: pale yellow sunflowers, with thin stems and oversized heads. A sudden flashback assaulted him: he was lying in his crib, crying. The television was blaring; his small, chubby hands were reaching for those pale flowers...

A sound distracted him: somebody was moving around downstairs. He heard crunching footsteps, a door banging open and then shut, and more footsteps slowly climbing the stairs.

Slowly, he backed towards the door. The sounds grew louder; whoever it was, they were heading for this exact spot. Fear gripped him, holding him in place. Who was this coming for him now? Who even knew that he was here, at the very heart of the story he'd been so reluctant to tell?

He turned around to face the door. A figure loomed into view. It was a man, average height, stocky build. He was wearing a black woollen balaclava over his face and carrying a wooden baseball bat. The man stood in the doorway, legs apart, and hefted the bat. One hand gripped the handle; the other opened to receive the wide end of the bat.

"I..." Marc didn't know what to say. This whole situation had become unreadable. He'd been flung from grimy reality into loathsome fantasy and then back again, and now he was so unmoored from the world that he felt unable to react to anything. "I'm sorry," he said, not even knowing what he meant, what he was apologising for, or to whom he was speaking.

"Erik Best says hello." The voice was flat, heavily-accented, and held the trace of a smile. More figures crowded behind the first, having reached the landing. They each had a similar bat in their hands.

"What do you mean?" Marc walked backwards, going deeper into the room.

The first figure stepped over the threshold, the bat swinging at waist level. He whacked it into the door frame and dust clouded at knee level, moving like a light mist. "Erik Best says hello," he said again, as if that explained everything.

And in a way, it did.

Hadn't Erik Best already threatened him once? He certainly didn't seem like the kind of man who would repeat himself, or who gave second chances. This was what he got for messing with the wrong woman. It was his payback for sleeping with Best's beloved. He should have seen it coming, but the truth was he'd been so caught up in events around the estate – and in particular those at Harry Rose's house – that he'd failed to see the signs. This was the only language these people knew; the dialect of violence, or revenge and repercussion. It was always the same: you do what you're told or you get smashed.

"I didn't mean it..."

The other man laughed, entertained by Marc's pathetic excuse. Marc laughed, too, getting the joke. But his laughter was mirthless. It was heavy with despair, the laughter of a doomed man.

There were three other men, and they too had entered the room. The four of them stood there, the bringers of some abstract apocalypse, and stared at Marc. They were calm, collected; clearly they were used to such acts of aggression.

"I can give you money."

The lead figure shook his head slowly. He raised the bat and swung it through the air, sending off a warning shot. He took another step forward. Marc took two steps back. It was like some idiot dance, a warm-up for the choreography of busted heads.

Shadows moved around the room, splashing the ceiling, staining the floors. Marc watched them as they shifted across the boards, climbed the plaster walls and made strange patterns on the remnants of old wallpaper. There was a strange humming sound in his ears. He wondered if everyone who was about to be killed heard this: a muffled sonic boom, the soul's implosion?

Then he realised the sound was an external one. It was coming from outside his head... outside the room.

He turned to the boarded window, his gaze drawn by the busy shadows. There was something out there, on the other side of the boards. He stared at the edges of the timber. The shadows bled through the gaps, like a thick fluid. The boards began to rattle, and then to shake. In what seemed like a couple of seconds, the boards were being torn away and a chaotic display of flapping wings surged into the room, filling all the spaces, swarming around his assailants and causing them to panic.

They were hummingbirds, and there were hundreds of them. But they stayed away from Marc, choosing instead to attack the other men in the room. He watched with difficulty through the screen of madly blurring creatures, amazed at the sight of the four grown men being pushed down to their knees. Hummingbirds pecked at them, pulling away strands of clothing and then of flesh. Screams mingled with the sounds of humming, and Marc turned away, appalled by the sight of so much madness.

When he turned back, the men were still. They lay on the floor, crumpled, broken and torn. The baseball bats were harmless now, discarded in the melee. The hummingbirds were silent – they hung in the air, unmoving, as if time had stopped, reality had frozen in place. Even their wings were motionless, as if someone had taken a photograph and this was the resultant image.

Marc walked forward and raised his arm. He opened his fingers and grasped at the flat, static image. He touched one of the birds near the front of the group, stroking its hard little beak with the tip of his forefinger. It felt like a stuffed bird: lifeless, essentially unnatural. He moved along the wall of birds, enraptured by their colours – at first they'd all seemed black, but now he could see that they were many-hued, things of beauty. He could hear no further sounds, even from outside the Needle.

When he reached the other side of the room, he stopped and turned around. As if drawn to the exact space where he was looking, four or five birds darted out of the frieze and flew headfirst at the back wall of the room. Sounds rushed in to fill the void; his ears popped. From outside there came deafening sounds of explosions, as if buildings were falling, roads and pavements were being torn up.

The birds hit the wall, backed up, and then flew at it again. Upon each kamikaze impact, the plaster cracked a little more; the cracks widened and set off a chain reaction. They crazed the wall, becoming deep zigzagging fissures. The wall split, the joints in the mortar turned to powder. Chunks of plaster, and then brickwork, fell away. Instead of revealing another room behind, the wall peeled away to show him something else, something that he could hardly believe. Thick tree roots mingled with the ruined brickwork, knotted and shredded.

He walked over to the damaged wall, stepping over the now dead birds that had sacrificed their lives to open up this wonder. He peered through the cracks and the dead roots and saw an expanse of flattened grass surrounded by the broad bases of huge oak trees. He bent over and stuck his head through the largest of the cracks, then stepped through, into the centre of the grove of ancient oaks that waited beyond.

As he climbed through, the trees spun away and he followed a trail of black leaves. The trees were replaced by what looked to be the base of a cliff. The cliff face was littered with openings which led into dark caves, and inside the mouth of one of these caves there stood four young girls dressed in raggedy clothes. He knew who they were immediately. They were the Gone Away Girls, and they were waiting for him.

He approached them in silence, hearing only the crisp black leaves crackling against the soles of his shoes. The earth had a heartbeat; he could feel it vibrating against the skin of his feet. There was power here, but it was old, tired, and unfocused. Like an ageing man at the point of death, it was troubled, confused, did not know what it was supposed to do or what it had done in the long-ago past.

Up close, he could see that the girls were dressed in animal skins, but the fur resembled nothing he had ever seen before. There seemed to be scales amid the pelt, and he was sure that he caught sight of eyes blinking at him from the garments, as if these were not the pelts of slain animals but living things, protective vestments that would attack if the girls were in danger.

Then, abruptly, they were once again just four girls dressed in torn but *normal* clothes.

They turned and entered the cave. Marc followed them, not knowing what else to do. He had not asked to be here, but it seemed that his presence was required. The girls were his welcoming party, and they were unthreatening, simply acting as his guides.

The cave walls were covered with strange paintings, but he could barely make them out because of the lack of light. He focused ahead, trusting the girls to lead him. He listened to their footsteps and kept going in a straight line, his arms held out at his sides to ensure that he didn't collide with the cave walls. Before long, dusty light began to glimmer in the air before him.

The ground was smooth underfoot. The air was moist but not unpleasant.

Up ahead, the cave broadened out to form a cavern. Along the far wall were the entrances to other caves, but in front of these was a broken stone plinth upon which two hummingbirds fought. But, no, that wasn't it. The birds were not fighting; they were balancing some kind of gemstone between the tips of their beaks. Their wings were a blur; they were soundless inside the cave.

"That's the first tear ever shed here, in Loculus." Abby stepped out of the shadows to his right and placed a hand on his arm. Her face was battered and bloody. She smiled. He had not seen her smile before, and it made her look beautiful, despite the terrible marks upon her face. Here, in this place, she looked different than she did in the Concrete Grove. She was less shabby, more substantial.

"What happened to you?"

"It doesn't matter."

"Why are we here?"

"Because we followed the Path of Black Leaves."

One of the girls – Abby's daughter, Tessa; he recognised her from her photograph – broke away from the pack and held her mother's hand. Her face was a porcelain mask; it held no expression. The eyes were flat and shiny. She was like a life-size doll.

"What do you mean?"

"We've been talking, my daughter and me. She's been telling me stories, lots of stories.

"Things started to happen a long time ago, and this is the outcome. Different people started to interfere with this place, tried to gain entry so they could use the power here for their own reasons. There's pollution under the ground and it gets stronger with each negative emotion that ends up here – the pollution came from us, from humankind. There used to be balance. Now that balance is misaligned. That's why they're struggling..." She indicated the hummingbirds with a raised hand. "If they drop the teardrop, it'll shatter. I don't know what happens then, but it can't be good. Not for any of us. But the Path of Black Leaves will grow longer and wider... other things will use it to leave Loculus and find their way back there, to our world."

"What about Terryn Mowbray?"

She didn't reply.

"Captain Clickety."

She nodded. "Oh, him."

"Yeah, him."

Abby sighed. "As far as I can tell, he's a... what's the word? A tulpa?"

"Yeah, that word would fit."

"You think about him, and he comes. It's like opening a door for him. Last year three men spent a lot of time thinking about him. He got his claws in. He broke through. They dealt with him, I think, and what we've seen is the leftovers... the remains. Not much, but enough to try and cling on, to use my pain and my memories of Tessa to try and stay there, in the Concrete Grove."

Marc turned to face her, finding it difficult to take his eyes off the birds. "So what are we supposed to do about all this?"

"The girls were brought here to watch over this cave, and what's inside it. They came to bear witness to the struggle for balance. Because that's all that's ever required, for somebody to see what's happening. Our world forgot about this place, absorbed it into our myths and our legends. The first dreams mankind ever had ended up here, strands of power. The last dreams we ever have will come here, too. This place... it's just concentrated Creation. But you'd be surprised how easy it is for creation to become destruction, when the balance isn't right."

"What about the girls?"

She shook her head. "They're tired. They were too weak for the task. They were inadequate replacements. You were promised and prepared a long time ago, to act as a permanent witness, but your parents reneged on the deal and that's when the balance really began to tip. You were always meant to be here. You were born to be here. I'm sorry... Clickety knew that. He tried to repair the damage. If the balance tips, he fades. He is a product of the status quo."

"So he isn't a monster?"

She nodded. "Yes, he's a monster. But one who knows what's good for him."

He thought of the life he was being asked to leave behind, and how it had always seemed hollow and insubstantial. He'd always felt that he was destined for something else, something better or more important, but he'd never been able to discover what it was he was meant to do. And now here it was: his purpose. He was nothing more than a witness.

"What happens if I say no?"

Abby smiled, but sadly. "Who knows? There are no rules here. It's just another form of chaos."

"What's in those other caves?" He motioned to the cave mouths beyond the plinth and its birds.

"They lead to other places. Maybe even other worlds or other times... probably both. This place we're in is just a way station. I have no idea what other routes might be available, but there are hundreds of them scattered throughout these caves and tunnels. All those hummingbirds originally belonged somewhere in there. Now they're lost in Loculus, just like the rest of us."

Without another thought, Marc nodded, stepped forward and knelt down at the foot of the plinth. It seemed natural, as if long ago – perhaps in another lifetime – he'd been trained to do exactly this. He wasn't sure, but the two birds seemed to respond to his approach. Their wings beat harder, their beaks looked stronger, and their colours were far brighter than they had been only seconds before. The shattered stone plinth began to mend itself.

He felt the weight of a hand on his shoulder, and then another as it enclosed the first. Five hands clutched him, thanking him and saying goodbye. He did not turn around. There was no need. This was his station – he belonged here, in this little place. He always had.

For the first time in his life, Marc felt useful. He was glad.

He'd hate to have made another mistake.

CHAPTER TWENTY-NINE

Royle felt immense pressure in his lower back as he held onto the small, soft hand. When Abby Hansen had dropped into the hole, he'd bent over and reached out instinctively, trying to save her. His flailing grasping fingers had come into contact with something, so he'd tightened his grip. But the hand he held did not feel right… there was something wrong with it.

When he looked down now, braced above the opening with one foot on either side of the hole, he wasn't sure whose hand he had hold of. He shifted his position, gripped tightly with both hands, and pulled. A small, dark shape began to rise up from the depths of the hole, covered in black leaves. The leaves formed a layer – a skin. They coated the figure, making it seem even smaller, compressed.

He tugged as hard as he could and the figure emerged, popping out like something being born. He thought of Vanessa, and the unborn child they had made together… he felt sick, wasted. His energy dipped dramatically.

He stepped away from the hole, hauling the body out and shoving it aside. It was damp, slimy. Unclean.

He looked at his hands. They were covered in those mulch-like black leaves. He wiped them on his trouser legs. The body stirred. Leaves came away, falling to the floor and making a soft, slippery sound. Royle went down onto his knees and stared at the figure. It was inchoate, not quite complete: a stunted child's body with an oversized, beaked head. The limbs were thin and wasted; the hands were three-fingered claws. He reached out and grabbed the mask, tearing it away... there was nothing beneath: just a shapeless mush of black leaves and a lot of tiny, fragile bones, as if a flock of birds had died in that mess.

The figure began to shred, parts of it slithering away and liquefying. Royle sat down and watched as it was reduced to a thick, black slime on the carpet. The last thing it did was reach out and hold his hand.

"You didn't make it," he said. "You couldn't get through. We stopped you... somehow they stopped you."

He stood and turned away, then, as an afterthought more than a calculated act, he turned back and kicked at the remains of the mound at the centre of the room, destroying the structure that Abby Hansen had so painstakingly made in honour of her missing child. There was no longer a hole in the floor. He could see no evidence of the route by which Abby Hansen had travelled... she was gone; her point of access had closed up, like a wound scabbing over. He wondered if she would ever return, if he would ever see her again.

Erik Best's body lay a few feet away, its ruined face turned away from him. He shook his head. "You stupid bastard..." He walked away, left the room, and went downstairs.

Outside, Royle stood in the street and surveyed the damage. It was chaos out there. Sirens were going off, emergency vehicles were entering the estate from all angles; alarms blared, creating more panic. People were running, standing in groups, or cowering in gardens and doorways. A well-known local drunk was standing in his doorway, waving an empty bottle and ranting about sea cows.

All around, huge, thick-bodied trees had burst through the earth, houses and buildings had tumbled, walls had shattered, exploded out into the street, and cars were overturned and ablaze. Water sluiced across the road, discharging from a burst water main. He spotted a few dead bodies: in the gutters, in gardens, even one slumped over the bonnet of a car.

It would take a long time – perhaps years – to figure out exactly what had happened here, but whatever had occurred, it was over. It was done. Something had tried to come through, and it had failed.

Uniformed officers were running around in a panic; they were not trained to deal with something like this. The news crew was trying to film everything and nothing. The whole place resembled a battlefield immediately after the fighting had ceased, or the site of some terrorist atrocity. He'd missed it all, but in some ways he'd witnessed more than anyone else. He just wished that he understood the things he had seen.

He glanced up at the ever-present shape of the Needle. The sky was clear; the birds had flown. A few of them had gathered around the tip of the tower block, as if they were waiting for something to happen. The outline of the building seemed to tremble for a moment, as if a detonation had occurred inside.

From the corner of his eye, he saw a quick, dark shape scurry across the road, but when he looked directly at it there was nothing there but what seemed like a dusty shadow. Nearby, a scarecrow lay in the gutter, its torso shredded, the stick that had supported it snapped in two. It was crawling slowly along the side of the road, heading towards him. Royle stood with his legs shoulder-width apart, wishing that he had a gun. Everything out here was like a medieval nightmare, an image from a biblical painting of demons and monstrosities, of impossible things.

The scarecrow was close now. He couldn't move. He felt like kneeling down and waiting for it to take him. His legs began to shake. Tears filled his eyes.

The black shape he'd glimpsed earlier shot across the road and hit the scarecrow, rolling it on the road surface. He couldn't make out what it was, despite the fact that it was only a few feet away from him. The creature's form was not solid, as if it were made of thought rather than matter. He thought of dusty rooms, empty larders, and buildings where old people went to die, lining up patiently to see the Reaper...

The scarecrow was torn apart as he watched. Then, as he turned away, he caught sight of the thing that had killed it – the thing was visible only at the edge of his vision, not head-on. It resembled old, ancient, papyrus tatters invested with a form of energy. Then, all too soon, it was gone, vanished into the air like a memory. People ran and screamed. The drunken sea cow man – now sitting on his doorstep – started to laugh hysterically.

Whatever that thing was, it had saved him.

Detective Superintendent Sillitoe ran up to Royle. He was hatless, with a shocked expression on his face. "What happened here?" He looked to Royle for some form of explanation, but it was futile. Nobody knew anything.

"I don't know," he said, as his superior officer moved away, running towards a squad car with its roof punched in and short, sharp tree branches poking out through the rips in the bodywork, waving around like monstrous spidery limbs.

Royle turned again to stare at the Needle. It drew his gaze, calling to him. He knew that he should be heading back to the hospital, to be at Vanessa's side, but there was something else he had to do first. There was unfinished business; the final act of this messy epic.

He started to jog in the direction of the centre of the estate, passing injured people, while others walked around in a daze. He couldn't stop to help. There was something more important to do. Ambulance men and paramedics tended to the fallen, soothing them, bandaging their wounds, trying to impose a sense of organisation onto the scene.

He heard the noise when he reached the Roundpath, and it grew louder as he approached the hoarding that ran around the Needle. A single soft note, as if hundreds of people were humming under their breath.

The fence around the building was torn and pulled away in places, so he had no difficulty accessing the site. He stood and stared up at the tower, and in that instant he knew that it was about to fall. He could feel it in the trembling ground beneath his feet; insistent tremors that travelled up through his legs and into his belly, making his innards sing. The loud humming noise was meant as a warning.

He looked at the ground, closed his eyes, and prayed that he wasn't too late – but too late for what? He had no idea. All he knew was that he'd been summoned here. He opened his eyes again and looked at the Needle, challenging it to show him why he'd been called. Thick tree roots were wound around its base. The walls were cracked, and leaves and branches showed through the widening fissures.

The main doors flew open. A figure staggered out, almost falling to the ground. It was Abby Hansen. Black leaves clung to her arms, her legs, and her body. More of them formed a narrow pathway ahead of her, out of the building. Her hair was wet. Behind her, four other figures – these ones much smaller, and dressed in rags – moved in a sombre line, exiting the tower and standing around her, reaching out to help her.

When he started to move towards the group, he realised who the other figures were. He recognised their clothes first – despite being torn and dirty, they were the same outfits they'd been wearing when they disappeared.

He knew these girls as well as he knew his own wife, despite the fact that he'd never met them:

Connie Millstone, aged seven.

Alice Jacobs, aged eight.

Fiona Warren, aged nine.

Tessa Hansen, aged ten.

The Gone Away Girls.

They were the same ages as when they'd vanished. This did not seem as insane as it should, and Royle simply accepted that it was true. Of all the things he'd witnessed today, this was probably the easiest to understand. They'd been gone for years, but hardly any time at all had passed since they'd gone away.

"Abby..." He grabbed her arm and helped her away from the building. "This way. We have to get out of here before it falls."

She blinked, her battered face showing comprehension. "It's going to fall?"

He nodded. "Don't ask me how I know, but yes it is."

They made it over to the fence line before it happened. Royle sat Abby down on the ground, and then he gathered the girls together. They said nothing; their faces were dirty and blank. Their eyes seemed to stare inward. He wondered if they had any idea what was going on, or if, like him, they were simply spectators to some greater event.

"You were shot... are you okay?"

She nodded, and smiled, as if enjoying a private joke. "Just a flesh wound."

He turned to take another look at the Needle, and it began to fall.

The lower floors sheared away, as if a great explosion had shunted them to the side. The floors above fell straight downwards. He was reminded of the World Trade Centre towers back in 2001, September the 11th. It was a date imprinted on the memory of the Western world, when terrorists had shaken the foundations of society. This tower fell in a similar manner, and its destruction was just as symbolic.

It seemed to take a matter of seconds, and when the billowing dust cloud began to clear, all that remained was the rubble. For an instant, Royle glimpsed a vision of a grove of massive oak trees, shimmering brightly, as if they were on fire. But the image lasted only a fraction of a second, and he could not be sure if he'd really seen it at all. All he was left with was a retinal burn; a visual tattoo, which soon faded to a small black spot – shaped not unlike a single leaf – in his vision. He'd stared directly into the sun, and it had not blinded him. He could still see, but the sights were much less beautiful than before. The falling of the tower had signified the end of something. Perhaps it was also the start of something else.

"What'll happen here now?"

He looked down at Abby. She was sitting on the ground with her legs tucked up under her body. She was shaking.

"I'm not sure." He reached down and stroked her head, ran his fingers across her battered cheek. "The people will have to move out of the estate. Or maybe they'll stay, living like savages among those trees and wrecked buildings. Who knows? Who even cares?"

Abby nodded. The Gone Away Girls stood staring at the ruins of the Needle, as if watching a miracle. Each of them was weeping, but silently. He had a feeling they would never say anything again.

"Let's go," he said, reaching down to help Abby to her feet. "There's a lot to be done. And a lot of other people to help."

"Your wife..." She stood shakily, grabbing hold of him for support. "I think she's okay. The baby, too. They're both fine."

Royle didn't question this wisdom; he simply accepted it, just as he knew he must accept everything else that had happened over the past few weeks – and even longer, because hadn't this been going on for centuries? If he doubted any of this for even a moment, he was afraid that he might lose his mind.

He held Abby's hand as they left the Needle, heading towards the sound of sirens. Around them, new shoots began to grow. Saplings took root in the ruins; they rose towards the sky, growing quicker and stronger than any natural tree. By the time they had reached the way out, the entire area was knee-high in new trees. They walked away from this struggling new life. They did not look back.

The Gone Away Girls followed close behind them, a tight little bunch of lost souls that had somehow been found.

EPILOGUE

ONE YEAR LATER

SOMETIMES WHEN SHE won't sleep, Royle puts his tiny fretting daughter in the car and drives out here. It's a short journey, and one that causes him to experience mixed emotions. At one time he used to feel his skin crawling at the very thought of coming to this place, but now he embraces the darkness that waits for him here. As he drives through the empty streets at the outskirts of the Concrete Grove, past the crumbling buildings wrapped up in the calcified remains of trees, over the road surfaces cracked and treacherous, he remembers a time when this estate was filled with life... and when it was occupied by the Crawl, the horrible sensation that has not plagued him since the birth of his daughter.

He nods as he passes each checkpoint, flashing his official ID. The faces he sees here are impassive. The eyes are cold and hard, focused on nothing, and understand little of the strange environment over which they stand guard. There is a solemnity here, a sense of respectful awe.

He drives to the massive, circular concrete wall erected around what is now known as the 'Green Zone' and parks his car near the twenty-four-hour security station. The wall guards know him well; he was recently promoted to the newly created role of Green Zone Task Force Commander. The title makes the role sound far grander than it actually is. He is simply an attaché. But he has a good relationship with most of the guards, and sometimes he plays a game of cards or just sits for a cup of tea and a chat.

The baby always falls asleep during the drive. He wonders if it is the movement of the car or some other, deeper feeling that sends the baby into a slumber.

The security lights are bright. It feels right that light is shone constantly onto the estate. Beyond the high walls and the razor wire, beyond even the reach of those arc lights, a vast darkness deeper than any other he has ever known lies in wait. Nobody is sure if the security guards are protecting this area from the outside or protecting the outside from its influence. The official stance is that they are just "keeping an eye on things".

Sometimes, when conversation lulls in the security station, or if he decides to walk along the walls for an inspection, he can hear the muted rustling of leaves and undergrowth, the creaking of branches. Occasionally he thinks that he hears a faint clicking sound, like chattering teeth...

He has not seen behind those walls since they were erected, but he has been told that there is now a forest in there – and at its heart there stands a grove of ancient oaks whose leaves have turned black. The roads and houses outside the perimeter are half-buried relics; the concrete ruins are like the remains of a lost civilisation, choked by the calcified remains of trees. No flight paths are allowed in the airspace above the wall. Whatever is in there, they are still trying to keep it hidden, at least for as long as they can.

The wall follows the line of what used to be known as the Roundpath. It contains the plot where the Needle once stood. It's just a small patch of land, and yet he has heard reports that the area contained within it goes on for miles. Part of him knows this cannot be possible; another part of him believes it implicitly.

Within the next few months, an expedition will be sent behind the wall. He hopes this isn't a mistake. Whenever he stands here, looking up at the wall, he is reminded of the film *King Kong*... Skull Island, another massive wall, and a hungry monster living in the landscape beyond.

All the survivors of what happened a year ago were relocated. Many of them sold their stories to newspapers and magazines and appeared on TV chat shows and documentaries. Handheld footage from mobile phones appeared on YouTube. Blurred digital photographs were reproduced in newspapers and magazines around the world. Over the last twelve months so much has been said and written about those events in the Concrete Grove that sometimes he feels like it's a fiction – and he is merely a character in a book that's still being written, or has yet to be written.

Some of those survivors are dying. The official verdict is that it's a form of cancer, but he isn't so sure. He's heard rumours of tumours formed on the skin like bunches of black leaves. Of bones transforming into what seem to be blackened twigs and branches and breaking through the flesh.

Whatever this is, it isn't over. In fact, it might have just begun...

He thinks of the dead and what he owes them.

Most of all, he remembers Erik Best and Marc Price – who still has not been found.

And he thinks of Abby Hansen and how she now protects the ageless Gone Away Girls, taking care of them in an old orphanage up in Scotland, where the press and the public cannot touch them. He thinks fondly of the Girls themselves, and how they never age, never speak of what they have seen and done. They just sit there, staring patiently into the distance, as if they are waiting for something.

There are so many unanswered questions. A new world order is waiting to slide into place. Mankind can no longer feign ignorance of the numinous.

Perhaps one day the answers to all questions will be found beyond those thick, high walls – one of the regular expedition groups might even find something of use in that dense primeval land.

Whenever he drives back home from these nocturnal visits, usually with the first faint rays of the sun kissing the horizon, he returns to bed and holds his wife. He hangs on to her as if she is a lifeline. He doesn't want to ever let go.

Every once in a while she mumbles something in her sleep: a word that he thinks sounds a lot like their daughter's name. They called their baby Hope, because that's what she represents.

He kisses his wife's shoulder, her neck, and then whispers secret, wordless promises into her ear as she sleeps.

And he waits quietly for the darkness to pass.